PRAISE FOR THE

"One of the freshest voices in fantasy romance! [illegible] it all: spice, humor, and a world I want to get lost in!"

—*New York Times* bestselling author Katee Robert

"A hilarious, down-to-earth romance with magic, adventure, and intrigue. What's not to love?"

—*New York Times* bestselling author Talia Hibbert

"Sexy, witty, and fun as hell—*That Time I Got Drunk and Saved a Demon* is the instant mood boost we all need."

—*New York Times* bestselling author Hannah Whitten

"Hilarious, hot, and full of heart, *That Time I Got Drunk and Saved a Demon* is exactly what you need in your life. Right now. Go pick it up because it is the cure to any reading funk and might even clear up acne. I'm serious. It's that good."

—*USA Today* and *Wall Street Journal* bestselling author Avery Flynn

"Delightfully spicy and full of heart, this is the perfect escapist fantasy rom-com—a must-read series for readers who always roll to seduce when they play D&D. Cozy fantasy fans, look no further." —Nadia El-Fassi, author of *Best Hex Ever*

"Hilarious banter, cheeky anachronisms, and hot and heavy lovemaking punctuate this full-throttle adventure. It's good fun."

—*Publishers Weekly*

"Delightfully over-the-top and raunchy, this fantasy romance takes the laugh-out-loud rom-com sensibilities (and explicit sex scenes) of Talia Hibbert or Ali Hazelwood and wraps them up in a loving send-up of some of the fantasy genre's favorite tropes. Readers who appreciate its irreverent silliness will be glad that there are already two more volumes."

—*Booklist*

"A quirky, steamy fantasy that's just what the romance genre needs." —*Kirkus Reviews*

ALSO BY KIMBERLY LEMMING

THAT TIME I GOT DRUNK AND SAVED A DEMON

THAT TIME I GOT DRUNK AND YEETED
A LOVE POTION AT A WEREWOLF

THAT TIME I GOT DRUNK AND SAVED A HUMAN

I GOT ABDUCTED BY ALIENS AND NOW I'M TRAPPED IN A ROM-COM

KIMBERLY LEMMING

BERKLEY ROMANCE
NEW YORK

BERKLEY ROMANCE
Published by Berkley
An imprint of Penguin Random House LLC
1745 Broadway, New York, NY 10019
penguinrandomhouse.com

Map illustration by Kimberly Lemming
Book design by George Towne

Library of Congress Cataloging-in-Publication Data

Names: Lemming, Kimberly, author.
Title: I got abducted by aliens and now I'm trapped in a rom-com / Kimberly Lemming.
Description: First edition. | New York: Berkley Romance, 2025.
Identifiers: LCCN 2024029114 (print) | LCCN 2024029115 (ebook) | ISBN 9780593818633 (trade paperback) | ISBN 9780593818640 (ebook)
Subjects: LCGFT: Romance fiction. | Science fiction. | Novels.
Classification: LCC PS3612.E4563 I33 2025 (print) | LCC PS3612.E4563 (ebook) | DDC 813/.6—dc23/eng/20240724
LC record available at https://lccn.loc.gov/2024029114
LC ebook record available at https://lccn.loc.gov/2024029115

First Edition: February 2025

Printed in the United States of America
1st Printing

The authorized representative in the EU for product safety and compliance is Penguin Random House Ireland, Morrison Chambers, 32 Nassau Street, Dublin D02 YH68, Ireland, https://eu-contact.penguin.ie.

Dear Reader,

This book deals with emotionally difficult topics, including dubious consent under the form of a love serum, hostage situations, violence, and sexually explicit content that could trigger certain audiences. Reader discretion is advised.

—Kimberly Lemming

POWDERED DONUTS
PUMPKIN SPICE
BLOODCRY CLAN
GLUTTONY POOL
EGGS IN PURGATORY
VERVAIN
CHURCH OF CHEESE
FUJILLY ROCK
MIRAGE MOUNTAINS
FUCHSIA GROVE
HOT COFFEE
DULBA
NIGHT RIDGE CLAN

WAFFLES
BLUESTARS
MOUNTAIN AND GRAVY
BCI
RESEARCH
CENTER
FRITTATA
BENEDICT BEACH
SUNVALE
BRUNCH PASS
CENTER BAGEL

I GOT ABDUCTED BY ALIENS AND NOW I'M TRAPPED IN A ROM-COM

CHAPTER 1

"THICKEN NUGGET, YOU EVIL BITCH, STOP MURDERING half the desert," I muttered from behind my camera. As expected, Thicken Nugget ignored my request.

Instead, the fierce meerkat matriarch of the Venus tribe charged into enemy territory. The Venus tribe was thirty meerkats strong, and judging by her protruding belly, Nugget planned on growing those numbers soon. Which might explain why she'd been on such a murderous rampage.

For the past few days, Nugget had been on a warpath clearing out the neighborhood. This time, her sights were set on her grown daughter. Tulip, aka Train Wreck, had recently come into power in the Pluto tribe after murdering their last matriarch. Like mother, like daughter, I suppose.

Success was still not without its pitfalls. Nugget was a supremely successful dominant female and had been leading this group for the past six years. Nearly unheard of in the meerkat world. She was so successful that I and the rest of the research team were growing concerned that we might need to take her out, as she was narrowing down the gene pool. But hey, that's how you know she's made it. Girl's got an entire research team plotting her assassination.

I shifted from my spot in the brush and crept closer, readying my camera to record the incoming carnage. This kind of development would give my research team the season finale we needed to get funded for another season. More importantly, I'd be the one to capture it. Not that blowhard John. "Oh, I can't wait to see the look on his 1970s pornstache-lookin'-ass face when he sees this."

Rhythmic chanting about an evil overlord hit my ear, and I fumbled around my camera to answer my phone, lest the noise interrupt the oncoming battle. "Mom," I whispered, "What did I tell you about calling me while I'm in the field?"

"Don't use that tone with me. I'm still your mother," she chided. The sound of plates clattering and muffled conversations rose from the other end of the phone. "Anyway, I'm having lunch with Cassandra. You remember Cassandra from church."

"Mom, I'm kinda—"

"A lady never interrupts, Dorothy. Where was I? Right, Cassandra was just telling me that her son finally graduated from Harvard!" she gushed.

My stomach twisted. I was already well aware of where this was going. Having a daughter more interested in animals and bugs than in etiquette classes and social status has always been a sore spot for her. My older sisters were more than happy to brave the cruel and unforgiving world of pageant society, but apparently two out of three perfect mini–Amelia Valentines weren't enough.

I'd bet my next paycheck that the sight of my solar-powered, heavy-duty phone case would have her fainting faster than her pastor after his wife and girlfriend both showed up to Sunday sermon. Which, to this day, is the most fun I've ever had in church. However, unlike Pastor Dan, she'd jump right back up only to lament how my unsightly cargo pants were made by the devil himself. If so, dear devil, I thank you for these marvelously deep pockets.

"Top of his class, mind you!" Cassandra piped up.

"Yes! Top of his class. You know I always said that boy was smart."

False, you always said he thought he was more important than the turkey at Thanksgiving.

"You know, he's coming back home to visit his mama next week. Why don't you fly in too? I know you're a *career lady*, and there's nothing wrong with that," she said, in a tone that implied that there was obviously something very wrong with that. "But I'm sure he'd love to see you."

And you'd love to play matchmaker so you can brag about your daughter snagging a Harvard grad. "Oh, of course. How does he feel about meerkat slaughter? If he's pro, I'm about to have a great story to tell him."

An aggravated sigh. "Dorothy Ann Valentine, don't be crass."

"Mom, I can't just fly home at the last minute. I'm needed here."

Also, flight prices are insane this time of year.

"I won't hear it, missy. You are coming home to visit and you'll wear something nice. No, your hiking boots do not count as nice," she said in warning.

"I sprang for the red Timberlands; you said those were stylish," I shot back.

"And I'm sure all of your animal-nerd friends were very impressed."

"Wow."

"Listen, your father and I paid for you to go to that fancy animal school in full, and you still didn't come back with a man on your arm. Who's going to take care of you when you're done with your little research project?"

"Aside from the literal PhD I'm about to get?"

An even deeper sigh. "Dory, at some point you'll need to settle—"

"Oh shoot, Mom, you're breaking up!" I said, mimicking the sound of static. "This damn desert has the worst signal. Well, just in case, I love you."

"Dory, you don't fool me! Don't you dare hang up—"

My thumb slipped of its own accord and ended the call. Terrible accident, really; could have been anyone. Funny how life works.

Anyway, I tucked my phone away and readied my camera. For some reason a death match between a mother and daughter felt even more interesting than it had been a few minutes ago.

The relentless Kalahari sun had my shirt stuck to my back. Sand packed itself into literally everyplace you didn't want sand to go. But such is life. No one said your dream job would be no guts, all glory. Careful so as not to interrupt the battle, I plucked a twig out of my way and settled in.

Nugget raised her tail high and began her war dance, an adorable little hopping fiasco to anyone unaware of the bloodlust meerkats were known for. But after studying these little guys for the past year, I knew this would end in one of two ways. Tulip could either surrender and flee or gather her forces for battle.

I turned the camera to Tulip, waiting for her decision. She scanned the war band before her. Her mate, Celestial Beast, came to her side. His reassurance seemed to help her decide. Tulip broke into a dance of her own, riling up the Pluto clan into a rage before charging at her mother.

Oh shit, she's really going for it. It was a ballsy move to be sure. Her clan may have rivaled her mother's in terms of numbers, but Nugget was a vicious fighter.

I shifted the camera back to Nugget, just in time to see her stumble back, no doubt just as surprised as I was at her daughter's defiance. Against a clan as numerous as hers, most other meerkats avoided confrontation, a strategy she was no doubt counting on.

The old gal recovered quickly. With a war cry, Nugget launched herself at Tulip. Dust kicked up around them as the two clans clashed. A flurry of tiny paws and fangs tumbled. Neither side was willing to yield.

I heard a piercing shriek and shifted just in time to capture Celestial Beast bite down on the back of Satan, Nugget's eldest son. Tulip joined him in the assault, no doubt looking to remove her mother's greatest fighter.

A sudden knowing fear sliced through me like ice, sinking into every bone until I shivered from the cold. The world grew still. Sounds rumbled to a low pitch . . .

Death was to my left.

Time snapped together at once. I rolled to my side, peering through the camera to see a lion heading straight for me.

CHAPTER 2

"FUCK, I'M DEAD?" I SNARLED, GAZING DOWN AT THE DESert. A bright light was pulling me farther into the sky. Which was probably good, right? I'm not the religious type, but I think the general consensus is that up is good.

"All right, not all bad, I guess?" I turned to have a look around, taking in the sights before— "THE FUCKING LION!" I screamed, trying to kick away my murderer. The sandy-brown fur of its mouth was stained a telltale red. I put a hand to my throat, flinching when pain erupted. My hand came back covered in blood. "All right, so you definitely didn't miss. What is going on?"

The lion ignored me; instead his eyes remained transfixed by what he saw above us. I stilled and looked up to see the clouds shimmering. A darker spot opened up in the sky. A greenish light sparkled out of it until the force pulling me sped up to a breakneck pace. The light became blinding, and I . . . I must have fainted.

The next thing I knew, I was in a tank. My body felt too

heavy to move. There was a tickling sensation on my neck. Reaching out, I tried to touch the glass front of the tank but couldn't reach it. When I cried out, bubbles floated uselessly out of my mouth. I wasn't sure how long I was floating as I drifted in and out of consciousness.

Muffled chirping met my ears. I struggled to open my eyes, but the room was so damn bright.

Why . . . why do I smell cotton candy? Am I having a stroke? I thought that was burnt toast. Dammit. I knew I should have taken that CPR class. What smell meant you were having a stroke?

A sharp zap to my neck shocked me awake. Birds were chirping all around me. I struggled to get up. Something dug into my arms, so I thrashed. Strings lined with suction cups snapped off my arm with little pops. The birds' chirping grew angrier as I pulled my other arm free. I blinked and looked around to see what looked like . . . owls?

"What the fuck?" I asked. Mutant-looking owls with large fluffy ears fluttered around me, chirping and fussing. Their feathers ranged in color from simple blacks and grays to the colorful blue and orange plumage you would normally find on a tropical bird. Which, frankly, is a wild range of colors for one species to have. I wonder if it's gender based.

Focus.

Macaw-like beaks took up a third of their face. Their flapping wings ended in tiny three-fingered hands. One of them was dressed in a white robe and it was trying to probe me with some horseshoe-looking gun thing.

I smacked it away from me and got to my feet. "One of you better start chirping in English," I warned. Fear and rage caused the threat to come out in a stuttered shout.

The birds were unaffected.

Unfortunate.

I touched my neck, unsure if I'd truly died and gone to some bird hell. But all I felt was smooth skin. When I inspected my hand, not a drop of blood was found. I checked the other side; still nothing. "If I'm not dead, how am I healed?"

The room was lined with rows of cylindrical tanks filled with green liquid. I peered closer at their contents to see the face of a sleeping woman floating in the tank. Her round face looked serene. Long braids fanned out around her face. A few tapped their beaded ends against the glass. The hair rose on the back of my neck as I took in each tank, noting that every one of them held a person. I rubbed my eyes, trying to wake up from the nightmare. Yet when I looked around again, the pods and their occupants remained. Worse still, I noticed that all of them were women.

Reality sank to the pit of my stomach. I was on an alien spaceship. Those aliens only felt the need to capture women, and I'd just woken up on an operating table. If this wasn't hell, it was about to be.

Screaming, I stumbled away from the nearest alien, then snatched a tray off the counter next to the table where I'd woken up. Glass vials and unsettling-looking tools crashed to the floor when I flung it at the nearest alien. Two slightly bigger Owlish came at me with what looked like cattle prods. I grabbed hold of one and kicked off its owner, then swung wildly at its partner. The bird's squawk was cut short when my stick hit the side of its head, sending the creature flying back. Not knowing what else to do, I just swung at any of the little aliens that came within striking distance.

Farther into the room was a dome-like door leading to a hallway. I leapt over two of the Owlish, caught my foot on one, then tripped and fell on my ass. The fall knocked the stick out of my hand; it ricocheted off the ceiling and slammed into a glass case lining the wall. Blue goop spilled out all over my hair. It weighed down my wild red curls until they felt like rivers of slime. "No! No strange alien goop in my hair, dammit!" I wailed, scrambling back onto my feet. "Fuck, my ass is gonna die. I'm so gonna die."

One of the Owlish squawked like a penguin and stomped closer to me. I jumped up, shoving it aside before I sped down the hallway. My vision blurred, causing me to stumble against the wall. The slime dripping down my head grew hot, and the skin where it touched tingled. "Oh, gross. This better not be poison," I said, wiping it away quickly.

I burst into the first room I encountered to see that it was full of bigger penguin-looking bird aliens and slammed the door shut. "Nope."

I swore all the way down to the next room and locked myself behind the door. Then I looked around to see that I had made a poor, poor decision, as this room was full of so many more Owlish, some with the cattle prods, and, of course, the motherfucking lion.

My murderer was floating in a ray of light on a table, completely unaware of his surroundings. Flapping noises beat on the door at my back and the Owlish in the room began chattering angrily. Those with cattle prods advanced.

. . . *Fuck this.*

"You know what? If I have to die"—I raised a finger to all the bird fuckers in the room—"we're all gonna die." I grabbed the nearest Owlish and threw it at the others charging forward. The creature squawked as it hit its comrades.

I darted around them and advanced to the table that held the floating lion. My boots skittered to a halt next to the control panel. Wasting no time, I pressed literally every button I could get my hands on. Red, green, blue, yellow, didn't matter, I pressed the shit out of it.

Light flashed all over the room. The green ray of light holding the lion swayed, the enormous head of the beast bobbing along before the light faded. As soon as it died out, the lion dropped to the ground with a thud, startling him awake. The Owlish flew into a frenzy and began flapping around and pointing their cattle prods at the lion.

Now, to be clear, I'd been studying meerkats the past year, not lions, but I'm pretty sure pointing a shock stick at one is a great way to piss it off. My theory proved correct when the beast launched all five hundred pounds of himself on the first Owlish. Purple blood sprayed into the air.

My vision blurred; a wave of nausea had me stumbling against the control panel. I rubbed my eyes and ducked low. After a few seconds the nausea faded. The cacophony of chirping warped into words. "Lion, obtain."

A reddish Owlish fluttered toward another room. "Forget that, get to the escape pods!"

"We can contain them just fine!" a green Owlish screeched behind me. "They're just dumb animals; we'll have them under heel in no time."

"Well, this animal knows what 'escape pod' means," I muttered to myself. With a snarl the lion pounced on another Owlish. When the little creatures flocked toward the larger predator, I bolted, using the opportunity to shove my way down the hall where the other Owlish motioned to the escape pods.

I forced my way in to see three oval-looking pods lining the room. Each looked wide enough to accommodate roughly six people. I made my way to the center pod and ducked in.

The interior floor was covered with a fuzzy blush-colored carpet. A window lined one half of the dome, while the remaining sides were kept bare, save for a green button that flashed on the far side of the wall.

Panting heavily, I stumbled over and pressed it. "Holy shit, I didn't think I'd make it this far. Yay me!" When the pod started up, relieved giggles burst out of my throat. Soon, I was slumped on the carpet laughing like a nervous maniac. Heartbeat hammering in my ears, I leaned against the wall, gulping in air.

"Okay, Dory, deep breaths. So, we're on an alien spaceship. But hey, look at you, girl, you made it to the escape pod. Maybe you're done."

A roar made my body freeze. The doors of the escape pod slowly began closing as if they didn't hear a fucking lion running toward us.

"No, no, no!" Panic had me racing over to shove at the door, trying to speed up the process. However, there was no handle to be found and my hands slipped uselessly against the smooth metal. "Close, damn you! Please, any and all gods, just close this motherfucking door!"

My cries fell on deaf ears as the lion jumped through the door at the last second. His claws tore at the carpet as the pod lurched away from the spaceship. The lion righted himself and locked eyes with me.

This time no stillness came over me. No ice chilled my veins. Instead, a hopeless rage had me sneering at the big cat. "You know, this never would have happened if you just let me film my meerkats in peace. Do you even know how long it took me to get accepted into the Kalahari Research Centre's internship? Four years of my life, lion," I spat, balling my fists at my sides.

"Four years of schooling. This internship is the last thing I need to get my doctorate. I could have been on the streets hoeing myself out with my friends and having a great time. Could have taken a train to New York City and gallivanted around Broadway like my cousin Jubilee! Or just married that boring Harvard doctor or whatever the fuck he studied like my mom wanted. But noooo, I had to have dreams, I had to have aspirations of saving the stupid fucking planet. My research team gets funding to help protect your whole environment, and you just . . . you just kill me!"

My murderer tilted his head at me; red blood mingled with purple before it dripped from his mouth onto the proud ruff of his mane. Those little drops added insult to injury, as their source should have been the blood in my neck.

"I'm just—so done. I'm so done, and I hate you," I hissed, shaking my fist at the lion. "I hope you choke on my bones after you eat me! I hope they find this escape pod and probe your ass. May your entire family line be cursed with hip dysplasia! I hate you, lion!"

The world tilted. I slammed against the side of the oval. The lion sniffed and crawled closer, tucking himself against me. When I didn't feel his fangs sinking into my neck, I peered down to see his head nuzzled against my chest. "Um, sir?"

The lion untucked his head from my chest to look me in the eye. My gut sank, eyes watering at the beast's horrid breath. He grunted, then a large pink tongue shot out and licked me square on my mouth.

"Ew, that's so nasty," I said, wiping his spit off my face. He shook his head, his nose curling as if he tasted something he didn't like. When he licked his chops, I noticed his gums had turned blue before fading back into a healthy pink.

The escape pod picked up speed. Sharp claws pricked at

my side as the lion clung to me, keeping me tight against him as we slammed against the side of the ship. I pried his claws off me and scrambled up to look out the window. We were plummeting toward the rain forest below at a frightening pace. I screamed, trying to brace myself against the wall. The lion yowled and curled up against my feet, as if I could protect us from the bitch slap gravity was about to deliver.

By some miracle, the escape pod lurched up, narrowly avoiding a tree before it skittered across the surface of a lake. My body flung back like a rag doll in a washing machine. The lion and I rolled forward as the ship bobbed before balancing out to flow calmly amid the waves.

"Braying zebras. I almost shat myself," said a deep voice behind me.

I paused, then looked at the beast. "Did you . . . did you just talk?" I asked.

His ears perked up as he turned to face me. "Did *you* just talk?"

My mouth fell open as we stared at each other. "How—?" I began, but couldn't find the words.

"A talking human," he said, eyes widening with the same shock I'm sure I was showing. He closed the distance between us and sniffed at my pants.

"Stay away from me," I snapped, pushing myself against the wall. The ship rocked in the water, causing us both to stumble.

"Don't move around so much," the lion hissed.

"Fine. Just stay on your side."

"Why?" he asked, tilting his head.

"Why?" I parroted back. "You tried to eat me! That's why."

He snorted. "You're going to need to let that go. It's in the past."

"My blood is still on your mouth."

The lion groaned. "Look, you and I just went through a very traumatic experience together. An experience like that forms a bond. We're basically brothers now. More importantly"—he sat down and grinned—"I'm a lion. Meaning I don't know how to move this"—he looked around the ship before turning back to me—"box. The only reason I followed you is because I know your kind is good with this sort of thing. You're always riding around the desert, singing your songs and shouting," he said. Rearing back on his haunches, he waved his front paws in the air, no doubt mimicking an excited tourist. "Now, be a good brother and move us to shore."

"Sister."

He cocked his head, eyes shifting over my hair. "Oh, I assumed you were male because of your mane."

Instinctively, I tried patting down the wild curls. Both my mom and sisters kept their hair relaxed, but I vowed never to do that again after a terrible reaction to the chemicals left me bald at fourteen. It grew back in time, but teens are cruel. "Hey, it's hard to keep it moisturized in the field."

"Well, if you're a female, then this is perfect." The last word came out in a delighted hum before he puffed out his chest. "That means I'm top male. And I'm not gonna eat you. I promise."

"Oh well. I feel perfectly safe, then," I said, sarcastically.

Unfortunately, it would appear that talking lions don't understand sarcasm, as my new companion made that chuffing noise big cats do when they're pleased about something. "Good. You catch on quick—I like that. So, talking human, got a name?"

"Umm, my name is Dorothy."

"Good to meet you. I'm—" His sentence cut off into a growl.

I wrung my hands together, unsure if I should try to repeat it and butcher the name of a creature who'd only recently decided not to eat me. "I'm sorry, but I don't think I can pronounce that."

He snorted. "All right. Give me a human name, then. But make it strong."

Gods, I hate being put on the spot. Nor did I have the mental capacity to come up with a name a lion of all things would consider strong. Not after spending the day getting killed, then abducted by aliens. If anything, all I could think about was Dorothy from *The Wizard of Oz*.

My mom named me after Dorothy Vaughan, one of the three Black women who played a vital role in sending the first American astronaut into space. Don't be fooled—that, too, was for her image. Which was fine, but as a kid, I didn't care about space and math and latched on to *The Wizard of Oz*, as the main character and I share a name.

Having been beamed up by a spaceship and tossed about, I couldn't help but see the parallels between my abduction and Dorothy's tornado. Though thankfully it looked like they'd just dropped me somewhere in a rain forest, not a strange new world. I was pretty sure the lion in that book was just called Lion. But Dorothy had a little dog . . .

"How about Toto?" I asked.

He repeated the name, tasting it on his tongue, then nodded. "All right. I'm Toto."

I snorted.

"What's so funny?"

"Nothing."

"Well, now that we've gotten that out of the way, I say we join together until we can find a way out of this box and safely back on land. What do you say?"

Water slowly rocked against the ship in an almost soothing cadence. Toto waited patiently, his body relaxing enough to kick his foot out as I pondered my answer. Finally, I let out a breath. "Well, it's not like I have any better options."

"Now you're getting it," Toto said. He came over and nudged my side affectionately. "I'm sorry I tried to eat you."

"I'm sorry I cursed your whole family with hip dysplasia," I said, scratching his ear.

"You what?"

"It's in the past; we're moving on."

The lion chuckled and lay down. "You'll be able to move this thing on your own, right? I've seen your kind roll about the desert in the bigger ones. Just steer us back to shore and wake me when you're done."

"Do you mean our vans? I have my license but I don't think it will be the same as driving an alien escape pod."

Toto licked his paw. "Then how do you propose we swim past any crocodiles or hippos in the water?"

"Oh shit." I forgot. Bodies of water in the desert are full of animals that just really get a kick out of tearing you to shreds. Wait. I looked out the window into the endless sea of greenery on the shore. "Toto, I don't think we're in the Kalahari anymore."

He followed my gaze to shore. "That doesn't look like anyplace I've been."

"Do you think maybe they dropped us somewhere in the Congo?" Depending on how long I was asleep in that tube, we could be anywhere in the world. There were plenty of rain forests in Africa, so it was hard to tell which one this was. It all just looked like endless trees to me.

"You keep saying these human words like I'm going to know what they mean," Toto growled. "What is a Congo?"

"Sorry, that's the name of a big rain forest north of where you were."

"Right, and I know this is much lower on our list of problems, but I despise getting wet."

"We can't have that, then," I said. My fingers felt along the walls, checking for any kind of hidden panel that could lead to a steering wheel.

"What are you doing?"

"Looking for the controls. All I see is the green launch button. Well, it's red now," I said, gesturing to the blinking red button.

Toto looked at the button, then back to me. "What's red?"

"Wha— Right. You're a lion, you can't see that."

"Why not?" he roared. His tail flicked against the wall harshly.

"Calm down. Your eyes just don't possess the cones necessary to process the color red."

He snarled.

I peed a little.

Toto's claws dug into the carpet. His large body rumbled as he growled, "My eyes have the perfect amount of cones!"

". . . Correct," I said soothingly. "We're getting off track. There's gotta be another button around here somewhere. Help me look around?"

He snorted, but shifted to his feet, then began sniffing around. The murky water lapped against the metal walls. When the ship dipped, Toto froze from his sniffing. "What was that?" he asked.

A cacophony of teeth burst from the water, clamping down on the pod with a sickening crunch. I screamed, watching the bits of metal cave in under the monster's impressive strength. It shook us violently, tossing us back and forth.

Toto let out a terrified yowl as the monster gnawed into the metal. Water sprayed in from the cracks. Each new breach in the pod's walls caused my heartbeat to speed up until the organ banged violently in my chest.

Frantic, I slammed my fist on the red button, hoping for a way out before we were crushed. Finally, the window lining half the ship opened up. With Toto close behind me, I plunged into the murky depths. Salt water stung at the cuts caused by Toto's claws. A fin passed by me, dragging me farther into the water in its wake. I kicked and struggled, trying to force my way back up to the surface. But my heavy boots and saggy clothing didn't help. Panicked, I thrashed harder, kicking at the fin when it passed by me again.

Something grabbed my arm, and I screamed, precious air floating out of my mouth in a sea of bubbles. I nearly tried to kick it away until I felt the brush of fur. Toto hoisted me out of the water and then spat my arm out of his mouth. "I can't drag you the whole way," he snarled. "Go, or I leave you!"

Needing no further invitation, I swam for dear life, coughing up a bit of water from my lungs. The escape pod flung over our heads to smash on a rock formation near the shore. I turned back around to see our attacker.

"Is that a fucking mosasaur?" I screamed. The massive finned lizard twisted its body around with a roar. The surrounding water sprang off in tidal waves that damn near took me under once again. Catching sight of us, the beast sank under the water.

"Mosa-whatever or giant crocodile god, I don't know," Toto roared, not looking back. "Just keep swimming!"

"Oh shit, oh shit!" Tears welled in my eyes. Toto and I paddled frantically through the water as the mosasaur surged toward us, its jaws gaping wide enough to swallow us whole.

I could feel the water churn beneath us as the monster closed in, its massive body slicing through the water like a knife. "We're going to die!" I wailed. "We're gonna die and I'm never going to get my PhD!"

A ball of flame shot past us and struck the mosasaur in the eye. The monster howled in pain, its jaws snapping shut just short of my foot. Toto yelped next to me but kept moving.

I caught a glimpse of a figure running on the sandy shore. The dark figure raced onto a cliff, using the higher ground to shoot fireballs at the mosasaur with deadly precision. Each time he struck it, the monster writhed in agony, its resolve weakening with each passing strike.

Toto and I swam as fast as we could toward the shore. The mosasaur continued to thrash and flail in the water, sending waves crashing toward us.

Finally, after several direct hits, the monstrous lizard gave up and retreated into the depths. We collapsed onto the shore, panting and exhausted.

"Great fireball in the sky!" Toto wailed, dragging himself farther away from the water. "It's all over me. My MANE!" The distressed lion let out a pitiful cry and shook like a dog, water spraying all over the sand.

I rolled to my back, letting the tears of relief fall freely. "This can't be happening." Mind reeling, I sat back up and rubbed my eyes, blinking away bits of sand before I scanned the water for the monster. Sure enough, the long tail of a fucking mosasaur rose above the waves. "That thing is supposed to be extinct," I said, getting to my feet.

"Well, why don't you go tell it that?" Toto said petulantly.

"A video!" I shouted, digging around my soaked pants for my phone. Despite our swim to freedom, my phone lit up with no issues and I pulled up my camera and hit RECORD. "I knew

I was right to spring for the waterproof tactical case! Wait, dammit, I should have gotten a video of the aliens too."

By some sheer stroke of luck, the mosasaur breached for air, giving me a clear shot. "Holy shit, this is the greatest discovery of a lifetime!" I gushed. When the beast dropped below the surface again, I cut the video and pulled up TikTok. "Fuck, no signal. All right, no problem. I'll just post it when we get back to civilization."

"Hey, do you know that gray human?" Toto asked.

I followed his gaze to see a man walking toward us on the beach. "Oh right, the flamethrower guy. I got so distracted by the dino I forgot about him. Hey!" I called, waving to him.

He paused, then lifted a hand in turn and continued toward us. Something about his gait seemed off. The lower part of his legs looked bent back, while something swayed behind him. He wore a long dark coat with green and red patterns along the side. Light tan pants ended above what looked like furred boots. Odd, seeing as it was hot as balls. As he grew closer, I noticed a pair of long arching horns rising out of a head of orange hair.

At my side, Toto growled low in his throat. "That doesn't smell like a human."

I swallowed, taking a nervous step back. "He doesn't look like one either. Should we run?"

"Can't," he said solemnly. I looked over to him and noticed he was favoring his back leg. Blood gushed from a cut above his ankle. Toto set his paw down, trying to put weight on it, then growled and lifted it again.

"Shit."

The lion's eyes turned murderous as he crouched low. "If he thinks I'll be easy prey, he's got another think coming."

"Wait, hold on," I said, holding my hands up. "He just saved us from the mosasaur; maybe he's on our side."

"Denalbu," the stranger called. He pointed toward the water and shouted something I couldn't understand.

"Take another step and I'll rip out your throat!" Toto snarled.

"Wait, let's see what he wants before we start a fight," I pleaded, stepping in front of Toto. I turned back to the stranger and gave a friendly grin. "Hey there." My grin died when I took in the size of him. I didn't even reach his shoulders and I'm five eight. *Please be friendly.*

The gray man stopped a few feet from us. Gold eyes narrowed as he looked us over. His face looked relatively human. Actually kinda hot as far as strange alien faces went. He had high cheekbones and a brow that was a little more prominent than normal. Sharp golden eyes flicked over me, no doubt trying to sort me out as well. A line of gold paint ran from his lower lip to his chin. Bits of another gold pattern adorned his forehead, but most of it was covered by his hair.

Oh, and he had a tail. *Great, of course he does.*

I looked down to see that his legs were in fact bent back and his boots weren't boots at all, but hooves.

Fucking *hooves.*

"What are you, an alien satyr?" I asked, dumbfounded.

He growled something in another language, then looked at Toto. His lip curled when he noticed his bum leg. The alien dug into the bag on his hip, then said something else to me.

Frustrated, I wrung my hands together. "I'm sorry, but I don't understand you."

He clicked his tongue, then approached Toto, who snarled in response. Unfazed, the alien grabbed hold of the lion and flipped him onto his back. I screamed and Toto flailed around, trying to rake his claws against the stranger. Before he could land a blow, the stranger wrapped his tail around Toto's front legs, then put a hoof to his throat to keep him still.

"GET HIM OFF ME!" Toto roared, thrashing.

I froze, too terrified to do anything but stand there like an idiot. The alien snarled, showing dangerous-looking fangs. His warning only enraged the lion more and Toto thrashed harder. "You gray bastard, I'll eat your heart and shit out your dreams. Let go of me!"

The alien sighed and pulled something out of the bag and poured it on Toto's wound. The lion hissed and resumed his threats. "YOU RUNT OF THE LITTER, I'LL KILL YOU!"

I came around to see what the alien was doing. When he reached into his bag again and pulled out what looked like a salve, I calmed down. "Toto, Toto, wait, man, I think he's just healing your leg."

The snarling ceased, and Toto tilted his head to look at his leg. "Oh?" he asked through panting breaths. His body relaxed as he watched the careful way the alien bandaged his leg. "Hmm, well, he could have warned me."

When Toto's leg was safely wrapped up, the alien released him. Toto stood and tested his leg. "Not bad. Fine, I'll forgive you this time. Next time you grab me, I take a hand."

The stranger regarded us both with a menacing scowl, then barked out another word and turned to walk away.

"Hey, wait, where's he going?" Toto asked.

"Wait, come back!" I called. When he kept moving, I jogged over to him and placed a hand on his arm. Damn, he smelled good. A mix of wood, vanilla, and gingerbread. Almost like tonka beans.

He flinched and looked down. "We have no idea where we

are," I began. "I know you can't really understand me, but is there any way you can guide us to the nearest town? Hell, I don't even know if we're on Earth anymore. First the alien birds, then a freaking dinosaur tried to eat us, and now you. I'm sorry, but I can't just have you save us, then walk off into the wilderness."

"Right," Toto said, walking up behind me. "You can't just save us and not adopt us. What's that word humans use for those animals that always stick around them? Pets? Yeah, that's it. We're your pets now, so you're stuck with us. Feed me."

"What, are you forming a gang or something?" I asked.

"Yes," he said. With a look that implied I was very simple, Toto nodded up at the alien.

I held up a hand. "Now, hold on, I haven't agreed to be anybody's pet." Turning back to the gray man, I gave a polite smile. "Though if you have any food I would not say no if you wanted to share. I kinda rushed through breakfast. And lunch."

Fuck, did I eat today?

He patted my hand, then continued down a path into the jungle. We followed closely, hoping he'd take pity and lead us to a taco shack or something. Movement in the trees caught my attention, and I turned to see a bright green creature zip past us.

"I've never seen a lizard that big," Toto remarked.

"Okay." I sighed, doing my best to keep my shit together. Several more green raptors shot past us before they darted after the first. Terror pricked its icy needles under my skin. I swallowed and flexed my hands to keep them from going numb. "That was definitely another dinosaur." My breathing grew rushed. "I'm following a strange alien with a talking lion—"

"Hey, from my perspective, you're the one talking."

"And there are dinosaurs everywhere. Great, perfect. Totally normal. Starting to think I'm not on Earth anymore. But it's cool, it's fine. We're rolling with it. Cool, cool, cool."

Toto eyed me warily. "You're looking lighter brown than you usually do. You're not gonna—"

My voice trembled before a sob escaped. Giving in, I shielded my face with my hands and just broke down.

"Yup, there it is." The lion sighed.

The alien turned back to me and stiffened. He shouted something in his rough language, then grabbed my hands and pulled them away from my face. Taking my chin in his hand, he turned my face back and forth. When I kept crying, he lifted my arm to inspect my side.

I screamed in anger and shoved him away. "I'm not fucking hurt, I'm freaking out. Don't touch me!"

"There, there," Toto soothed. He came to brush against my hip. The wetness of his fur chilled my side, but the comfort was nice. "You're wailing like a cub. Knock it off."

"Excuse me for not being able to roll with the punches after I got kidnapped by aliens," I snapped.

"Yeah, but look on the bright side."

"What's the bright side?" I asked.

Toto grinned and nudged me. "I could've eaten you."

Laughter escaped through my tears. The sharp panic ball sitting on my chest felt a little lighter at his teasing. "Yeah, you could have eaten me."

CHAPTER 3

MAYBE HE SHOULD HAVE JUST EATEN ME. IT WOULD'VE been better than trekking through this madhouse of a jungle on an empty stomach. Our fearless alien leader hadn't stopped for what seemed like hours. The sun was setting in the distance, yet the big guy showed no signs of tiring. On the other hand, my feet were on fire. My throat was dry, and I just wanted to sleep for a week.

It wasn't even just the endless walking. The years I spent studying wildlife biology at SUNY ESF had trained me to recognize all types of flora and fauna. Most of my training pertained to modern-day Earth, but put a bunch of animal nerds in one place and it's only a matter of time until someone brings up dinosaurs. Tie it with the fact that one of my professors was an insanely hot paleontologist who would get all starry-eyed as soon as someone uttered the words "Cretaceous period." Gods, the rabbit holes of research I used to go down just to get that man to glance in my direction.

Anyway, I knew a lot about dinosaurs and animals. Which

is how I knew for a fact that this fauna did not match its flora. Like, at all. Case in point, the stegosaurs eating dandelions along the path. "Toto, I'm losing my mind," I said.

He followed my gaze to the giant herbivore and sniffed. "I know what you mean; that's the ugliest rhino I've ever seen."

"It's not." I sighed, then pinched the bridge of my nose in an attempt to stall the oncoming migraine. "That is a stegosaur, a creature of the Jurassic period, and it's eating flowers."

"So?"

"Flowers didn't exist back then. Well, I should say that it's hotly debated that there might've been Nanjinganthus, but sure as hell not the dandelions he's munching on. Never mind the fact that we just escaped a mosasaur, which is from the Late Cretaceous period."

"You're saying a lot of human words again." He groaned.

"I know, just . . . I just don't understand what's going on and it's driving me insane." My breathing sped up as my voice grew more and more frantic. "None of this makes any sense. Why would a bunch of aliens bring us to a weird dinosaur land?" I took deep breaths, trying to calm down. "And where did he come from?" I yelled, pointing to the alien.

The man in question turned back to me, scowled, then motioned to keep walking. I tried to keep my chin up, really I did. It worked for a few minutes. For a few measly minutes I was able to shut my brain off and ignore the fact that a pterodactyl from the Jurassic period calmly flew overhead, while tiny alwalkeria from the Triassic period scurried along the jungle floor. When a feathered dino I didn't recognize leapt from tree to tree, I looked the other way.

But when we passed by a giant ground sloth, I lost my shit.

"YOU DON'T BELONG HERE!" I screamed at the elephant-sized megafauna. The sloth in question paused his avocado pilfering to look back at me. "You belong in open woodlands during the ice age. Why? Why are you in a jungle with fucking dinosaurs and an ocean with a goddamn mosasaur?"

Slowly, the creature brought an arm up to scratch at its face, then decided I wasn't worth the trouble and kept eating.

Toto came to stand at my side. "Yeah . . . I don't think he knows, Dory."

When the alien came to hurry us along, I kept moving. We walked and walked, and just for a change of pace, he carried me over a river for a bit when I refused to get in. But can you blame me? I don't know what's in the water on this planet. Could have been a giant snake.

Pass.

As we charged through the dense foliage, my senses were overwhelmed by unfamiliar sights, sounds, and scents. Each step felt like I had cinder blocks tied to my legs; they were so tired. The alien, seemingly impatient with my slow pace, kept urging us forward.

Finally, after what seemed like an eternity, we stumbled upon a small clearing. The dense canopy overhead allowed rays of sunlight to filter through, casting a soft, dappled glow on the forest floor. There, in the midst of the natural oasis, sat a car of all things.

It wasn't even weathered and rustic like you would normally think an abandoned car would look in the middle of a random jungle. No, it looked like someone had just parked their brand-new sedan, with shining red paint and glittering windows, in the middle of a random jungle. Vines were snapped and crumpled under wheels, yet no tire tracks could be found around it.

"Odd," I said, curiosity tugging me forward. I approached

the abandoned vehicle cautiously, stopping only when the alien grabbed my arm.

As usual, he was frowning. He pointed back onto the path we were following and said something in a biting tone.

"Yes, yes, I know, we need to keep moving to wherever it is you're dragging me off to. We'd get there a lot faster if we had a car, though, so . . ." I said, shrugging him off.

He huffed dramatically, swishing his tail back and forth in a similar fashion to my aunty's cat when she didn't get her way. "Volbrukan ru lo," he said, pointing to the sky.

I looked up into the clear blue sky, waiting for some kind of signal. Finding none, I repeated the words back to him to see what he'd do. His face brightened into a smile as he motioned back toward the path.

"Hmm, you're kinda cute when you smile," I said, grinning back at him. "Too bad I've always favored curiosity to men."

The look of indignation on his face when I went back to the car was almost worth the alien abduction.

Far too exhausted to err on the side of caution, I marched up to the car and flung the door open, hoping against all odds that it wasn't a stick shift.

It was not a stick shift. It wasn't anything. Nothing but a hollow shell devoid of any seats or recognizable car parts.

"EMPTY?" I screamed. The sound carried through the canopy loud enough to scare tiny raptors from their nests. One fell from a tree onto the metal roof of the car before it scurried away, leaving tiny footprints of pollen on the red paint. "Wha—" I leaned in farther, peering into the depths of the car, hoping to find some hidden clue, a secret button that made all the seats and steering wheel appear. Or maybe a hidden camera where some celebrity asshat was watching me just before he jumped out of the trees to yell, "Punked!" Yet all I discovered was a barren expanse.

"Ugh, I quit," I said, slamming the door shut.

"Agreed," Toto growled. "Does Gray Man ever stop? I need to nap and my leg is really starting to hurt." The lion stretched, then moved to a shady patch of grass and plopped down with a groan. "I'm not moving. You can't make me."

"I would never try to," I said, walking over to him.

The alien paused when he noticed we weren't following and turned back. He stomped his way over to us, motioning back toward the path. "Buldan fu yanku," he said.

I stared up at him with tired eyes. "Whatever you just said, no. I'm done. I'm not meant for whatever bullshit this is. Just let me die here."

"So dramatic," Toto said.

"Call me whatever you want. Honestly, I don't understand how you're not freaking out."

"Eh, a jungle, a jungle. I'm sure I'll find my way back to the desert eventually. Or maybe there are a few lionesses around here. I was hunting for a new pride anyway. This morning I found a small pride of three females. They had a male, but he looked small, so I could have taken him. You were actually going to be a gift to them after I killed their mate."

"Charming," I drawled.

"I know. I had it all planned out. Very romantic."

"Toto, I don't think we're on Earth anymore. You're not going to be finding lionesses. We're in some strange land or a new world with freaking dinosaurs, aliens, and who knows what else. I know you've never seen a movie, but trust me when I say the Black woman always dies first. Why not just save myself the trouble and give up here?" I lay down next to

Toto, my muscles screaming with the exhaustion of the day. "I quit," I shouted petulantly. "Spread my ashes by the seaside with a tasteful eulogy."

The lion snorted at my antics, then rolled onto his back. "Take a nap, cranky thing."

A pair of dark gray hooves stopped by my head. I peeked an eye open to see the alien staring down at me with his fists on his hips. "Net hullden," he said.

"Do you mind? I'm trying to die."

The alien looked to the sky, then ran a hand along one of his horns. Whatever he saw must've been unpleasant. He glared back down at me before he slapped his tail against the ground and repeated himself.

I blinked up at him, then turned onto my side and got comfortable. When neither of us made a move to stand, the alien stomped off. If I'd still had any will to live, I would've gotten up and followed him. Yet when I so much as tried to move my legs, they screamed in protest. I couldn't take any more walking even if I wanted to. Lids heavy, I gave in to the exhaustion and closed my eyes.

The sound of clomping hooves returned, but I ignored him. Let him snarl and huff. Unless Gray Man came back with food and water, I wasn't interested. I supposed I could try sneaking a few avocados away from that ground sloth. On second thought, he was rocking some wicked claws on his forelegs. Never mind, I didn't even like avocados.

"RELEASE ME," Toto roared.

My head snapped up to see the alien tying a vine around Toto's legs. The lion bit into the alien's forearm. Gray Man hissed in pain and shook Toto off, then grabbed his snout and tied another vine around it.

Panicked, I shot to my feet and tried to get away. Yet a

large hand clamped around my ankle like a vise. I screamed, kicking at his solid chest. It did nothing, and soon I found myself bound and slung over his shoulder. He knelt low and picked up Toto, securing the thrashing lion in his arms before taking off at a run.

I wheezed when his shoulder knocked the breath from my lungs. Thanks to the vines binding my wrists, I could barely grip his coat for purchase. "What's the big idea, asshole?" I snarled.

Thunder rolled overhead. I looked up to see the sky suddenly turn black with ferocious-looking clouds. "Ohhh. That's the big idea."

Lightning flashed so bright that the world turned white. In the next second, it was pouring. Like monsoon-level pouring. Wind whipped so fast, I nearly blew off his shoulder. The body beneath me heated as the alien swore something in his strange language and ran faster.

Thunder boomed so loud it made my teeth clench. I shielded my eyes, trying to save them from another flash of blinding lightning. All at once, the rain stopped. Gray Man slowed to a halt inside a cave, where he laid Toto and me down. The large alien moved to lean on the side of the cave and catch his breath. Like the rest of us, he was completely soaked, the long jacket he wore sticking to his sides. His bun was half unraveled, leaving streaks of orange hair to fall around his face.

He shifted to take the tie out of his hair and shook it loose, sending droplets of water all over the floor. Next, he stripped himself of his coat and hung it on a hook on the wall. To my unexpected delight, the linen undershirt came off next.

"Wow, okay, several questions," I said to Toto. "One, why is the alien so hot? Second question, how on earth is our anatomy similar? I mean I've heard of convergent evolution, where two species develop similarly despite having no common ancestor, but his muscle structure is incredibly similar to that of a human male. Albeit a very cut human male."

And I did not hate it.

Toto murmured something, but it was muffled by his restraints.

Gray Man's muscular structure was a little more pronounced than that of the average human. Especially around the chest cavity. If I had to wager a guess, I'd say his lungs were probably oversized. His cloven hooves made me think of a mountain goat. It was possible the cloven hooves and larger lung capacity were an adaptation to a mountainous homeland. That long tail probably helped him keep his balance as well.

Orange spots, the same shade as his hair, dotted along his shoulders and back like large freckles. On closer inspection, it looked like his horns were smooth and covered in skin. If I hadn't been bound, I might've reached out a hand to touch them. The long, thick tail coming out his back had a row of large darker spots lining the top side of it, while the tip resembled a tube.

Fuck, I wished my friend Stacy was there. As a paleoanthropologist, she'd have a field day trying to record the similarities of our species. "Oh! Dammit, I should be recording everything," I yelled, mentally kicking myself for not thinking to jot down everything I'd seen. If there was any chance at all that I got back to Earth, any number of these discoveries would change the face of science as we knew it.

Gray Man shifted away from the wall and made his way over to us. Stopping a foot away, he crossed his arms over his chest and met my gaze, as if daring me to start fighting again.

"I'll be good," I said obediently. Then, upon remembering he couldn't speak English, I smiled brightly.

The alien sighed, unsheathed a knife from the holster on his belt, and cut me loose. I rubbed my wrists and watched as he did the same to Toto.

The lion growled low but didn't swipe at Gray Man when he was free. Instead, Toto snarled and slinked over to sit beside me. "Are you thinking what I'm thinking?"

"Doubtful," I replied. "What are you thinking?"

The lion lowered his head and fixed the alien with a hungry stare. "I'm thinking we should eat him."

"Wha— No! He saved us."

"From rain. He tied us up and threw us around because of the rain."

"More like a monsoon."

"It was rude and he should pay for his crimes. Besides, look at him. I've never eaten . . . whatever that is before."

"Is that why you tried to eat me?" I asked, voice rising with my ever-growing concern.

Toto ceased eyeing up the alien in favor of putting a paw on my leg. "No, it's not like that at all. I've mostly gone after people since my mouth started hurting. Humans are soft prey. No offense."

Yup. Not gonna think too hard on that.

"What's wrong with your mouth?"

His face scrunched. "Something is digging into my gum, but I can't get it out."

"Oh, want me to get it out?"

He gasped up at me, wide-eyed. "Would you?"

"Yes. If it means you don't fucking eat us."

"Of course. It's over here somewhere." Toto opened his mouth wide and tongued at something on the bottom right of his jaw. The area was inflamed and red. Something poked out from between his teeth.

A small tendril of fear wound its way up my spine. Steeling my nerves, I reached into the lion's mouth. Toto winced. The angry snarl he let out damn near made me scream, but I reeled it in. With one hard tug, a piece of aluminum came out. "Were you chewing on a soda can?" I asked.

The lion groaned before flopping to his side. "Sweet playing lionesses, that feels so much better. All right, Gray Man can live."

Outside, the storm raged harder. The trees swayed back and forth, one even snapping and coming down. When the rain picked up, I could barely see a few feet out of the cave. I clicked my tongue and turned back to Gray Man. "So, uh, thanks for getting us out of that."

He merely narrowed his eyes at me in response, clearly annoyed we had put up such a fuss when he was just trying to help us get out of the storm. In my defense, how the heck was I supposed to know that? He's not exactly a man of many words.

Still, I couldn't deny that I owed the man my life—several times over by this point. Swallowing my pride, I stood and flashed him a grin. "You and I got off on the wrong foot. Let's start again. Hi, I'm Dory." I tapped my chest and repeated my name, then pointed to him.

His mouth formed a thin line as his tail swished behind him. After a moment, he tapped his chest. "Sol."

"Sol," I repeated excitedly, then held out a hand. "Nice to meet you, Sol."

He stared at the offered hand, then glanced back at me. Feeling awkward, I chuckled and began to draw my hand away. "Right, you probably don't understand handshakes."

Sol dug around in his bag and then placed a biscuit in my hand. Then he took a pouch from his belt and offered that up as well. I heard liquid sloshing inside and I nearly cried from joy. "You had water this whole time?" I asked, snatching the bag. Opening it quickly, I greedily drank my fill, groaning in relief when the water soothed my aching throat. "Oh Mylanta, I could kiss you! As a matter of fact—" Overcome with relief, I slung my arms around his shoulders and gave him a quick kiss.

His eyes grew wide. "Oops, sorry," I said, scratching my head. "Got a little too excited."

"Whatchu got?" Toto demanded, peering at us over his shoulder.

"A biscuit and water," I said, breaking the biscuit in two. "Want half?" I asked, holding out one half for him.

"Is it meat?" he asked, eyes widening with interest.

"No, sadly, just wheat. Wait, lemme check." I bit into my half of the biscuit, checking to see if there was any meat filling. "Nope, just bread."

"Humph. Prey food," he said, turning away.

While I enjoyed my biscuit, Sol made his way to the back of the cave and brushed leaves and debris away from a small corner. Then he pulled out a stack of logs and a blanket. He moved to a spot where the rocks were sunken in farther and arranged the wood in a stack. With a flick of his wrist, he tossed the blanket next to me, then grabbed some leaves from the debris used to cover his bounty and stuffed them between the logs. The dark spots on his tail glowed orange before he spat a ball of fire on the wood.

"Holy shit, he breathes fire," I mumbled around my biscuit. "Guess that's how you saved us earlier? What a crazy adaptation; I wonder how he does it."

Still, the warmth of the fire was a welcome sight, as the rain had chilled me to the bone. It didn't help that my clothes were soaked as well. I took a note from my alien companion and stripped off my cargo pants and T-shirt, then hung them next to his coat.

Sol's gaze burned into my back, but I ignored him. It was only fair, seeing as I was checking him out just a moment ago. Besides, it would be weird if he wasn't a little curious about my body. We were completely separate species after all. A small twinge of self-consciousness wormed its way into my brain, and I stomped it out—the one trick my therapist managed to teach me before I fired her.

With my clothes hung up, I went to sit next to him by the fire and kicked off my shoes.

"GAHH!"

I turned to see the alien crab-walking away from me looking terrified. His back hit the wall of the cave before he pointed a finger at my feet. "What in the twin moons is wrong with your hooves, woman?" he hollered.

"He can talk now?" Toto gasped.

Shocked, I whirled around and asked, "Can you understand us?"

"I . . . yes?" he asked, gaze still locked on my feet. When he glanced up at me, his eyes grew sorrowful. "You poor thing, do you have hoof rot?"

"Hoof rot?" I asked, tilting my head. "Oh, you must mean my feet." Lifting my foot, I wiggled my toes at him. Only to stop when it looked like he might throw up.

Sol's body lurched, and he covered his mouth. "What are those disgusting appendages?" he asked, wiggling his fingers to match the movement of my toes.

Damn, I'd never been a big fan of feet myself. But from his

reaction, you'd think I just took off my shoes to reveal a three-headed slug. "It's not that bad," I said, wiggling them again.

The alien dry heaved and waved a hand at me. "Stop that!"

Giggling, I set my foot down. "Oh, come on, I didn't make a big deal out of your hooves. That's pretty weird for me."

Sol's body remained stiff, as if I'd leap and attack at any moment. His tail twitched behind him. "Are you sure you don't have hoof rot? I can't bring you back to my village if you're going to infect everyone." His eyes grew wide before he jerked to stand up, then put a fist over his chest. "Don't worry, we were able to save a few healers from the Calamity. We'll set up a hut for you on the outskirts until you're fully healed. We have warriors patrolling the perimeter. You'll be perfectly safe."

"Sol," I began slowly, "I do not have hoof rot. I have feet. And I'd appreciate it if you'd stop staring at them like they were going to jump off my legs and bite you."

"I might."

"Shut up, Toto."

"Right," Sol said, clearly unconvinced. "How can I suddenly understand your words? A moment ago both of you were speaking gibberish."

Shifting to one side, I put a hand on my hip and thought for a moment. "I think it's because I kissed you. Now that I think about it, the same thing happened when Toto licked my mouth."

"What is a kiss?" he asked.

"It's where you put your mouth on someone else. It's a sign of affection or in our case gratitude."

"Without biting?" he asked.

"Why would we bite out of gratitude? Who would do that?"

His brow furrowed. "I didn't know what you were doing. Suddenly you just launched at me."

"I . . . All right, fair. Well, on that note, what are you?" I asked.

Sol bumped his fist against his chest. "I'm a monster hunter of the Night Ridge clan. What are you?"

"Well, I'm a wildlife biologist from Georgia, but I meant your species," I said, gesturing to him. "My species is called human."

"My kind is called Sankado. Are humans the native species of this planet? We haven't seen any of you since we've been here."

His question caught me off guard. I bit the inside of my cheek. "Shouldn't I be asking you that question? This must be your home planet. I'm pretty sure it isn't Earth."

Sol crossed his arms, frowning. "No, what was left of my people was dropped here by small feathered creatures roughly ten years ago."

Toto leapt up. "Oh! The sour birds!"

"Sour?" Sol asked.

"Don't ask," I said, waving a dismissive hand. "To make a long story short, I'm pretty sure we were dropped here by the same feathered creatures that brought your people here. What do you mean by what's left of your people?"

The alien's face grew somber. "Most of us were lost in the Calamity. About a decade ago, my home planet was struck by a giant spaceship. In one fell swoop the continent of Dulrock was completely wiped out. If that wasn't enough, noxious fumes rose from the spaceship and poisoned our air. Those strong enough to withstand the fumes were left to die in the aftermath of a poisoned world. We thought all hope was lost, until those sour birds, as you call them, beamed us up into their spaceships and dropped us here."

My hand flew to my mouth as I imagined the horror he must've faced. "Sol, I . . . I'm so sorry."

He held his hand up. "We don't need to speak on it any further. Was your planet destroyed as well?"

"Not to my knowledge," I said, uncertain. "At least I hope that's not why I was beamed up." Slowly, a ball of dread formed in the pit of my stomach. "Nope. Not thinking like that," I said, shaking the dark thoughts away. "Still, if you aren't native to this world either, then that doesn't leave us with a lot of answers. Did the birds say anything to you when they dropped you here?"

"No, they didn't speak like you do. After we were dropped, most of us formed bands and split off. My clan settled near the lake about another six hours' walk from here. We have spent most of our time here clearing the area of those monsters."

"Right, we're in a dinosaur world."

His eyes brightened. "Then you know what they are. Those monsters came from your planet?"

"Technically yes," I said, tilting my head. "But they were before my time. Like millions of years before my species even existed. Today's the first time I've ever actually seen a living dinosaur."

"Hmm, that doesn't give us much information to go on if neither of us knows why we're here." Sol got up and joined me by the fire. "Were you and your beast the only ones they brought here?"

"Who are you calling a beast?" Toto snapped. "I am the top male of this pride!"

"I see." Sol's voice hardened as he eyed Toto. "You are her

mate, then? The differences between your species' sexes is . . . unique."

Toto and I looked at each other before roaring in laughter. Wheezing, I wiped the tears from my eyes. "Are you kidding? Of course we're not the same species. Hell, he tried to eat me this morning."

"It's true," Toto roared, laughing along. "Tore her throat right out, I did."

"You what?" In an instant, Sol was on his ~~feet~~ hooves and put his big body between me and Toto. The darker patches along his tail lit up into a bright orange. Whistling air came from the tip of his tail and the orange patches grew brighter, some shooting off small sparks of flame.

Toto recovered from his laughter enough to eke out a response. "It's fine, we've moved on and formed a pride."

"Yeah, that was so last morning, we're over it," I said.

Sol eyed the lion warily but relaxed enough to sit back down. "If you're sure."

"I am," I said. "To answer your previous question, no, there were other humans on the ship before we escaped. Toto and I were the only ones to make it on the escape pod, but I think I saw at least twenty of these tube things with humans in them. Though I don't know where they are now."

"This is deeply concerning," Sol said.

"You can say that again."

He quirked a brow at me. "Are you hard of hearing? I said it was deeply concerning."

"No, sorry, it's an expression." I scooted closer to the fire and held my hands up, trying to warm them. Worry and exhaustion weighed heavily on my body. Staring into the flames, I thought about the woman with the braids I saw in the tube. Was she even still alive? I was so caught up in all the panic I didn't think to even check. Not that there was anything I could have done even if she was. "Well, damn. Now what do I do?"

"You will sleep," Sol said firmly. "In the morning I will finish my task and return for you. Then I will bring you to my chief. He will know what to do."

Under normal circumstances, I would not allow a man to decide whether or not I slept. But who had time to be difficult after what I'd been through? If he wanted to get all caveman on me and protect me, then I wouldn't say no. It wasn't like I had much of a chance without him. "Your clan doesn't, like, eat women, right?"

"Do you honestly expect me to tell you if we did?" he asked.

"You know, you could just say, 'No, Dory, you're perfectly safe with me.'"

He raised his voice, mocking my higher pitch. "No, Dory, you're perfectly safe with me."

". . . Rude."

CHAPTER 4

"HEY, WAKE UP," SAID A VOICE ABOVE ME.

When I ignored it, something nudged at my side and I swatted it away. Everything hurt and I was so tired. The beds they had at the research center were little more than prison cots, and my back was always killing me. But today was worse than usual. Not that it mattered; I'd have to get up soon and check on the status of Nugget's troop and the power struggle. Bad back or no, we needed that footage for a dynamic season finale. Still, it could wait five minutes. "Go away."

"I'm hungry," the voice said.

"How is that my problem?"

"Fine, we can play your way." A booming roar shook me awake. I opened my eyes to see Toto's fangs about to descend on my face. Screaming, I backed away from him, my heart pounding in my chest. Confusion clouded my mind as I tried to gather my bearings. The lion erupted in laughter, rolling onto his back in his hysterics.

Memories of the alien abduction and dinosaurs all came rushing back. Blinking rapidly, I tried to make sense of my surroundings. In lieu of the **Stay Positive** poster of a shark eating a child holding a thumbs-up sign I kept next to my bed, my gaze landed on the rough, jagged walls of the cave I found myself in. The air felt heavy and humid, carrying a scent of rich vegetation. "What is wrong with you?" I snapped. "You scared me half to death."

Toto merely rolled upright and stretched like a cat. "Get up faster, then. I've been waiting all morning. Sleep any longer and we'll have to hunt in midday sun. I hate running in the heat."

"What hunt?" I asked, rubbing my eyes. As my senses started to awaken, I became aware of a symphony of sounds echoing through the cave. A cacophony of chirps, trills, and distant roars filled the air. The cave was dimly lit with morning sun. Sparks of amber still danced among the remnants of the fire we had. Its small heat provided a comforting warmth against the chilly air. I glanced around to see there was no sign of our new alien friend. "Where's Sol?"

The lion bent forward, stretching out his back legs before shaking his head. "He left much earlier. Said he would be back as soon as he finished hunting down something called the Gruulorak." Walking toward the front of the cave, he inclined his head and grinned. "By hunt, I mean you and me. You won't let me eat Sol and I already promised I wouldn't eat you. Normally I just do it myself, but I don't know the area and this leg is still giving me trouble," he said, shaking out the leg still wrapped in bandages. "So I suggest you help me hunt so I can keep that promise."

"Right," I said. "Let me just . . ." I trailed off, trying to gather my thoughts without the helping guide of coffee or energy drinks. "Damn, I don't exactly have a toothbrush or change of clothes. All right, whatever. Let me just grab my phone." Still feeling a bit unsteady, I managed to stand on wobbly legs. As I did, the lion paced back and forth, his tail swishing impatiently. His amber eyes flicked between me and the dense jungle beyond the cave entrance.

"Finally, let's go," Toto said.

I followed him out of the cave, pulling out my phone and opening a recording app. I pressed the big red RECORD button and held the phone up to my mouth. "Captain's Log, Day 2."

My companion turned back to me. "What did you call me? I thought my name was Toto."

"Hmm? Oh, not you. I'm making a captain's log of what we see here in case we get rescued."

The lion looked at the phone, confused for a moment, before deciding it wasn't worth the trouble. "You humans are strange. Just keep it down so you don't scare off any prey."

"I'll do my best," I said. Deleting the old recording, I started again. "Captain's Log, Day 2. My location is still unknown. We walked at least ten miles away from the crash site. No new sightings of any birdlike aliens. Contact has been made with a local from a species called the Sankado."

"He's not local, remember," Toto cut in. "They got brought here just like we did by the sour birds."

"Right, thank you." I corrected the statement and detailed the species I had seen the day before. With no way of knowing whether or not I'd get back to Earth, keeping a log made me feel like I was doing something. If I did get back, no one would believe the things I'd seen, so I made a note to take several pictures. After some convincing, I got Toto to pose in a selfie with me, which would immediately become my profile picture on every social media platform if I was returned home.

As we moved deeper into the jungle, the dense foliage became thicker, obscuring our view and making each step more challenging. Toto gracefully maneuvered through the tangle of vegetation, his movements fluid and deliberate. In comparison, my attempts to keep up with him looked more like a drunkard stumbling along.

Suddenly, Toto stopped in his tracks, his ears twitching as if picking up a distant sound. Instinctively, I slowed my pace, mirroring his alertness.

Without warning, Toto veered to the right past a cluster of bushes and out of sight. I climbed through as well, just to see him melt into the grassy clearing on the other side. His powerful body blended seamlessly with the tall grass. I followed closely, my eyes darting around, searching for any signs of danger. The grass tickled my legs as I pushed through, my heart pounding with a mix of excitement and anticipation.

But just as I was about to catch up to Toto, my foot caught on an unseen root hidden beneath the thick vegetation. I stumbled forward, my arms flailing, before I landed on the ground with a soft thud. The fall knocked the wind out of me, leaving me breathless.

When I moved to get up, Toto rushed to my side and put a paw on my head. "Stay down, there's food." His low voice came out hushed as his eyes remained transfixed on something ahead. "You're smaller and weak, so I'll deliver the killing blow. Flank it and scare it toward that large tree in the center."

Peering through the grass, I finally spotted what had caught his attention. What looked like a cotton ball mixed with a young stegosaur grazed peacefully halfway across the clearing. "What in the world . . . ? Is that stegosaur covered in wool?"

"Hush," Toto snapped. "Haven't you ever hunted before? I know humans eat meat. Listen up, lazy thing. I won't coddle you, so learn quickly. Swing wide around the grassy side. You'll be easier to spot against the trees. Charge at it from behind and try to steer it toward me. Go. Watch for rocks as you step." He then slinked off toward the large tree in the center of the clearing.

The squeamish part of me was grossed out at the concept of killing a baby dinosaur; however, the wildlife researcher in me was freaking out. I was hunting with an actual lion. A lion who was telling me how he hunted and why. My mind raced, trying to commit everything to memory. The little girl inside me who had been obsessed with animals since I could walk was screaming with joy. Unfortunately, the small rational part of my brain that still feared death had my stomach in knots.

Even though the calf was definitely a lot smaller than the non-fluffy stegosaur I saw yesterday, it was still the size of a donkey at least. Menacing-looking spikes adorned the end of its tail. One good swing and I'd be impaled. On the other hand, if I didn't pull this off, Toto might eat me.

Decisions, decisions.

I sent a silent apology to the fluffy guy and crept around him. The calf poked its head up to survey its surroundings and I ducked down. When its head sank below the grass to continue grazing, I charged. Yelling loudly, I flailed my arms over my head, trying to scare the thing toward the aforementioned tree.

The calf stumbled and ran. With an unexpected burst of energy, I charged after it. But just as I closed in, my foot landed on something soft, causing me to falter midstride. Before I could get my bearings, pain shot through my leg, and I found myself abruptly yanked backward, suspended in midair.

I let out a cry of surprise as I realized I'd been caught in a snare. The branch holding the rope creaked under my weight. "Are you fucking kidding me?" I screamed. "Poo on a stick! It's just one thing after another with this stupid planet."

Behind me, I heard a snarl and a dying cry cut short. Flailing, I was able to spin around to see Toto holding the calf by its neck. Damn, he was really good at that. I rubbed my own neck in silent solidarity with the now dead calf. "Better you than me, Fluffy."

Toto released his hold on his kill and tilted his head at me. "Whatcha doing up there, buddy?"

"Oh, shut up and get me down."

Laughing, Toto circled around me as he tried to figure out the trap. "What did I say about watching where you stepped?"

"You said watch for rocks. Not stupid traps!"

His lips pulled back into a Cheshire grin. "It was heavily implied."

Something rustled in the trees and we froze. "What was that?" I asked, the hair on the back of my neck beginning to rise.

Toto scanned the dense foliage, tensing when a twig snapped.

I swallowed the lump in my throat. "Toto. Toto, get me down."

"Right." Standing up on his hind legs, Toto grabbed me by the pant leg and pulled me to him. His sharp claws dug through the fabric, making me wince. The lion pulled me farther down until the branch arched.

In the distance, I could hear the rustling move closer.

Heart pounding in my chest, I reached for my ankle and tried to untie the knot. The damn thing must have been tied by this planet's most anal-retentive Boy Scout. It was so tight I couldn't even get a good grip on it. "Toto, hurry," I said.

The lion bit the rope, trying to slice through it. "I'm trying," he said.

"The rope's too thick; just untie it," I said, voice frantic.

"Woman, do I look like a mammal with opposable thumbs? Quit thrashing!" He bit down harder, shaking his head like he meant to snap the neck of a gazelle. The movement only caused me to bounce around.

My stomach rolled, and I nearly tossed up the meager biscuit I'd had the night before. "Oh god, I'm gonna be sick."

"This thing is more stubborn than a water buffalo. Break, damn you!" He gave another shake, pulling me close enough to the ground that my fingers could touch the tall grass.

"Denalbu!" came a deep voice.

Toto released the rope and looked toward the voice, sending me flying when the branch holding the end of the rope snapped back upright. "Fuck!" I cursed, flailing around.

"Oh, sorry," Toto said.

When my dizzied vision began to clear, I caught sight of a horned figure walking toward us. Blinking rapidly, I squinted, trying to make him out against the sun. "Sol?"

The large man approaching us was definitely a Sankado, but it sure as hell wasn't Sol. He was bigger. Deliciously so, with a face that made me think there was a conspiracy going on where all aliens on this planet had to be unfairly hot. Maybe I'd just been single too long.

While Sol's horns arched back like an ibex's, this alien sported a large pair of horns that twisted around. The base of his horns was decorated with red lines that matched the red arrow tattooed on his neck. As he drew closer, downcast silver eyes raked over the two of us in obvious confusion. They were framed by curly black hair that fell past broad shoulders. His left ear had a notch missing, as if someone had sliced through the pointed tip. His skin was dark purple, with freckles of yellow dotting along his shoulders before disappearing beneath his shirt. Two sets of sashes came over his shoulders to form a loincloth that fell past his knees, held firmly in place by a thick belt displaying various knives and trinkets. A spear with colorful feathers adorning the top of its shaft was strapped firmly to his back.

"Get away from her!" Toto snarled and took a swipe at the newcomer, who leapt away.

The Sankado muttered something in his native tongue and pulled out a knife from his belt. "Oh shit," I breathed. The man grinned before he twirled the knife through his knuckles and took a step forward. Which would have been unbearably sexy, if he wasn't about to murder my lion.

"No, no, stop!" I yelled. Both Sankado and lion paused to look back at me.

"What?" Toto snapped.

"Don't snarl at him like that; we don't even know if he's friendly yet. He could just be here to help."

Toto looked at the newcomer, then back to me. "He has a tiny spear."

"A knife, Toto. He has a knife. And he only drew it after you swiped at him. Gimme a chance to see what he wants before you try disemboweling him."

A petulant huff. "But I want to."

"Are you kidding me?" I asked, voice rising with growing indignation. "Why, man, why do you want to disembowel him?"

"Defending my kill, protecting you, the simple thrill of a fight to the death? I'm a fucking lion, take your pick."

I let out a breath, trying, and failing, to rein in my ever-growing hatred for this damn planet. "You know what? I'm just going to ignore you," I said firmly.

"How dare—"

"Hush," I snapped. I waved at the Sankado and did my best to sound friendly. "Hey there, stranger. Sorry about my friend; he's a little cranky without his breakfast. Do you mind lowering that knife?" I asked, then pointed to the blade and made a motion of tossing an invisible knife away from me.

He raised a brow at me and slowly lowered his knife, waiting for my reaction. "Yes!" I said, smiling. "If we could all just calm down, and maybe, ya know. Cut me down, if it's convenient. I'm sure we could all work this out."

The Sankado approached me, his silver eyes piercing through mine as he inspected me. I hung there, suspended in the snare, feeling vulnerable and exposed. The weight of his gaze made me squirm uncomfortably, and my ankle chafed against the ropes that held me captive.

He grabbed hold of my leg and raised his knife to the rope. Just as I braced myself for the imminent fall of being cut down, the Sankado's attention shifted. His eyes darted toward something in the distance. Before I could fully comprehend what was happening, a sudden explosion rocked the air.

A fiery projectile slammed into the Sankado's shoulder, knocking him off-balance and sending him sprawling away from me. I watched in shock as he tumbled through the air, his body crashing into the underbrush with a thud.

Sol came sprinting out of the trees. His tail rose and a whooshing came through the air. Each of the black spots running down its length glowed a fiery orange before he shot a fireball across the field.

I coughed at the trail of smoke behind it. Sol came to stand in front of me, staring daggers into the small brush fire containing his fucking murder victim.

"Dammit, I can't leave you alone for a second, can I?" Sol growled. "I knew I should have kept you tied up. Why did you leave the cave?"

Goose bumps raced along my arms. An icy chill touched my heart as his words sank in. "Oh fuck, you're a psychopath. You didn't take us to that cave to save us; you took me there to trap me for some Stockholm syndrome–type shit."

The psychopath had the audacity to look back at me as if I was the problem. Which frankly did not help his case. I know a murderous gaslighter when I see one. "Did you bash your head against that tree when you stepped in his snare?" he asked. "I don't even know what a Stockholm is."

"That's just what a crazy stalker would say. Right before they kept you locked in a storage unit, like that one guy did on the last episode of *True Crimes and Wine Times*. Dammit, I'm not into this. This is not my kink at all. I do not consent. Cut me down! But get away from me. Cut me down and get away from me!"

He shook the smoke off his hands and pulled a knife from his belt. He grabbed my leg and began sawing through the rope. "You make an incredible number of demands for a woman in constant need of saving."

"You just murdered someone in front of me!"

"He's not—" His words were cut off when the other Sankado rammed into him, knocking him back.

The stranger stood, then looked down at me with a grin.

In a fluid motion, he cut my leg free and flipped me upright to stand beside him. I stumbled to get my balance, then yelped when he pulled me to rest against him. He nodded toward Sol and asked me some kind of question.

"Right, this is gonna seem weird, but bend down, I need to kiss you." I reached up to grab the back of his head and pulled him to me. His brow rose, but he didn't protest. Just before our lips touched, Sol yanked me back by my shirt.

"Stay behind me," he barked, then took a swing at the stranger, who blocked his blow. Sol snarled, and his tail lit up. Sparks ignited in his palms. "What are you doing this far inland? You know this is Night Ridge territory."

The stranger snorted and waved around the clearing before barking something back at Sol. It must have been an insult, as the next thing I knew, the two were trading blows. The larger stranger clearly had the physical advantage, and Sol was sent flying by another headbutt. Undeterred, he used his superior speed to lob fireballs at the guy before darting farther back out of his reach.

Sol fired another shot at the stranger, catching him right in the chest. Smoke spilled around him, blocking him from my view. When Sol pushed away to catch his breath, a hand shot out of the smoke and grabbed him by the tail. With a roar, the stranger slammed him hard into the ground.

"Can . . . can we just talk about this?" I asked. My plea fell on deaf ears as the two began trading blows again. "Hello?" I asked. Instead of answering, Sol tripped the larger man and began punching him repeatedly in the face. I threw my hands up. "All right, fine!" I walked over to them, slapped Sol's fist out of the way, and kissed the stranger.

"What are you doing?" he snapped. "I told you to stay back. You can't trust a Roamcrest."

I crossed my arms but took a few safe steps back. "Well, I told you two to stop. Clearly, we both have issues following directions."

His eye twitched. "Will you just get back to the damn cave? I'm trying to protect you."

"Protect her from what?" the stranger asked. "All I was doing was cutting the poor thing down. You're the one that attacked me in neutral territory."

"This isn't neutral land. The Night Ridge clan's territory—"

"Ends at the Fujilly Rock." The stranger laid his head down against the ground and pointed a finger at a boulder with words painted on it in red. From the look on Sol's face, I'd guess it said "Fujilly Rock."

Sol cleared his throat. "Well, it seems I've made a mistake."

The stranger pulled his hands behind his head and relaxed, crossing one leg over the other. "So, are you just gonna get comfortable up there? I'll admit, I was hoping to convince that enticing creature there," he said, nodding to me, "to share a meal with me. But if she'd prefer an entourage, I'll make room."

I looked back and forth between Sol and the stranger, feeling the tension in the air dissipate as they both seemed to realize their misunderstanding. Sol released a deep breath and stood up, brushing the dirt from his clothes. The flames on his tail subsided, returning to their dormant state.

"I apologize for the confusion," Sol said, taking a step closer to me. His height blocked my view of the stranger, who blatantly walked back into my view. "My name is Sol, from the Night Ridge clan."

The stranger's eyes flicked back to Sol, then he grinned. "So I've gathered, Sol from the Night Ridge clan. Now that we've established that—" He shoved Sol out of the way and knelt in front of me, taking my hand in his. His hand was shockingly smooth. Like how you'd think the hands feel on those lotion commercials where the women are always smiling as if they'd just found the fountain of youth. "Hello there, my name's Lokbaatar, but you can call me Lok. Tell me, gorgeous, are you the one that fell from that star?"

"Star? Oh! The space pod, yes, that was Toto and me."

He grinned wide. "It seems wishing stars do exist. Tell me your name, Stardust."

What kind of isekai shit is this? I wasn't sure how many laws of nature I was breaking by being attracted to aliens, but his grin was a little sexy. "I'm Do—"

"She's just leaving," Sol cut in, then snagged me by the wrist and all but dragged me away from the man.

As Sol dragged me away from Lok, I stumbled along, trying to free my wrist from his tight grip. "Sol, wait! What are you doing?"

Sol didn't respond immediately, but his grip tightened even further, causing a sharp pain to shoot up my arm. He finally stopped, turning to face me with a stern expression. "Do you have any idea who that man is? He's a Roamcrest, Do—"

"I don't care if he's a Roamcrest or a unicorn from outer space," I interrupted, my patience wearing thin. "Let go of my damn wrist; you're hurting me."

Immediately, he let go, instead placing a hand on my back to ensure I kept moving. His body tensed, and he narrowed his eyes at me. "I apologize for grabbing you too roughly; there's no need to pinch me."

"I didn't."

A puzzled expression settled on his face before he looked down at his butt, his eyes widening in horror as he noticed a small dart protruding from his rear. He reached and plucked it out. Confusion turned to anger as he quickly turned his accusing gaze toward Lok. "You shot me with a dart?"

Lok wasn't paying attention to him. Instead, the larger alien was crouched low, eyes trained on something in the trees. His body tensed before he darted toward me and tackled me to the ground.

CHAPTER 5

I FELT A RUSH OF AIR PASS ABOVE US; THE SCENT OF COTton candy followed. A dart lodged itself in Lok's shoulder, right where I was just standing. My heart raced as I realized Lok had taken the hit meant for me.

"There's something in the sky," Lok shouted. I tried looking up, but he tucked my head under his arm, then hoisted us both up, sprinting toward the trees. He set me down once we were out of the clearing and pulled his spear from his back holster.

Sol's spots lit up as he scanned the sky. Something blurry floated past the tree with the snare. "There!" I shouted, pointing to it. Toto leapt up to smack it. A loud tink of claw on metal rang through the air. For a brief second, a sliver of gray appeared in the sky, then flickered away. The blur sped toward us, veering when Sol shot at it.

"What is that thing?" I shouted. Lok's eyes were locked on the approaching blur, his grip on his spear tightening. He positioned himself in front of me, ready to defend us both.

"I don't know," Lok replied, his voice steady and focused. "But it looks like it's got designs on you."

As the blur drew closer, I noticed the side where Toto had hit it glitch and shudder. It looked like a small space saucer. Lime-green lights flickered in a row along the middle, like the dashboard on my Nissan when it was time to change the headlights, its sleek metallic surface marred with the jagged lines of claw marks. The saucer weaved through the trees, narrowly missing branches as it closed in on us.

Lok aimed his spear, gauging the saucer's movements. He waited for the perfect moment, his body coiled with tension. As the spacecraft veered toward us, he threw his spear with precise accuracy. The weapon sailed through the air, striking the saucer's claw-marked side. A loud boom echoed through the forest as the saucer faltered, losing its cloaking ability.

The once-invisible vessel now shimmered into view, revealing its sleek and compact design. It began to spiral out of control, hurtling toward the ground. The sounds of snapping branches and breaking twigs filled the air as the saucer crash-landed, skidding across the forest floor like a skipping stone until it came to a stop.

Silence enveloped the clearing as we cautiously approached the crash site. Smoke billowed from the wreckage, obscuring our view. As the smoke cleared, a small hatch on the craft opened, and a tiny, electric-blue-colored Owlish emerged. He stood no taller than a foot, his large lime-green eyes blinking rapidly as they adjusted to sunlight. Several feathers fell from his wings as he fluttered out of his wrecked space pod and onto the ground. He shook himself out, then froze. The crest of darker feathers on his head fell flat against his skull. Slowly, the Owlish looked at the four of us before scrambling away. Toto slapped a paw down on the Owlish's tail feathers, holding him in place. The bright creature squawked, desperately trying to flap away.

Lok spoke up first. "What should we do with him?"

Toto licked his chops. "I say we should—"

"Toto, don't you dare say 'eat him,'" I deadpanned.

"It's a valid solution," he protested.

Stepping around the bits of broken spacecraft, I picked up the frantic Owlish and waved toward the calf the lion had taken down before. "You go eat; we'll handle this."

"Humph, fine," he said, before slinking off to his kill.

I held the tiny creature up to my face for a moment, assessing his sharp beak. The smell of cotton candy rolled off him, as if I was standing in the middle of a state fair. "Can you understand me?" I asked.

His eyes shifted in between mine. The feathers along his head flicked, but he made no move to speak.

"I'll take that as a no."

Sol peered over my shoulder. "Did the ones on the ship talk to you?"

"Not *to* me. But I could understand them after this blue goop got in my hair." I turned my attention back to the alien. "Hey, say something." I demanded.

The alien's only response was more prolonged eye contact.

"All right, maybe the translator has to be a two-way street. You better not bite me," I warned, then gave the alien a quick kiss. Wide green eyes stared back, unblinking. A sharp sting hit my leg, and I looked down to a dart in my thigh. The gun in the Owlish's tiny hand trailed wisps of smoke. "You little shit, you shot me!"

His beak fell open, and he emitted a frantic series of hoots. The bird's body seemed to shrink in my hands as his feathers fell flat. His neck elongated, as did his feet, while he continued his distressed hooting. Startled, I released the creature and backed up. "Get away from him," Sol shouted, grabbing me by the waist and pulling me to him.

"What the hell is he doing?" I asked, clinging to him.

Lok trained his spear on the creature, taking a cautious step forward. "Maybe we should just kill him."

The Owlish fluttered his wings at that, frantically hopping up and down and looking around. Slowly, his hoots and trills formed into words. "Hoo, hoo, hooo, fuck this is bad! This is very, very not good at ALL!"

"At least he can talk now," I said, relaxing a little. When the frantic blue thing continued hopping around screaming about how not good the situation was, I snapped my fingers in front of him to get his attention. "Hey, do you want to fill us in on what is so *not good* about the situation? What the hell is going on?"

He froze, somehow getting even skinnier and taller before he slowly turned his head around to look at me. "You can understand me." He shuddered.

"Yeah, it seems to happen when I kiss someone. I think it might have to do with this blue goop I spilled on myself while I was on your ship. Unless you guys implanted me with a translator chip or something?" I was never that big into sci-fi, but it seemed like a reasonable thing for an alien to do. You know, after they went around kidnapping innocent researchers.

The little bird turned his body around to face the same direction as his head. Then he approached the three of us, looking between Lok, Sol, and me with a wide-eyed, fearful expression. He swallowed thickly, then tilted his head up at Lok. "H-hello?"

Lok raised an eyebrow. "Hello."

His body shuddered before he fell to his back, wings akimbo. "You're a class A species," he said, voice hollow. "Not animals at all, you're a class A species. Stars above, the war crimes we've committed. The Galactic Federation is gonna have our heads. I'm going to get demoted to a waste collector, if the natives don't just kill me first."

Getting up, he paced back and forth, then shook his head so hard I feared he might pop it off. "I do not have the necessary training to handle a first-contact debrief with class A species." He froze, then dove into the wreckage of his ship. "Give me a moment, my com might have survived the crash," he said. Bits and bobs were tossed out of the craft in his frantic dumpster dive.

The Owlish snapped upright. His bright feathers puffed up until he resembled a distressed cotton ball with eyes. "No!" he cried, getting to his feet. Whirling around, he threw a metal ball on the ground. Its cracked screen revealed a web of fractured lines, mirroring the shattered hopes of the alien. With deep breaths, the Owlish snapped his attention back to us. Straightening his back, he waddled a few steps closer.

Clawed hands tapped nervously against his thighs. After a moment's hesitation, he lifted his beak to speak. "Hello, alien life-forms, I am a behavioral observation intern with the Biodiversity Conservation Initiative. I hail from a species called Biwban and . . . and . . ." He trailed off. The gears churning in his mind were practically visible as he tried to remember the rest of the practiced speech.

He broke in seconds. "None of this was my fault, you hear me? It was the director! He's the one embezzling our research funds to fund his stupid private estate. All I did was follow the data; in the data sheet you were a class C species completely nonrespondent to our language symbionts."

Lok elbowed Sol, gesturing to the panicked Biwban. "Any idea what he's going on about?"

"No idea," Sol replied. His face hardened as he reached down and grabbed the Biwban, bringing him up to his face. "Why don't you slow down and start from the beginning. When you're done, we'll consider what to do with you then."

His feathers went flat; the long, purple-tinted tail feathers shook. "Please, I'm just an intern," he begged. "I swear to you, I didn't have anything to do with the ship that destroyed your planet. My only task was to retrieve Subject 4 and bring her to the soft-release enclosure with the other females. But with two strong males already with her, I figured I'd take a chance and see if either of you would respond to the Nexus serum."

"Whoa, slow down. You're the ones that destroyed our planet?" Lok asked.

"Not me specifically. A Fuel X cargo ship laden with Voxen took a shortcut through a less-regulated part of the Pullvaton galaxy and was attacked by marauders. The ensuing battle caused the ship to veer off course and crash-land into one of your planet's oceans. Unfortunately, while Voxen can be turned into some of the purest fuel in the galaxy, its crude form is highly toxic when exposed to water. And, well . . . I'm sure I don't need to explain to you the details of what happens to the surrounding wildlife when that occurs."

Sol tightened his grip, and the intern's words became rushed. "But, I assure you, as soon as we noticed the crash, our government demanded that Fuel X pay for the necessary repairs, and we were able to fund a conservation corporation to save what we could of your planet's species and relocate you here to a newly terraformed world. Had we known that Krydon 4 was home to a class A species, the transport of

Voxen would've never been approved so close to it. Fuel shortage or not."

I narrowed my eyes on him. "Wait a minute. That substance is so volatile that you don't allow it to even travel *near* planets with sentient species?"

"Of course not," he chirped. "That would be incredibly dangerous. If a company wants to transfer dangerous chemicals outside of normal preapproved shipping routes, then they are required by law to test each planet within two parsecs of its route for a class B species at least."

"And you trusted companies to do this?" Sol spoke up. "You trusted the company that wanted to make money off the shipment of a dangerous chemical to properly test each planet for sentient life-forms and hope that, what—?" He paused, twirling a hand in the air around him. "That they would just follow the law instead of simply saying they found nothing to save money? That's the reason our planet was destroyed?"

Anger rolled off him like steam, causing the intern to retreat farther back. "Again . . . I am just an intern. Meaning I had nothing to do with that."

"Then why am I here?" I asked.

"Well . . . our field team didn't have a lot of time to study the Sankado species before we had to make the grab, so they made an educated guess on which specimens would have the highest chance for survival and only picked the largest 30 percent. They assumed that much like our own species, sexual coloration indicated which of you were females, not sexual dimorphism, and only males ended up being rescued. We ran a scanner through our database and found that human females could be a compatible replacement when given a few modifications."

"You modified me?" I screeched.

He shook, twisting his way out of Sol's grip to flutter onto a fallen branch outside my striking distance. "Just enough for you to be able to reproduce with them! We used our time displacer to only take females that were near death anyway; your disappearance shouldn't affect your planet any more than your natural death would."

My natural death . . .

The air rushed from my lungs. Across the field, Toto tore apart the fallen calf. The sound of tearing flesh filled the air as the lion's powerful canines ripped into the carcass. He burped, making my stomach drop. That was supposed to be my fate.

I'm supposed to be dead.

Feeling hollow, I looked around the new world, suddenly realizing I wouldn't wake up from this terrible dream. Even without the alien interference, I never would have finished my internship. I never would have gotten my PhD. All that hard work just to end up another sad blip on the news. My heart felt like a heavy stone in my chest. I wanted to fall to the ground and scream. Demand to know why my life was always reduced to another failure, why nothing could ever just go right for once. Yet even so, my tears refused to come. Not in front of a crowd. The one strength my mom succeeded in giving me.

I swallowed the lump in my throat and reached for that never-ending well of curiosity that always itched in the back of my mind and asked, "Why dinosaurs?"

The intern tilted his head. "You mean the animals we took from your planet? We sent a research team to gather DNA from your planet to re-create your natural habitat the best we could. Luckily, your planet stored a wide range of specimens in a few buildings they found."

My head fell to my hands. “Where did they get the DNA from?” I asked, already dreading the answer.

He waved a wing, and the space behind it warped into a screen. “Let me check my notes. I should have a few pictures,” he said, flipping through pages of alien scribbles.

Pictures of familiar museums came onto the screen, each one sinking a knife farther into my gut. “Are you joking?” I bit out. “Those are the Academy of Natural Sciences of Drexel University, the American Museum of Natural History, and the Wagner Free Institute of Science.”

“Oh, you know them?” he asked curiously.

Bringing my hands up to my face, I prayed for the strength not to drop-kick that fucking bird. “Yes, all of them are museums relatively close to the college I used to go to,” I began. Breathing deep, I tried to rein in the growing anger in my voice. “All museums that have a focus on *dinosaurs*.” I stressed the last word, failing spectacularly at keeping my anger in check.

The intern seemed to notice the change and fluttered to another branch a little farther back. His voice warbled as he spoke. “Are dinosaurs not animals from your planet?” His eyes widened as a look of realization crossed his face. “We made sure not to re-create any venomous animals we found. I assure you we’ve taken great lengths to ensure that this world is full of abundant resources for your species. We’ve even created a few more fruit trees with higher nutrients. Our research shows that humans love sweet fruit—”

“Intern, I don’t care about your stupid fruit,” I snapped. “Dinosaurs may be creatures from our planet, yes, but they were millions of years before the time of humans. We have no defenses against dinosaurs. Have you seen them? They’re massive! You say you made this planet with the ease of humans in mind. Yet I walked around this stupid planet for miles. Where is the damn grocery store? Hmm? Tell me, Intern, where is Target?"

He shifted uncomfortably on his perch. "Do humans require target practice?"

I lost my internal battle and raged. "I don't want target practice. I want a grocery store. Fully stocked with food I don't personally have to hunt down and kill. How long did you idiots even study humans?"

His tail feathers shaking, his answer came out in almost a whisper. "Well, what you have to understand is that we were very short on time because of the cost of fuel. Our initial funding was allocated for a month at least. But the director kept funneling our grant money into these useless state-of-the-art features for the research center. By the time we reached your planet, most of our funds were gone. Each day on Earth required a tremendous amount of fuel in order to operate the cloaking feature and the time-manipulation device; don't even get me started on how much energy the stasis pods take up."

"Intern, how long was your research period?"

". . . Three Earth days."

"Lok," I called, turning to him. The man snapped to attention as if he feared I'd turn my wrath on him. "Give me your spear. I'll kill him myself."

The Biwban grew frenzied, almost falling off his perch in his attempt to get away after I snatched the weapon. Just before he landed on his face, he remembered he had wings and corrected himself before hopping farther away from me. "Subject 4, please remain calm!"

"DORY."

"Yes!" he half screamed back. "Dory, my apologies. If you need a target, I'm sure we could help build you one."

"I don't want a target," I hissed through clenched teeth. "I want to go home. NOW, INTERN."

He flattened himself against a tree, whimpering when the spear brushed against the feathers of his belly. "And trust me Sub—Dory, I'd love to do that for you. But . . ."

I pressed the spear into his belly, not enough to break the skin, but enough to make him shiver. "But *what*?"

"We . . . we just don't have the funding for that."

For a moment, we just stared at each other. Then I lowered the spear. He sighed in relief.

"Toto," I hollered over my shoulder. "Get over here; we're eating him after all."

The intern screamed as he jumped, using the tree trunk behind him to spring higher over my head. The dash to freedom was squashed when Sol snatched him up like a rag doll.

"If you are not responsible for the destruction of my planet, tell me who is," Sol snarled through clenched teeth. His gaze narrowed with an almost predatory intensity. The Biwban trapped in his grip shook, as if he was held by the grim reaper himself.

"I . . . I don't know," said the intern. "Krylix Krynn is the owner of Fuel X, so probably him. I imagine he's off on some pleasure cruiser light-years away from here. But you could talk to his son, Vexil. He's the department head of the BCI."

If looks could kill, the intern would be dead thrice over. "The son of the company president responsible for the destruction of my planet is the HEAD of the department in charge of fixing it?"

"Well . . ."

"No one thought that was a conflict of interest?" Lok spoke up.

His beak quivered as he spoke. "Listen, as much as I'd love

to give you answers that don't get me killed, I can't. This isn't even a paid internship. I'm just here for job experience."

Hmm. That hits close to home.

Sol pulled a knife from his belt and held it to the intern's throat. "Try harder. I don't see the son of this company head in front of me. I see you. And I've got a lot of anger to take out right now."

As much as I understood his rage, as a fellow intern, my heart went out to the little bird. Moving to Sol's side, I placed a hand on his arm. "Sol, why don't we all take it down a notch?"

My gaze fell to my hand on his arm. Noticing the firm muscle underneath, I gave it a little squeeze. His enthralling scent hit my nose like a beckoning finger. Its gentle warmth tingled across my skin, settling into a pleasant thrill that had my toes curling.

Fuck, he feels good. Nope, nope, focus. Remember the last gym rat we dated. Sexy muscles are always attached to narcissistic cheaters.

Jerking my hand away, I reached over to pluck the Biwban from his murderous grip. Sol's tail flicked behind him, ready to lash out at any provocation. The muscles in his neck and shoulders visibly tensed when I took the intern in my hands.

"Put him down. I don't enjoy seeing you hold him," he said with a measured tone.

I narrowed my eyes at him, ready to tear him a new asshole for ordering me around. The Biwban shifted uncomfortably, his eyes darting between Sol and me. Then he placed a hand on my arm and craned his neck to give me a pleading look. "Please put me down. I don't want to be touching his mate when the serum takes effect."

For once in my life, I had no words. I stared at the little

blue alien, dumbfounded, before finding my voice again. "I'm sorry, his *what*?"

Sparks erupted from Sol's tail, causing the intern to squawk and thrash his way out of my arms. He darted behind Lok, who was just staring at me with a dopey look on his face.

Sol stepped in front of me, blocking Lok's gaze. In an instant, the larger Sankado's demeanor shifted. His easygoing posture faded as he stiffened, glaring at Sol.

"Why do you keep looking at her like that?" Sol asked. "She's already been cut down. I'll take it from here. Be on your way."

"Sol, what the hell?" I asked.

Lok didn't back down. Instead, he stood taller, using his superior height to dwarf Sol before flashing a wicked grin. "Awfully pushy, aren't we? Why don't we let the lady decide who she wants to go with?"

Right before my eyes, Sol's body seemed to grow a little bigger. The horns adorning his head elongated. A bioluminescent golden stripe appeared to run down their length, stopping in a band at the base.

I backed away from him. "What in the world?"

"I won't tell you again, Roamcrest," Sol growled. "Leave."

Lok's smile grew, showing off long canines as he, too, grew bigger. His ram-like horns grew long enough to coil at the end, before silver bands crisscrossed down their length. "Why don't you try and make me?"

"Can we not do whatever macho shit this is?" I asked, holding up a hand.

Behind Lok, the Biwban trilled excitedly. "Oh, this is excellent!"

"What is excellent about this? They look like they're about to kill each other!"

Lok chuckled and boldly stepped around Sol to come to my side. The rings on his horns seemed to pulse. On most people it might have looked ridiculous. But something about when it was combined with those teeth and that big burly form was making me question why I ever sullied my body with whatever the hell I thought was sexy when I was stupid and twenty. He smiled, taking the strength out of my knees. "No need for the concerned face, gorgeous. I'll be fine."

Gods, he was a big gorgeous beast of a man. His maddening scent wrapped my mind in a fog of lust until I had to fight the urge to drop to my knees and beg for a taste of his cock.

Fuck, I want him so raw.

I shook my head, trying to clear my thoughts. Yet the motion only drew Sol to me.

"Are you all right?" He reached up to touch my face, then paused, his hand inches away. A tilt of my head would have my cheek in his waiting palm. His fingers twitched before he drew his hand away, balling it into a fist at his side.

Whatever this sudden intense attraction was, he felt it too.

All right, that settles it. I've died and been reincarnated in some stupid anime. If there are any gods at all, please don't make this a full-blown "why choose." Just keep it to us three. Lord, you know I don't have the stamina.

"Hey, Intern, did that serum have something to do with you calling me his mate?"

"Why, yes!" he chirped, obviously having a grand time now.

"It's an aphrodisiac, isn't it?"

"Oh, it's much more than that." His feathers poofed happily as he waved a wing. The space behind it warped into a screen.

"You see, when a Sankado is put under a lot of stress, such

as a near-death experience or a complete exhaustion of the body, their brain triggers—"

"You know what, let me rephrase that question. Based on what you've told us, is it safe to assume this is a breeding program?

"Yes."

"How long do the pairings last?"

"Our records don't show any bonded specimens straying from their union until death."

My legs decided it was time to sit. I scooted back against a tree, resting my arms on my knees. With my nose buried against my pants, I could almost block out the scent of the two men. My *mates.*

"Fuck you, Intern," I hissed.

"Pardon? Our species isn't compatible w—"

"Oh hush! Go somewhere." I waved a dismissive hand at the lot of them. It was all too much. I needed to have a good cry and I couldn't do that with a damn crowd. Waves of unabashed lust rolled through my body. I squeezed my thighs together, trying to ignore my purring pussy. "All of you go somewhere and give me a minute."

Sol took a step closer. "Hold on."

"Sol, I will curse you with my dying breath if you don't give me a fucking minute. Go. Somewhere."

He frowned at me, but Lok grabbed him by the forearm and pulled him away. I watched them go, hating how much I was panting after the broad expanse of Lok's back as he hauled the other man away.

I buried my head in my knees, listening to their retreating footsteps until I was sure I was alone. Then came the tears. I was exhausted, frustrated, and egregiously horny on an alien planet with no way home. Even then, if I wasn't taken to help some alien race with my species-saving coochie, I'd have fucking died in that lion attack.

All my life I'd fought for a place in the world that wasn't under my mother's thumb. Years of meditation, distracting hobbies, endless fad diets, and three sessions of pouring my heart out to a therapist in an attempt to undo the damage of her beauty pageants and the notion that I was only worth as much as the man I'd marry.

The therapist called the hobbies a "Band-Aid" and said that I'd need to do more than crochet my troubles into little giraffes, but their cuteness added extra spice to my application for the Kalahari research program, so what did she know? Hobbies work. That's why I fired her. No respect for the craft.

Just a few more months of that internship and I would have gotten the credits I needed to get my PhD. I came so fucking close, only for it to be ripped away at the finish line. Now what? I was going to be stuck popping out alien babies for two strangers? A part of me felt bad for even mourning my life. Compared to the destruction of an entire planet, my own life felt meaningless.

Maybe it was. But it was still *my* life, and I had the right to mourn it.

Not to mention, I had no idea what that serum was going to do to me, aside from making me ridiculously randy. Both Lok and Sol grew bigger in a matter of minutes. Yet, as far as I could tell, I hadn't grown at all. Not that I wanted to.

A hissing came through the trees, accompanied by rustling leaves and hot breath that blew over my face. "No," I snapped, not bothering to look at whatever ridiculous creature decided to show up this time. "Get lost, I need a minute."

The creature loudly sniffed at my side. Annoyed, I slapped it. "What did I just say?"

It let out a deep huff, and I turned to see a fat bright pink T. rex staring back at me.

Oh shit.

My heart took a leap of faith and shot out of my ass. Endless survival scenarios poured through my head. Make yourself look bigger to a big cat, punch a shark in the gills, shout and make a ton of noise for a grizzly bear. None of which prepped me on what to do when a fucking chonk of an ancient predator sniffs your pants. I glanced to the other end of the clearing, but neither man was looking my way. Instead, they were fighting with each other. If I screamed, they'd never reach me in time.

The colossal beast bent farther down and sniffed my hair. Wild red strands snaked their way up her nose, causing the T. rex to back up and sneeze so hard the folds on her neck jiggled with the force of it. It was then I noticed her right arm was missing. The wound was still scabbed over, meaning it couldn't have been long since she lost it. She rubbed her snout against a nearby tree, glared back at me, then walked off.

When the last of her pink form disappeared back into the trees, my heart rate slowed. Finally alone, I sighed and stared up at the sky. Then I retrieved my phone from my pocket, pulled up the log app, and hit RECORD. "Captain's Log, Day 2. Everything is fucked."

Hitting the END button, I stuffed the phone back in my pocket and let my head fall to my knees. Then I pulled the phone back out. "By the way, T. rexes are pink. Fucking pink. We all had it wrong."

Through my tears, I could see Toto stride up to me. He carried the severed leg of the stegosaur in his mouth before unceremoniously dropping it at my feet. The lion puffed out his chest, brimming with pride. "I saved you a leg," he stated.

I blinked down at the bloody appendage. "So you did." His tail flicked; he was obviously waiting for praise. I obliged. "I've never seen a lion take down an animal so quickly. You must be a mighty hunter."

"I am," he stated matter-of-factly. He scooted the leg closer to me. "Eat. Scavengers will come soon, and your mates are too busy fighting each other to guard the kill."

Sighing, I glanced over to Lok and Sol. The two idiots were bickering about something at the far end of the clearing. Lok caught my stare and smiled back at me, before he was shoved by Sol. Blows came shortly after.

"You know, I'm just not that hungry at the moment. A lot on my mind, ya know?"

"No," he said, coming to sit next to me. "You have two strong males competing for your affections and food you refuse to eat in front of you. What else do you want?"

"An internet connection, coffee, my fucking life back?"

He studied me quizzically. "You are very much alive, Dory."

"That's not it," I groaned, rubbing at my temples. "I just don't know what to do. I spent my life working toward becoming a wildlife biologist and making a name for myself on my own. Everything was going according to plan, and now all that hard work is up in flames. All thanks to an underfunded research department of all things, the irony of which is NOT lost on me!

"I am stuck! Stuck on a crazy, poorly planned planet where I'm probably gonna die via getting eaten by a dinosaur or trying to push out one of their giant horned babies!" Hot tears spilled down my face. The ache in my chest burned as I thought about the life I was supposed to have.

A sudden weight squished into my side, and I nearly fell over. Toto stretched out against me, his big head lolling into my lap as he got comfortable. “Dory, Dory, my constantly chattering friend.”

“Ouch.”

“Stop worrying about what’s going to happen. Think about where we are right now. Think about what we’ve already done. You say you want to make a name for yourself; well, how many humans have swum past a river monster and lived to tell the tale?”

“We almost died, Toto.”

“So what?”

“What do you mean ‘so what’? I don’t want to die.”

The lion snorted. “Everyone dies. You could catch your last drink at the river before becoming a crocodile’s meal. A hunt gone wrong could leave you trampled. Or maybe you become one of the lucky ones that lasts long enough to see your mane turn gray. If you wanna find some meaning to life, then fine, but maybe it’s just not that serious. Look around you; you’ll be all right. We’ve been here less than two sunrises and look at all that’s happened. Even if we die tomorrow, we’ve walked where no one else has and seen more than most do in a lifetime. *If* we live to see tomorrow, great. There will be more to see and do. But for now, at least our bellies are full. Stop worrying about your life’s plan and sunbathe with me. It’s a good day.”

“But I’ve done everything according to my life’s plan.”

He grinned up at me. “Yeah? How’s that working out for you?”

“Not great,” I admitted, scratching his ear. “I just don’t know what to do.”

“For starters, you keep scratching my ear. Next, you can embrace this for what it is: an adventure. Let’s see how far we can get.”

“I strive to be as unbothered as you, Toto.”

He chuffed happily, leaning into my petting. "Everyone should strive to be more like me."

True to his lion nature, Toto had no shortage of self-confidence. I tried to imagine what it must have been like to live one's life so sure of one's place in the world and found myself envying him a little. Even so, I drank in his comfort like a lifeline.

When I was a kid, a large gray tomcat lived in my dad's shed. He was a pissy, half-feral creature that refused any of my many attempts to tame him. He was so wild that my sisters named him Catzilla and refused to go near him. If he weren't so effective at keeping the shed free of mice, I doubt my mom would have hesitated to get rid of him. Yet whenever I was sad, I'd go out to the shed and hide my tears. Without fail, Catzilla would come find me and clamber his big self into my lap and stay there until I couldn't cry anymore.

I ran my fingers through Toto's mane, losing the tension in my shoulders to the soothing rhythm of his breathing. "I'm glad you're here with me, Toto."

"Of course you are. Aside from the obvious, if you don't want to eat, what do you want to do now?"

"Now?" I thought for a moment. "Aside from my growing need to be split like a banana, right now I think I want to find that incompetent department head and punch him right in the face. Then, I don't know, maybe try to steal one of their ships and see if there's an equivalent to Google Maps that can take me back to Earth? Hell. If I managed to get back, I'd probably get a fortune for all the pics on my phone. Not to mention any videos I could get of the aliens." There was no way anyone in my family could look down on my work if I came back with a discovery like this. No one could. Just one video on any news station and I could shut them up forever.

An intoxicating thought.

Though the logistics of that plan grew more abysmal the more I thought about it. "Who am I kidding? I couldn't even figure out how to land one of their escape pods, let alone pilot a stolen ship. Or figure out how to refuel. Are there gas stations in space?"

My head fell. "If nothing else, I'd still settle for punching that asshole in the face."

"Ah, vengeance. Now, that is something I can sink my teeth into. Let's do that."

"Just like that?" I asked, chuckling.

Toto rolled off me and stood. "Why not? You hate him; your bickering mates probably do too. I say we make you a new life plan. You give in to the call of nature and mate with them," he said, nodding to the two fighting Sankado.

"I don't actually want to mate with them!" I protested.

He leveled me with an apathetic glance. "Dory, don't lie to me. Anyone with a nose can smell you're in heat."

"Gross. And bullshit. It's gross, and it's bullshit. I overcame my fear of needles just to get this stupid birth control implant, and now it's"—I paused, running my fingers over my upper left arm where my Nexplanon should be. To my surprise, it was still there. "Hold on." I pressed against the skin, checking the little matchstick-shaped implant for any damage. "No way."

"What way?"

"Oh Mylanta," I said, giggling. "Those idiots didn't take out my implant. I can't get pregnant!"

Toto glanced down at me, searching my face. "Are you happy or sad? It's hard to tell with human faces."

I laughed, thanking the stars above for small miracles. "Happy. Thrilled."

"Good." He nodded. "Then, as I was saying, you give into the call of nature, then we force that sour bird to tell us where the research center is, and we punch the department head right in his feathered face. Then, if you find out if there are gas stations in space, you drive us home. If not, we stay here and run off into the sunset, happily ever after."

". . . I could get behind a life plan like that."

"Yeah?" he asked sweetly. "All right, let's go get you your pride."

CHAPTER 6

GETTING A PEP TALK FROM A LION WAS NOT HOW I EXpected my day to go. Yet Toto made a lot of sense. Chances were, I couldn't go home. This wasn't *The Wizard of Oz*, and tapping my heels together three times wasn't going to fix everything.

Unless . . .

My heels clicked together thrice. Sadly, no whirling tornado came in to take me home.

Shoot.

"Okay, Dory, so your life's gone up in flames. Shit happens."

"Why are you talking to yourself?" Toto asked. "I'm right here."

I pinched the bridge of my nose. "Man, can you just . . . Can I get a sec to get my shit together? This has been a deeply traumatic experience for me."

"All right, fine, look crazy if you want to," he huffed.

"I will."

Toto cast a judgmental side-eye before turning to leave.

"I'll head back to the cave for a nap. Come get me when you're done with your mates."

Now that the weight of pregnancy was off my shoulders, my entire body felt lighter. Almost giddy. Though that could just be the serum convincing me to throw caution (and my panties) to the wind. The ache I felt before was steadily growing into a roaring inferno. Another hour and I'd probably be on all fours howling at the moon for dick. I was still fit to be tied about being trapped in some half-baked alien breeding program. Vengeance was still very much owed.

But at the very least I could blow off steam, so long as my new boyfriends were up for it. A small part of me still held out hope that I'd be able to find a way back home, and I grabbed on to that little bit of hope with the delusional resolve of a mediocre man in an interview for a job he had no business even applying for. If it could work for my old boss, John, it could work for me. If nothing else, I deserved a fun fling full of hot alien sex.

Steeling my resolve, I got up and headed toward them. Sol turned to face me, and even halfway across the field, I felt the gold in his eyes melt into lava. The blood in my veins answered in kind. It started slowly at first, a dull roar that grew louder with each step. Then it was like a fire lit in my belly, desperate and howling to burn its way out, but it couldn't reach my skin. I was cold. So fucking cold I wanted to dive into the heat of both of them and drown.

My tits ached, my breathing sped up, and I couldn't think of anything but Lok and Sol. Sol and that sexy scowl and that tall, lithe body. Lok and that massive frame. I swallowed, trying to fight off the urge to leap onto his shoulders, grab him by the horns, and grind my pussy on his face like a shameless trollop.

"Dory." Sol's breath hitched at my name. He squeezed his eyes shut, running a hand down his face. "Fuck."

"My sentiments exactly," I mused.

Lok slapped a hand on the man's shoulder. "Ah, now look at what you've done, Stardust. You've made the poor man all flustered. Not that I blame him. If your beauty was kept from me much longer, I'm afraid I would have hunted you down."

That . . . probably shouldn't have turned me on. Whatever, blame it on the serum.

Sol scowled and shook off his hand. "She doesn't want to hear your cheap pickup lines."

I kinda do.

"Don't be so threatened, Sol. We can share. Art is meant to be admired, not locked away. Besides—" Lok chuckled, and his narrow flirtatious eyes threatened to eat me alive on the spot. His touch on my side was graceful, like I was something priceless—not a strange woman who crash-landed in a stolen space pod the day prior. "It was more of a promise."

Despite the fire in my veins, I couldn't help but giggle at his words. "You don't beat around the bush much, do ya, Lok?"

He grunted, then traced my lower lip with his thumb. "Some things are worth the rush." His gaze dipped to my lips before flicking back to me. "That thing where you pressed your mouth to mine earlier, I'd like to do it again."

"For the last time, Lok, you can't go rutting her into the grass, so get your hands off her before you lose them." Sol pulled Lok away.

I bit my lip, replaying Toto's pep talk in my head to work up the courage to speak up and go for it. My voice was strained, barely above a whisper. "Actually, I do kinda want to be rutted into the grass, if that's an option."

When the ground didn't open up to swallow me whole at my brash words, some of my bravery returned. "Don't get me wrong, there's like a billion things wrong with this situation. But I know I'm not the only one who's going a little crazy with . . . whatever this serum has done."

The intern piped up. "The Sankado Nexus serum works by targeting a specific brain region called the neurosynaptic cohesion center in the Sankado species. It contains neurochemicals and nanobots that stimulate neural receptors, triggering intense bonding and emotional connections. This process replicates the effects of extreme stress, forging a permanent mating bond between individuals. Additionally, the Sankado bonding process boosts growth-hormone production in the male, resulting in accelerated healing, physical development, and increased size and strength. Simultaneously, the serum's composition activates—"

"THANK YOU, INTERN," I said. My face heated; suddenly the idea of getting eaten by the T. rex didn't seem so bad. "You know what? This is stupid." I turned to walk away.

In an instant, Sol grabbed me by the throat, spun me around, and devoured my lips in a kiss. His touch was electrifying, completely devoid of the restraint I'd seen before. His hunger was palpable, wild and mind-numbingly ferocious.

Practically begging for more of his touch, I moaned, and he used the opportunity to snake his tongue against my own. Its texture was firmer than I was expecting, with ridges lining the top of it. It was at that moment that I realized my life's dream was to have that tongue on my clit.

Lok growled behind me, making me shiver. I felt his large body flush against my back, his fingers fumbling with the waistband of my pants. A groan escaped me when he drew my hair back and traced his tongue along my neck. Impatient, I fumbled with my pants, frantic to get them off and get their hands on me in every which way.

I whimpered as Lok traced his lips up the curve of my neck to whisper in my ear. "On your knees, Stardust."

My knees hit the ground before I could even pretend to have an ounce of remaining feminism. The new position put me at eye level with the bulge in Sol's pants. A part of me wanted to tease him. Trace my fingers along his thighs, just brushing against where he needed me. The rest of me had to touch him; I had to taste him and it had to be right the fuck now.

I buried my nose against him and breathed deep, closing my lips over his bulge and giving it a suck.

Sol gasped, knees shaking, before he fisted my hair. He yanked, forcing me to meet his gaze. The slight pain hardened my nipples. I reached up to stroke them, but Lok knocked my hands out of the way and replaced them with his own. My eyes fluttered closed on a moan as he toyed with the peaks. One big hand came up to rest on my throat, keeping my head locked in place. "Focus, Stardust, he's talking to you."

As if to emphasize his point, Sol gave another sharp tug until I looked back at him. "I need you to tell me you want this," he growled. "Say it, and know I won't stop until we're done if you do."

"Yes," I rasped, contemplating what to name the new river in my panties. "If one of you doesn't start licking my clit soon, I will riot."

A slow grin spread across his face, revealing the sharp canines that poked just slightly into his lower lip. But it was Lok who answered, "Good girl."

Lok slid his hand down my body, exploring the thick expanse of my thigh before coming up to cup my sex. "Don't leave him waiting, gorgeous," he said lazily, kissing my temple. "Let me see how pretty your lips look wrapped around his cock."

Eager hands tugged on the black straps of his pants, lust spiraling me into madness at the sight of the ridged cock beneath. The base flared wide, ending in a fold of skin. Panting, I wrapped my hand around his girth, noticing with no small glee that my fingers didn't touch. Never had I considered myself a size queen, but some things just made a girl happy. I gripped tightly, running my tongue along the ridges lining the bottom of his length, before sucking on the bulge at the base.

"Ah! Yes. Like that, just like that," Sol whimpered.

"Mmm, look at you, gorgeous. You've barely begun and you've already got him simpering beneath your touch." Fed by Lok's praise, my fingers wrapped more firmly around Sol's girth, lust and longing threatening to eat me alive. "Press your thumb against his tip and run your tongue from base to crown. See how he shivers? Fuck, you're so good to him, aren't you?"

I lapped at the bead from the slit of his crown, almost orgasming at the heady taste on my tongue. Sol gasped, his fingers tightening in my hair, guiding my head to take more of him. My tongue wove over the wide flare of his crown before taking in as much of him as I could. He shuddered, the ridges lining the top and bottom of his cock flaring out, making me choke. I drew back, coughing.

"Open, let me fuck your throat. Please." Grabbing my chin, he drew my mouth open with his thumb, like a fish on a hook. He thrust his cock in, slowly feeding each ridge past my strained lips. Just before it became too much, he withdrew, admiring the string of spit conjoining us before whipping it against my lips. Groaning, he thrust back in. “That’s it. What a pretty little mess you are.”

Lok’s fingers dipped just inside my pussy, making me shiver. “Where’s your clit, Stardust? Show me.”

I grabbed his hand and led it to the swollen bud. Just the brush of his thumb had me seeing stars, and I cried out around the cock ravaging my throat. He took over, gliding his thick fingers against my folds before circling my clit. My hips jerked, desperate for release.

“Ahh, this is what my woman needs.” Lok brushed the hair from my face, leaning in as his tail brushed against my inner thigh. “I know you asked for tongue, but you’re taking our mate so well, I can’t help but want to spoil you rotten.”

“Our?” Sol grunted.

“Don’t be difficult.”

The end of Lok’s tail brushed against my folds, and he grabbed it and positioned it over my clit. With a kiss to my temple, he spread my lips with his fingers, settling the end of his tail securely in place.

At least I think that’s what happened. It was hard to tell after the end of his tail latched on and sucked the soul out of my body. I screamed, shoving Sol out of my mouth before my body convulsed. That damned tail, spawned by the devil himself, continued to suck on my clit, prolonging the rapture until I was making noises no living human should make. My hands tried to pull it away; my thighs said, “Fuck you, live fast, die young,” and clamped around it for dear life.

“F-fuck, Lok, I can’t!” I sobbed, grinding helplessly against him.

He hooked a hand around my thigh and flipped me on my back, caging my head in between his arms until all I knew was him. “Oh, gorgeous, I’m not going to give you a choice. Didn’t you hear him before? You'll get no rest until we're good and done." The head of his cock brushed against my weeping pussy. He reached down and fed the thick tip inside me, straining the aching flesh apart for him until I could feel every ridge.

"Do you understand how badly I want to break you? I want you desperate, I want you needy, I want you so well used that you'll never doubt who you fell from the sky for." Lok kept up the pressure on my clit as he fucked me into the ground. Again, I came. He swallowed my scream as I convulsed, slowly pushing his thick cock into my pliant body.

"Oh shit," I whispered, clawing at the grass in an attempt to stave off a third orgasm.

"Get back here," he growled, digging his fingers into my hips. "Isn't this what you asked of me? To rut you into the grass? Take me, gorgeous. See how devoted your mate is."

Shaking, crying, and somehow coming again, I wrapped my legs around my alien and held on for dear life. With a groan, he ground down, brushing against something deep inside that had me screaming his name.

The world spun as he rolled us, lifting me up to bounce on his cock. Strong hands came to spread my ass cheeks before Sol spat against my hole. The first finger was a tight fit, and the man beneath me kept me distracted through rolling waves of pleasure. "Fuck, this hole is way too tight," Sol panted. Something cold poured onto my ass and I looked back to see Sol draining a vial of blue liquid. My skin tingled where it touched. He gathered some of it onto his fingers and slowly worked them inside me. I moaned when the tingling sensation gave way to pleasure. "That's it, let the oil loosen you up for me. I'll take care of you."

My body relaxed and I couldn't help but thrust against

him. He drew back, using his cock to feed some of the cooling liquid into my ass. Throwing the vial aside, he thrust into me with a groan. The small bit of me that was always too chicken to try anal was promptly smacked down by the unshakable greed I felt for the both of them. I needed them both inside me. Needed to take and take from them until the three of us were reduced to nothing but shuddering cries in the wind.

I moaned, relishing the time Lok took to lavish my breasts. His full lips circled the brown nipple into his mouth, the tongue swirling around it until the bud grew painfully hard. He nipped at the other, making me gasp.

The sound was cut short as Sol grabbed me by the throat, pulling me toward him until my back arched. "You're loving this, aren't you?" He chuckled. "Here I was thinking I needed to protect you from him. I see now, we're the ones in danger, aren't we, Dory?"

I only moaned in response.

He answered with a grunt and guided me along his cock. Everything was too much, too full, yet it didn't stop me from rolling my hips each time with his thrusts, working his cock deeper into my ass.

"Yes," Lok breathed. "Look at you, gorgeous, you take us so well."

Sol's fangs brushed against my neck, teasing the vein running along the side, before nipping at my ear. "Fuck, you feel so good. So eager, so obedient." He changed his thrusts to offset Lok, sending my brain into orbit. "Yes . . . say my name. Now!"

A sob escaped my lips before I could even think of protesting. "Sol!"

"Stars above, it feels like you were made for me." Hard thrusts turned to aggressive pounding as he panted.

"Use me," I begged. "Use me." It was too much; it was everything; I wanted to marry and kill them both. I grabbed the tail trapped against me and ground down, screaming as a deep stroke pinned me between my two aliens.

Beneath me, Lok gasped and I felt the base of his cock twitch. It swelled, putting pressure on my clit, and I greedily ground down against it. "Fuck," he panted. Lok dug his fingers into my hips, rocking me against him. He shivered, looking into my eyes with a frenzied plea. "Please, Stardust, I need to knot you."

Need to what? These aliens must have been fucking me stupid, 'cause I coulda sworn he just asked to knot me.

Knot.

Like on a wolf? I had so many questions. I thought they might have descended from herbivores because of the hooves; why would a herbivore evolve a knot? Were they canids? They had fangs, but all I saw Sol eat was a biscuit. Oh, this was gonna drive me crazy.

Before I could ask what he meant, Sol tilted his hips. The new position drove him deeper inside me. My knees shook. Lok's breath hitched, and he bit down on his lip, squeezing his eyes shut. "Please," he begged.

The sight of such a big man quivering beneath me, begging me of all people for release, was beyond addicting. In the morning there would be a million and one questions about the logistics of this. In the moment I could not have given less of a fuck. "Yes," I said, digging my hand into his hair. "Both of you can for all I care. Just don't stop touching me."

Sol cried out, his thrusts fumbling before I felt the base of his cock begin to swell too. A hand gripped my hair before Lok kissed me. My pussy stretched around him, almost painfully straining to accommodate his girth.

"Oh gods," I moaned. "Yes, grind into me just like that." The building white-hot pleasure tore at my insides like a wild animal desperate to get out. Never in my life had I been so full, yet dammit all, the only thought on my mind was *More! Please, don't stop. Fuck me more!*

Sol's warm breath caressed my ear. "Come with me, Dory. Let me feel you break."

I shuddered into a final climax, feeling hot ropes of seed fill both my holes. I made a choked sound before collapsing on top of Lok, my pussy fluttering around his knot as he lazily rocked his hips. Sol shuddered behind me, tracing comforting fingers along my back. He kissed my shoulder before resting on top of me.

Behind us was the faint sound of typing. I tilted my head to see the intern tapping away on a little screen. Rows of blocky-looking text filled the air in front of him before he pressed a button that caused the screen to turn green with a happy little ding.

He smiled brightly, putting the screen away. "Well, this was excellent data!"

My mouth fell open. "Wha . . . Were you watching this whole time?"

"Of course!" The floating screen shifted into a video of the three of us entwined. "This is the first recorded mating of a human and Sankado. Headquarters will want to use this as important training material. On that note, Sol, would you mind leaning back? I'd like to get a clear shot of how your knot fits into her anus. We hadn't planned on that."

"Hmm?" Sol regarded him with a dazed expression. Then, much to my horror, he did as he was asked.

"No, don't listen to him!" I snapped, pulling him forward.

"You know what? Just get off me." I shoved at his chest, but he didn't budge. Frustrated, I whipped around to glare at the intern. "You!"

"Me?"

"Delete that video now!"

"But the data!" he cried, clutching at a particular feather on his wing. The screen shuddered before fading away.

"Fuck your data," I growled. "You are not using my alien sex tape as a training module. Delete it." I gave Sol another shove, but he merely grunted in response. "Would you get off?" I yelled.

"He can't." Lok replied. He lifted his hips, grinding his knot against my inner walls. "I'm afraid we're stuck like this for now, gorgeous."

"This can't be happening."

Sol rested his head on my shoulder. "Do your males not have knots?"

"No!"

He chuckled and asked, "Then why did you say yes?"

Embarrassment heated my cheeks. "I . . . It doesn't matter. How long are we stuck like this?"

The intern peered at one of his feathers before answering. "If my data is correct, it should be roughly ten Earth minutes."

"Great." I sighed. "So what, we all just lie here?"

Lok chuckled, running his warm hands along my thighs. "I take it you aren't much of a cuddler?"

"I'm afraid there's no time for that," Sol said. "We've got company."

I followed his gaze to the tree line. A faint rustling sound reached my ears, barely audible against the stillness of the forest. Then I saw them. "Oh great. Just a couple of glowing yellow eyes. Just what I was hoping for." The forest lit up with yellow. "Perfect. Folks at home, don't worry. They've added more eyes!"

"Who are you talking to?" Lok asked.

"The cameraman for whatever bullshit interstellar reality TV show this is."

One of the creatures in the forest let out a guttural call that seemed to vibrate through the clearing. Soon, its friends responded in a mix of clicks, trills, and hisses, creating an eerie symphony that echoed through the trees.

CHAPTER 7

"RUN FASTER!" I YELLED. MY FOOT CONNECTED WITH THE neck of a velociraptor, sending the dog-sized beast crashing into a tree. Those behind her leapt over their fallen comrade, using their superior speed to gain on Lok.

The big Sankado shifted Sol and me higher, straining the knot still firmly plugged inside me. When I didn't pull free, he cursed and kept running. "I can't!"

The lead raptor hissed, showing off rows of sharp teeth. Sol fed it a fireball, causing its cry to be cut short before its blood painted the remaining three in red. Undeterred, they shot after us.

Lok sprinted toward the painted rock, wincing when a particular step caused me to bump down hard against his balls. "Sorry," I said.

Intern screamed, flailing when a raptor bit off one of his tail feathers. The little bird clung to Lok's hair, desperately trying to hold on. "What do we do?"

“Don’t you have a ray gun or something?” I asked. “Shoot them!”

“You think I have the clearance for that? I told you, I’m just an intern!”

“Both of you shut up. I’m trying to concentrate,” Sol growled. His body heated to a fever pitch, causing warmth to spread up my ass. My stupid insatiable body reveled at the touch and I had to bite my lip to keep from moaning in Lok’s ear.

A ball of fire shot at our pursuers. But the one in the middle dropped low, avoiding the attack. Another launched itself at us, biting down on Lok’s thigh. He cried out, nearly falling before he righted himself. I kicked at the raptor’s side, but it wouldn’t budge. Instead, it closed its eyes to shield them from my blows. Its long talon rose, ready to gut Lok’s side.

I grabbed its foot, cursing when the long talon sank into the back of my wrist. Ignoring the pain, I twisted its foot until its joint popped. The raptor screeched, releasing its hold on Lok. I let go, letting it crash into its packmate.

Sol blasted the remaining one. Its leg blew clean off, sending the beast crashing to the ground with a pained wail. He shot at the two raptors struggling to get up but misfired when Lok jumped on top of the painted rock. He fell back on his ass, breathing heavily. “Sol, take care of the last one,” he panted.

Sol raised his hand and aimed at the raptor charging toward us. Sparks danced over his palm before falling uselessly to the ground.

“Shit,” Lok growled.

“Shit?” I parroted. “Wh-why shit? What’s happening?”

The fire-haired Sankado thrust his hand out again, only to have the same result. “I’m out of fire.”

"You wouldn't be if you hadn't spent so much time trying to incinerate me just for helping Stardust," Lok sneered.

Sol scowled but said nothing. Instead, he pulled a knife from his waist belt. The velociraptor tried jumping up onto the rock but fell short. Its sharp talons raked across the stone with an awful screech. The creature hissed, then looked around before running around to the back side of the rock, where smaller boulders could be used to jump up. It leapt onto the first before turning toward us and shimmying like a cat ready to pounce. It leapt with a shriek, its long talon extended.

I screamed and closed my eyes. A snarl caught my ears, followed by a sickening crunch. I peeked an eye open to see Toto standing next to us, the dead raptor clamped firmly in his jaws.

"Oh, Toto, thank goodness. I thought we were goners. Thank you so much," I said.

The lion preened under the praise, dramatically tossing his kill off the rock. "That was nothing. I once killed four hyenas in one sitting. Those hunchbacked scavengers always think their numbers make them invincible. Just be happy I could hear you screeching halfway to the cave."

"I killed three," Sol grumbled.

"Two," Toto replied.

"No, it was—"

"Two. The one you shot in the leg didn't die." Toto grinned, looking unbelievably smug. "Don't worry, I got it for you."

Sol tensed at my back, glaring at the lion. I patted him on the shoulder. "Ladies, please. You're both pretty, and really good at killing things. Can we relax now?"

"Right, sorry," said Sol.

Toto lowered his head, looking contrite. "Of course. We

were being childish." He lifted his gaze, one corner of his mouth lifting in a smirk. "I am better, though."

"Oh for fuck's sake," I said, giving a test lift against Lok. When I didn't feel stuck, I pulled myself off him, letting his and Sol's cocks slide out of me. Gods, what a mess. I'd give my left tit for a hot shower and a sugar rub. I pinched the bridge of my nose, doing my best to count down from ten instead of screaming my frustrations into the sky. "All right, Intern," I began, putting a hand on my hip. "Where is the research center? I'm assuming it's somewhere on this planet, right? Or are you guys just up there in orbit?"

The little Biwban sat up, twisting his head around to scan the area. "Oh no, an on-the-ground facility is far more cost-effective than a space station. Let's see, I flew past the Gullbaton pass, soooo, ah!" His feathers poofed, and then he scrambled up and pointed to a mountain ridge in the distance. "It's in the valley between those mountains there."

"Right." I cast a glance at Sol and Lok before making my way down the rock. "Goodbye, then."

"What, where are you going?" Sol asked.

"To grab my clothes and then to the research center," I said. "Where else?" I got on all fours and tried to reach the next rock down without falling on my face. "That damn department head needs a good kick in the ass, and I'm going to give it to him." My foot was just a few inches short. I stood up, taking a deep breath before I swung my arms and jumped. Lok caught me by the arm and tossed me over his shoulder. "Hey!"

He jumped off the rock before sliding me down to the ground. "Oh," I said, dusting myself off. "Thank you."

He grinned down at me before sweeping into a bow. "At

your service. Well, lead the way, Stardust. If we hustle, we might just make it there in a few days."

We made our way to the pile of discarded clothes and quickly dressed. "You're coming too?"

Lok hopped up and down as he shoved his leg through his pants. "Of course I'm coming. Did you think I'd leave my pretty mate to fend for herself?"

"Oh" was all I could manage to say. It had been a while since I'd had anything longer than a one-night stand. After breaking up with my cheating ex a year ago, I hadn't had much interest in men and their lies. Well, beyond a good fling, I mean.

"So, you actually wanna try that whole weird serum mate bond? I'm fine now that we got it out of our systems a little." The need to climb him like a tree was still there, lurking somewhere in the back of my mind, but for now at least, I felt sated.

He laughed, crossing his arms over his chest before looking down at me like I'd said something ridiculously funny. "That 'weird serum mate bond' triggered my Zhali. I don't care how it happened. The stars opened up and saw fit to give me a gorgeous woman of my own. You're stuck with me, Dory."

"And a Zhali is what now?" I asked.

Sol finished dressing and dusted himself off. "The Zhali is the call inside all of us that chooses our sacred partner. Normally, it could only be triggered by those willing to face the trial of the gods and scale the holy mountain of our home world. If you succeeded in reaching the mountain's summit, the gods would unlock your Zhali, which can turn even the scrawniest men into fierce warriors."

"Well, that explains the physical change you both went through. But what's that got to do with a mate bond?"

"Ah, but that's the best part." Lok grinned. He threw an arm around my shoulders and pulled me close. "You see, the very first Sankado to scale the holy mountain only did so to save his love. It is said that back when the world was new, two lovers, Gravara and Lythron, were set upon by a pack of Void-howlers. Gravara was gravely injured. Lythron, overcome with grief at seeing his mate at death's door, scaled the holy mountain with her strapped to his back and pleaded with the gods to save his love. Before him, no one else had ever reached the summit. Impressed by his perseverance, the gods not only healed Gravara but granted him the gift of Zhali."

Lok paused, then took my hands in his. His playful smile faded away. He searched my eyes as he spoke, as if trying to find the secrets of the world behind them. "Zhali bonds you to the one meant to walk with you through this life and the next, and grants you the strength to protect them above all others. When our world burned, I thought my chance of ever finding my mate went with it. Then I saw your ship fall from the sky and something in me knew to come find you. I don't care if it's the result of meddlesome aliens. From this moment on, where you walk, I follow."

"I . . ." My throat caught. A bead of sweat slid from my forehead and trailed down my face. *Holy alien gods matchmaking service. That is a* lot *to put on a gal.* "Are you sure I'm really your Zhali mate? We're not even the same species. This could just be a fluke."

"Of course it's not a real bond," Sol scoffed. "You can't take an ancient rite from the gods and put it into a serum."

"You can if it's caused by a chemical reaction in the brain," Intern said. He brought up his screen, showing what looked like strands of DNA dancing in a petri dish. "The chosen mate part took a bit of guesswork to figure out who would be compatible with who, but our algorithm has shown a 96 percent success rate in triggering the desired response. Would you like me to run through the numbers?"

Sol looked murderous. I pulled a hand free from Lok's grasp to wave the intern's screen away. "Now's not really the time for that," I whispered.

Smoke pooled from the fire-haired Sankado's tail. "I don't care what kind of tests were run. You idiots didn't even bother to check which of us were females before you grabbed us. There's no way I'm trusting anything that came from you. For all we know, this serum could wear off before the week is out."

"Good." Lok spoke up. He gave Sol an encouraging smile and pulled me closer to him. "If you're not interested in her, then I will be Stardust's one and only. Be on your way and I'll take her to the research center."

"As if I'd trust my woman in the care of a Roamcrest," Sol growled.

Lok raised a brow, and his voice took on a taunting tone as he spoke. "'My'? I thought you weren't going to trust the Biwban's serum."

"I said I don't trust it. Not that I'll hand her over to you. Until we know for sure, she's not leaving my side. For now we will take her to the Druid Onchu. He'll be able to tap into our Zhali and see if it's genuine."

"You expect me to let you take her into hostile territory? Who's to say your kin won't run me through as soon as they see me? No. I don't need your druid to tell me what's right in front of me. Go test your Zhali on your own. Stardust and I have a date at the research center. Now, if you'll excuse us."

He turned to walk away but Sol grabbed him by the shoulder and spun him back around. "Wait—"

"NO!" I raised my arms, breaking free of Lok's hold, then backed away from both of them. "I'm not listening to another second of your arguing. This day has been weird enough as it is. I'm going to the research center."

"But—"

"NO BUTS! I'm going. With or without either of you. Lok." I turned toward the larger Sankado, who stood straighter under my scrutiny.

"Yes?"

"I don't know a damn thing about a Zhali, but I do know I just met you. We don't have whatever soul-bond-type thing this is on my home planet, so don't expect any undying love confessions from me anytime soon. But I am willing to try. Mostly because I'm not sure if I have a choice with this serum."

"You don't," Intern said matter-of-factly.

I shook my head, choosing to ignore him. "Can you work with that?"

Lok smiled wide. "Absolutely."

Nodding, I turned my attention to Sol. "My mind is made up, but you are welcome to join us."

He gritted his teeth, his eyes shifting between Lok and me. Clearly he was trying to fight back his dire need to argue about every little thing. After a moment, the man must have decided to concede defeat and let out a breath. "Fine. We'll try it your way."

"Good." I clasped my hands together and smiled. "Now that we've got that out of the way, Intern, lead the way."

"Right." The intern flew up to rest on Lok's shoulder and

pointed to the mountains lining the horizon. "Let's be off, then."

"This group is entirely too comfortable using me as a beast of burden," Lok said. He tried to manage a pointed scowl, but it soon broke into a chuckle. Reaching to his belt, he unhooked a long bone horn and brought it to his lips. Its sound blared across the clearing like a trumpet, one long note followed by three short honks. Once finished, Lok returned the horn to its holster.

"What was that?" Sol snapped, his body tensing as his hand inched closer to the knife on his belt. "Who did you call?"

Lok rolled his eyes. "Blossom."

"And just who is—"

A blaring call interrupted his question. Fast trills rose from somewhere in the distant tall grass. I followed the sound to see a duck-billed dinosaur galloping toward us. The ground thudded beneath her heavy stomps. At the sight of Lok, the creature threw back her head and a loud, triumphant blare escaped the long red crest adorning her skull. The rest of her body was a greenish beige, with black stripes peeking out from beneath the saddle on her back.

Spreading his arms wide, Lok braced himself for impact as Blossom charged at him. Her front legs hit the brakes a few yards from him, but the rest of her body was far too full of excitement and didn't get the memo. I winced as the dinosaur slammed into him. Intern squawked, frantically flapping his way to safety.

Lok merely took the hit with a smile and petted her. "Blossom, my big girl!"

"Big" was an understatement. His *big girl* dwarfed the

man entirely. Even standing on all fours, Blossom had to be at least nine feet tall and thrice as long. The duckbill leaned into his hand, then snorted and nudged at his gut with her hoof. Taking the hint, Lok pulled a brown flower-shaped treat from his pocket and offered it to her. His hand disappeared into her mouth, then reappeared flowerless. Thankfully with all his fingers intact.

Amazed, I stepped closer to the dinosaur, instinctively reaching for my phone. Swiping away its LOW BATTERY notification, I pulled up my camera and took several pictures. "You tamed a dinosaur? I thought Sol said you've only been on this planet for ten years."

"Yes?" Lok cocked his head as if confused and said, "It doesn't take that long to make a friend. Blossom here will do just about anything for a sugar flower." He produced another flower from his pocket, then dodged Blossom's lunge and tossed it to me.

I caught it with a completely normal amount of awkward flailing. The sugar flower was about the size of my palm. On top of the flower sat six petite petals reaching outward, each one resembling a dainty heart-shaped leaf.

My hand is gone.

Just. Gone.

Oh, it came back, thank the gods.

Body frozen, I chanced a glance at Blossom, who held my gaze, happily chewing her prize. Pinky, ring, middle, pointer, thumb. Praise the Absolute, her prize did not include my fingers.

"And now she won't nip at you when you ride her." Lok scratched her behind her crest, then took her by the reins and gently but firmly led her back a few steps, out of my space. She flicked her head in irritation but was soothed quickly enough.

It was at that moment I knew Lok was dangerous.

Not in the sense that I half expected him to take the spear from his back and drive it into my gut, which I suppose he could have done if he was so inclined. No, Lok was something much more menacing to my heart.

He was a man who was good with animals.

Be it firemen posing with adorable kittens on calendars, Steve Irwin calling a crocodile rightfully trying to murder him beautiful, or apparently even alien men petting dinosaurs, something about it made me weak in the knees every time.

Blossom tried to jerk out of his hold and step toward me again. Lok's grip on her reins tightened, flexing the prominent veins on his forearm. As if my already weak-minded self needed another reason to find him ridiculously attractive. He tucked a strand of his long black hair behind his ear and gave me an apologetic smile. "Sorry, I'm still teaching her manners."

I bit the inside of my cheek and tried not to drool. "She's perfect."

"Isn't she?" His face brightened, a direct attack on my heartstrings. He slapped her side. "Blossom, call your boyfriend."

She shifted her weight back on her feet and blared a tune into the sky. Lok produced another flower from his pocket and tossed it to Sol. "You get him, good luck."

CHAPTER 8

"YOU SON OF THE RED PLANET, SLOW DOWN!" SOL'S EXASperated command cut through the dusty air as we traversed the rugged dirt road that cut through the vast grasslands. The relentless sun overhead cast a fiery glow upon the landscape, intensifying the vivid colors of the wildflowers scattered along the path.

In response to Sol's plea, the cantankerous dinosaur beneath him showed blatant disregard. The ornery duckbill, aptly named Beast, glared at the Sankado clinging to the saddle on his back before blowing a series of rumbling notes from his crest that sounded suspiciously like an insult meant to address not only him but all of his ancestors as well. When his rider attempted to pull back on his reins, the ill-tempered dinosaur decided that meant it was time to rear back on his hind legs and roar his displeasure. With a thunderous pounding of his hooves, Beast bolted in the complete opposite direction, causing a startled Toto to leap out of their path. The lion shook his head and trotted faster to catch up to Lok and me.

From my vantage point atop the much more docile Blossom, I watched the chaotic scene unfold with mounting concern. Blossom plodded along serenely, leading a small herd of fluffy stegosaurs in her wake. Sol's signature scowl gave way to a parade of new emotions I'd yet to see from him. Rage, determination, and, if I squinted, a slight tremor of abject terror when Beast nearly flung him loose. "Should we . . . help him?"

"Hmm?" Lok shifted his weight, his powerful thighs brushing against my own. "Oh, I suppose." He raised a hand to shield his mouth from the dust kicked up by the stampeding duo and shouted, "Stop fighting him. He knows where he wants to go."

"That's the problem!" Sol shouted back, his voice barely audible over the chaos. "This wretched flackshaw wants to go the wrong way."

"What's a flackshaw?" I murmured to Lok.

"A gelatinous bug with anger issues that's known to bring misfortune," he answered, before turning his attention back to Sol. "He'll stop having a go at you when you stop trying to control him. Even beasts have their pride, you know. Let go of the reins and sit." When Sol kept his hands firmly on the reins, Lok sighed heavily. "Or just keep pissing him off. I'm sure that will work eventually."

Amid the turmoil, I couldn't help but wonder aloud, "How do you know Beast will follow us? Seems like he's pretty keen to do anything but."

"Easy." He smirked. "Blossom is going this way. He's a man, you know. Show him a pretty woman and he's a mere slave to her whim."

"That simple, huh?"

He leaned in, pressing his body flush against my back

before burying his nose in my hair, his nearness wreaking havoc on my senses. The cool silk of his clothes brushed against my heated skin. "Aye, we're that simple."

Lok inhaled, his hand leaving the reins to caress my thigh, sending tremors of excitement down my spine. However, given the fact that I'd spent the better part of the last few days running around from both velociraptors and general mayhem, coupled with the fact that I'd been fucked within an inch of my life not even two hours prior, I was in no state to try to jump in for another round. Not without a shower at least. I'd even settle for a bath given the circumstances. Normally I hated baths. The thought of sitting around in a puddle of my own filth sounded disgusting, but beggars can't be choosers.

I took his hand from my thigh and rested it on my lap, lacing our fingers together. "You have soap on this planet, right?"

He chuckled, his tone lightening in mock offense. "Is this your way of telling me I stink?"

"No, I do. Badly. Any chance we'll cross paths with a stream or something on the way there?"

"No need!" the intern chirped, landing on Blossom's shoulder. He hopped around excitedly, tail feathers shaking. "It just so happens that we're headed right for one of our human cu . . . cul . . ." The intern clenched his tiny fists, willing the foreign words out of his beak. "Cul-de-sacs!"

"You built a cul-de-sac?"

"Of course! We wanted to expedite human acclimation as soon as possible. A part of that was ensuring we brought numerous human enrichment items and scattered them throughout the planet. We weren't sure how far your home territories tend to be, so we tried to place them about thirty Earth miles apart just to be sure. My map tells me we'll make it there in about three hours at our current pace. Which will let us arrive just before nightfall. Oh, you must tell me if we re-created them right!"

"You're pretty psyched about these houses, Intern." Not that I was complaining. I assumed I'd been doomed to a life of the outdoors. Maybe these Biwbans weren't completely incompetent. Just mostly. Though a hot shower wasn't enough to save that Vexil guy from the Punch of Justice I owed him.

"Psyched?" he asked, his head tilted to the side like a confused dog.

"Sorry, I mean excited. Do you mind if I take a look at your map? I want to see where we are."

Intern ran a gentle claw under one of the long feathers on his wing. The feather twisted with a click, and he pulled it free and handed it to me. The tip of the shaft was made of metal, with a little notch to hook back onto his wing. I ran a finger down the vein in the same fashion I'd seen him do, and the map materialized in the space above the feather. I couldn't understand the language the map was written in, so I decided to replace each of the place names with breakfast foods to better keep track. A blinking green dot indicated our location in a grassland hereby known as Hot Coffee. Hot Coffee was not far from a marker near Fujilly Rock. An arrow pointed east toward Mountain and Gravy, the center of which held a red destination marker.

To the west of Fujilly Rock was Vervain, and if I squinted hard enough, I somewhat recognized the beach where Toto and I had washed up yesterday. I balked when I noticed just how far it was from Fujilly Rock. We must have been following Sol for a good ten miles at least. No wonder my feet were killing me. Each step felt like a vendetta against my knees. I'm not ready to have bad knees. Wasn't that supposed to wait until your thirties? The more I thought about it, the more I didn't like the answer.

I've definitely earned some R and R in a real house. More importantly, a quiet bed where I can finally unwind and get my thoughts together. "These houses have running hot water, right?"

He raised his beak proudly. "Of course! I was on the human enrichment team that focused on your living areas."

"You're not the one responsible for that car with nothing in it, are you?" I asked, handing the feather back to him.

He lifted his wing and clipped the feather back in place and strummed his fingers down the length of the wing. "Car?"

"Never mind, I'll see for myself when we get there."

With a trill, he fluttered around Blossom's shoulders before sliding down to rest in the crook of her neck. "This is so exciting!"

Well, I'm glad one of us is having fun.

We fell into silence, minus the various grunts and stomps that were par for the course when traveling with a herd of dinosaurs. "Lok, can I ask why we're being followed by a herd of fluffy stegosaurs?"

He looked around at the herd, confused for a moment. "Do you mean the yix? They are a part of my flock and I trained them to follow the marker on the back of Blossom's saddle. We're still headed to the research center, but I can't leave them stranded out here on their own. The lot of them combined have the intelligence of a sinking stone. They'll be predator food by nightfall if left on their own. Luckily, I was already set to rejoin the main herd about a day's ride from here. It's on the way, so we can drop them off with my men tomorrow morning and head out right after."

"Not today?"

He shook his head. "We've only got a few hours of daylight left. Trust me, you don't want to be traveling in the dark. Especially not in storm season. Even if we tried to keep moving, the yix would stop dead in the rain and hunker down. They're fickle, stubborn creatures; the wisest herders know not to fight them on that."

"Ah, so you're a herder. Wait, does that mean that your home planet had fluffy steggos, or yix, I mean?"

He blew out a breath. "Well, no, the yix back home looked nothing like this. They were about half the size, with six spindly legs and tusks. When we were dropped into this world, we didn't find any yix, but we noticed some of the monsters here had their same wool. We Roamcrest are nothing without our herds, so we made do. Now I can't imagine going back to the yix of my home. Those barely had any meat on 'em. And they smelled *terrible*."

I leaned over to reach out and touch the densely packed wool of the nearest yix. To my surprise, it didn't feel like wool at all, but silk. My hand sank into the coils of hair as if disappearing into a chilly cloud. I righted myself and ran my hands along Lok's clothing, finding the texture to be similar. "Fascinating. But why do only some of the stegosaurs have yix wool?"

"Oh, I can answer that!" Intern said. "The yix we got from their planet were incompatible with the increased level of oxygen we needed to maintain the larger Earth species. Our brilliant scientists came up with a way to splice their DNA into select stegosaur embryos to create a suitable hybrid. Much like we did with you, Dory."

My face scrunched, and I once again found myself fighting off the urge to kick that damn bird. "I need you to stop looking so joyful every time you talk about how you modified me. In case you haven't noticed, I'm still pissed at you for that."

His ear tufts fell flat. "Right. Well . . . at least you can reproduce more efficiently now. The maternal mortality rate of your species is frankly horrific."

I shook my head. "Not helping."

"Right." He flew away.

"Coward."

I relaxed against Lok and allowed myself to be lulled by the lazy cadence of Blossom's steps. We'd been plodding along for two hours, and the adrenaline from running from those raptors finally wore off. My body was exhausted, and a nap was just what the doctor ordered. When I closed my eyes, my stupid brain whirled with more questions. More importantly, it finally dawned on me that Lok was a yix herder. Like that calf we found this morning. "Oh fuck, did we kill your calf?"

He barely managed to choke back his laughter, turning the sound into more of a strangled cough. "Yes."

Mortified, I sat up and shifted to face him. "I'm so sorry! We didn't know."

His gaze moved from my face to my hands, before he closed his own hand over them to stop the nervous wringing I didn't even realize I was doing. A terrible habit I'd been trying to fight off since my beauty pageant days. In the back of my mind, I could still see my mom's face in the crowd. Tight-lipped, eyes brimming with the "Dorothy the Disappointment" lecture that awaited me as soon as I exited the stage. Despite myself, I felt my chest tighten. Not two days on this planet and I'd already killed someone's pet. Gods, what if he—

"It's just a calf." The way his eyes flitted over my face as he watched me made me feel so . . . seen. Not in the way countless judges scrutinized how perfectly my hair was coiffed or whether or not my thighs were parallel to the floor during a grand plié. He just looked concerned. With an easy grin, he continued. "A damn stubborn one too. I didn't even bother to name it with how often it wandered off. Yix that don't stay with the herd don't last long in this area. I've lost two adults already. Swear something's been following us, but I haven't seen anything around big enough to take them down yet."

Beating down my mounting anxiety with a stick, I smiled at him. "You can't be considerate and good with animals. It's not fair."

"To who, Sol?"

"No, my heart. I just got here, man. Cut a girl a break."

He gave me a lopsided grin. "Oh, I'm afraid I can't do that. You're mine, after all. If you're not completely obsessed with me by nightfall, I'll die of a broken heart."

"Mm-hmm, you should savor your last day, then."

His voice grew husky as his hand caressed my thigh. The warmth of his touch licked a trail of flames along my skin that coiled in my belly. "Is that an invitation?"

I bit my lip, trying (and failing) to keep my voice steady as I asked, "You can't be serious for a second, can you?"

His lips curved into a grin against the shell of my ear. "How could I not be serious with a fallen star pressed against me? The world could sink into oblivion and I'd still have the honor of dying the happiest man alive."

"Such flowery praise for a woman who's a stranger to you."

"Then let's get better acquainted," he whispered. My breath caught as his hand grew bolder, sliding along my inner thigh before squeezing. His breath shuddered as if he was surprised at the sight of his fingers sinking into the clothed skin.

It was a miracle my pants didn't disintegrate under the burn of his touch.

Reins forgotten, his free hand slid under my shirt to trace up my belly. My eyes fluttered closed when I felt the brush of his fingers against my breast, and I gasped.

"No, no, don't do that." His voice was a low drawl. One that you sank into like the sea at night. Its water wrapped around you, keeping you safe and warm as it pulled you deeper into the dark. He brushed my hair to the side and kissed my neck. "See, if you go around making noises like that, I'll need to draw more of them out of you." His lips trailed across my skin in featherlight touches. Each little kiss was a tease that had my body thrumming with need. "And if I get more of them out of you, I'll need to see those pretty brown eyes wet with tears as I fuck you again. Ah, but if you cry I'll need to comfort you, won't I? Gods above. We'll be here all day."

He cupped my breast before sliding the rough pad of his thumb over the nipple, making me whimper.

Lok tsked. "Now, see? There you go again."

My eyes flew open when I felt him unbutton my pants. He traced the hem of my panties in a gentle, maddening rhythm. When gooseflesh pebbled along my arms, he grew bolder still and spread my pussy lips with his fingers and stroked along the center. I cried out and drew my knees together.

"Bad girl," he teased.

"I need a bath first."

"You smell fine."

"You evil debaucher, I absolutely do not."

He buried his nose in my curls and inhaled. "You smell like sex, honey, and mine. I want more of it."

"Oh *fuck*."

"Open your legs, Stardust."

My deceitful heretic of a body burned with compliance. My legs spread, earning a groan from the man behind me as he cupped my sex. Well, if he didn't care, then who was I to stop him?

"I've missed this," Lok said. He dipped a thick finger just in my well, groaning in approval at the wetness he found, before flicking his thumb against my clit.

"Ah!" I clung to his arm, unable to stop my legs from quivering under his touch. He thrust the digit inside me, letting it curl against my inner walls.

"Not a day has gone by since I've had this bliss wrapped around my cock, yet already I feel like a man starved. What am I going to do with you, Stardust?"

I smiled and rested my head against his shoulder. "Keep teasing me and I'll get Sol over here and ride with him. From the looks of it, he's finally getting the hang of it."

He laughed, a dark sound that would have given me pause, if he wasn't strumming my body like an acoustic guitar. "You think he'll save you?"

"Of course he will. If nothing else, just to get me away from you. He strikes me as the jealous type."

"Oh you sweet, innocent thing." He pulled away from me, letting the unexpected cold air slap against my skin. His heel kicked at Blossom's side, bringing the creature to a halt, then he brought his fingers to his lips and whistled.

Through the haze of my mounting lust, I heard thundering footsteps approach. Lok lifted us from the saddle and jumped down. My feet had barely hit the ground before he spun me around and kissed me. I moaned into him, my body seeking his in a dizzying dance of need. He hand slipped past my pants to grab a fistful of my ass.

Any trace of satisfaction I felt before died as he kissed my neck. Lok tugged my pants down and I kicked them off, letting him turn me around to rest with my back against him. He nudged my legs apart, wasting no time in burying his fingers in my pussy. I shuddered when his thumb flicked against my clit. He worked the swollen bud mercilessly until I was a panting mess against him.

"Here comes your hero, Stardust," he said. I looked over to see Sol jump down from Beast. His eyes widened at the sight of us.

I swallowed down a moan, too proud to feed Lok's ego even further. My restraint earned me a thrust of his fingers, before he curled them inside me, his long strokes teasing that sensitive spot until I was forced to bite my lip instead of crying out. "Now you try to hide it?" he asked. "As if I can't feel your heartbeat jump at my touch? How this greedy little flower weeps for me every time I tease you here?"

He thrust harder against my sweet spot, and I gasped. "Mmm, yes. There's my needy pet. Well, don't just stand there, Sol. Our woman needs your help."

Sol's lips parted, eyes trained on the way Lok's fingers worked my slit as he approached. He started to speak, but Lok interrupted him.

"You see, Stardust here has gotten it into her head that you're the brave hero that will save her from my dastardly ways." He drew my hair back and kissed my temple. His fingers continued their delicious rhythm. "But I think I know you better than that. I think seeing this wet cunt in front of you drives you just as mad as it does me." As if to prove his point, he hooked his arms around my thighs, lifted me against him, then guided a hand to my lower lips and spread them for Sol to see.

A muscle jumped in Sol's jaw, then was quickly ushered away behind a controlled glower. "And if it does?"

Deep and carnal, Lok's voice flitted through the air like a devil signing a deal. "Then you're going to fuck the hope right out of her."

The words hung in the air. Sol didn't trust Lok. Wanted to kill him, if the disdain in his glare was any indication, but there was more to it than that. Something about the Roamcrest deeply unnerved him.

But there was a fever in all of us. A burning sickness that could only be healed with their skin on mine, and when his breath stalled, by the gods I felt him ache with it.

"Fuck it."

Sol leaned over and settled a hand possessively on my neck. Molten eyes glinted as he searched my face. Then the hand slid downward along with his gaze, feathering light touches against my skin that burned a plea from my lips. "Please."

He grinned. "What a pretty sound."

Pride long gone, I almost said it again, but the word fell silent when he kissed me. An unsure press of the lips at first, like he might have second-guessed himself. The indecision was brief, then he nipped at my lower lip, licked the sting away, and marauded his way deeper, sliding his tongue against mine. A sense of urgency drove my hands into his hair, pulling him as close as I could to satiate the pounding of my heart.

Sliding his hand under my shirt, he cupped my breast. When he broke the kiss to rip the shirt with his teeth, my gasp was both indignant and appallingly aroused.

"I'll get you another one," he said against my nipple. Then he bit it.

He's right. Fuck the shirt.

Kneeling between my legs, Sol ran his hands along my thighs before kissing the sensitive skin he found between them. He looked up at me, letting the warmth of his breath fan over my sex. Anticipation nearly killed me.

My breathing sped up as I watched him. Just before I felt the tip of his tongue, Lok's tail cracked him on the side of his face.

Contempt laced his question. "Did I say you could taste that before me?"

My mouth hung open; I was far too stunned to speak.

Furthering my dismay, Sol merely laughed and said, "Greedy prick." Then he stood, sliding his hand up my thigh. He dug his thumb in my pussy, earning a gasp. He withdrew and rubbed circles around my clit before thrusting his fingers in. "Not like she needs it either way. Look at you dripping all over my hooves." His gaze raked over my body as his free hand closed around my throat. "Gods, what a mess you make."

I closed my eyes, getting lost in the feeling.

"Look at me," he whispered, and gave me a sharp slap between my legs.

I cried out and squirmed in surprise at the throbbing need pulsing through my body. My heart was pounding; my body was shaking. So much I couldn't stand it. I managed a withering glare.

His smile was crooked; I bet his heart was too. Then he shoved my legs apart and buried his cock deep inside me like he'd die if he didn't.

I cried out his name, body jerking like it couldn't get enough. When he started to pound into me, my nails clawed at his back.

"Yes, keep crying for me, I love that."

Panting, I held his face as he fucked me, unforgivingly

rough. His throaty grunts mingled with the slap of his hips on mine and it was fucking music to my ears. Wetness soaked my inner thighs and dropped to the grass below.

"Oh gods, yes, that feels so good." He fucked me until my head was spinning. I felt high, drunk on the fever that kept me begging him for more. Low moans delved into desperate mewling as my orgasm came closer.

"Is this what you wanted?" he asked Lok.

His chest rumbled at my back as he replied. "Close." I felt the brush of Lok's tail before it slid down Sol's back. A gasp fell from his lips before he glared at Lok. His thrusts halted.

"Ah-ah," Lok scolded. "I told you to fuck her. Don't you dare stop."

Sol's body tightened, before his eyes fluttered closed on a heavy breath. Lok's tail pushed farther into him, before starting a slow, gentle rhythm. The cock inside me twitched. With a shuddering gasp, Sol grabbed my hips and thrust into me.

"Good boy," Lok crooned. He fisted his hand in Sol's hair and kissed him. When they broke apart, Lok's voice was a graveled murmur. "Put your tail on her clit and suck."

Sol's obedience ripped a scream from me. Searing pleasure bordered on madness when Lok grabbed the tail and ground it farther down. "Tell us who this belongs to, Stardust."

I whimpered. Words were impossible. Lok pinched his fingers around the tail sucking at my clit, and whimpers escalated to screams as my orgasm hit me like a freight train.

Sol gripped my throat with one hand, and he bared his fangs on a groan as he thrust deep. "Say it. Sing for me and I'll let you come again on my knot."

I felt the barest prick of his nails on my pulse. My core contracted around him as I squirmed, unable to hold still in the face of the incessant orgasm that just wouldn't end. "Yes!"

"Yes, what?" Lok asked.

"Yes, it's yours. I swear it's yours, please just don't stop!" The words sounded desperate. But the pleased shiver Sol gave was worth it.

"That's my girl." Lok put a hand on Sol's shoulder, halting his movements. He grabbed a blanket off Blossom's saddle and threw it on the grass before setting me down, quickly positioning Sol in front of me before he took his place behind him. Wasting no time, Sol kissed me senseless and buried himself back inside me.

I was panting, but it felt like I couldn't breathe.

"That's it, hold it in her. Hold yourself inside her while I push into you." Tremors rocked through Sol at the thrust of Lok's hips. Eyes closed, lips parted, he was the most beautiful creature I'd ever seen.

This was so good. Too good. Be it the serum or some cosmic twist of fate, the need to get lost in them was euphoric.

Sol ground into me, his tail working my swollen clit. He leaned down and nipped at my neck, my blood throbbing in the veins just underneath. His knee pushed against my thigh, spreading me farther before he sank to the hilt inside me. The base of his cock pulsed, putting more pressure against my sweet spot.

"Oh fuck. Oh fuck. Yes!" I jerked up against him, begging for the knot he promised.

Lok reached down and cradled the back of my head. I braced myself on my elbows to meet him, and the kiss was deep, dominant.

Binding.

If your beauty was kept from me much longer, I'm afraid I would have hunted you down.

The memory of his words pulled at my mind like the water

that dragged me toward the mosasaur after it opened its mouth.

From this moment on, where you walk, I follow.

I swam as fast as I could, but I still felt its fangs at my heels.

You're mine, after all.

Escape was impossible without Sol's outside interference.

You think he'll save you?

"Oh gods." My body thrummed as Sol worked his knot past my slit. His hands were rough, his breathing rougher. The orgasm was as blinding as the revelation.

Lok had staked his claim. Help wasn't coming.

He'd make sure of that.

CHAPTER 9

SOME WOULD CALL IGNORING YOUR PROBLEMS UN-healthy. I call it an art form. Lose out on that scholarship? Crochet a jellyfish. Ring cam showed your overbearing mom on your doorstep with some lawyer's son? Go for a hike until they leave. Crazy possessive alien mate problems? Distract, deflect, ignore!

"What is going on with these billboards?" I asked. Intern followed my gaze, as if the stream of billboards randomly scattered about the rolling hills was supposed to be an every-day occurrence.

His beak clicked before he slowly sounded out the word. "Billboards." With a delighted tail shake, he hopped from the crook of Blossom's neck to her back and proudly waved at the menagerie of confusing advertisements. "Ah, your human note cards! More enrichment items to help with your transition to this planet. Do you like them?"

The closest boasted a spoon rising out of a graveyard sur-rounded by bats under the full moon, while 1980s horror-movie-style text read **SPOONKILLER SERENADE: JAZZERCISE WITH UTENSILS.** Not far from it sat another billboard that had a picture of a smiling woman holding a clipboard that read **Who will add your enemies to the list? Call Kiran today!**

"Intern, tell me what you think billboards are."

His cheer faltered, and he looked at Kiran's billboard before tilting his head. "Um . . . Hmm. Don't humans use them to mark their way? We saw them all over the roads leading to your homes."

Case studies could be done on how little research these fuckers put in before they grabbed us.

"All right, first of all, no, we don't use them to mark the way. We use them to advertise goods and products. Second, these aren't even in a line on the road. Or, well, dirt path, I should say." Exactly one of them was actually on the beaten path we'd been following all day. And by that I mean it was directly in the center of the path, and Blossom had to veer around it. The others had no rhyme or reason to their placement. Some were smack dab in the middle of the river, some jammed straight through trees, and a cluster of them formed a bush that could have passed as an art exhibit called *Capitalist Jamboree.* "Third, do you even know what they say?"

He blinked as if the meaning behind the words never occurred to him. "No, we assumed your language was too primitive to bother studying. Our translator symbionts couldn't even make sense of it when we ran our initial tests. These billboards were all done by AI. It's a marvel that the symbiont you absorbed on the ship was capable of altering itself to fit your rudimentary human brain. OW!" He held a tiny hand to his forehead, rubbing the spot where I'd flicked him. "What was that for?"

"Just my rudimentary human brain getting the better of me, I guess."

As we kept on the path, the rolling hills disappeared into thickets of kudzu. The aggressive little vine had even climbed its way up a few of the billboards in its quest for world domination. "Even alien planets aren't safe from your conquest," I muttered.

"Whose conquest?" Sol asked, from behind me. After our tryst in the grass, Lok had offered up Blossom to the other Sankado and mounted Beast instead. Maybe he did it as a reward for Sol being agreeable for once. Or maybe he just wanted to show off the fact that he was capable of riding the ornery duckbill without getting bucked off. Either way, I was glad for it after his little possessive snit.

"Hmm? Oh, I meant that thicket choking up the billboards over there. It's called kudzu. Also known as 'the vine that ate the South' due to how absurdly fast growing and invasive it is. Entire jobs have been created just to fight its eternal crusade. It's a little funny to see it still doing its thing on an alien planet."

"Your people dedicate part of their workforce to fight a vine? Must be incredibly deadly. We'll be sure to steer clear."

"No, it's not deadly. Just highly invasive."

"Does it matter?"

"Of course it does. Kudzu can destroy a thriving ecosystem and turn it into a monoculture. All the native wildlife gets swallowed up into the thicket, which means less food for wildlife, erosion control issues, and a host of other problems."

"Hmm, I never expected such a fuss over a vine."

"I am a never-ending sea of useless plant knowledge."

He gave the kudzu an appreciative glance. "Doesn't seem all that useless to me."

Blossom groaned her complaints as the path bled into a

steep hill. The incline forced me to shift my weight back to maintain my balance, and I found myself pressed against Sol.

My breath hitched as I felt the powerful muscles of Sol's chest behind me; the heat of his body seeped through the layers of fabric separating us. My heart raced as I became all too aware of the strong arm wrapped protectively around my waist. Which by all accounts was fucking ridiculous. We'd just had sex. Twice already today.

I let out an aggravated sigh and waited for the onslaught of lust. When my kitty cat didn't start singing the song of her people, I let myself relax against him a bit. *Maybe I'm just feeling the residual effects of the serum.*

Sol rested his chin on my head, causing a tingling feeling to spread throughout my body. I swallowed thickly and tried to push the feeling down. It wasn't lust, thank small miracles, yet his nearness all but had me twirling my hair and kicking my feet like some blushing schoolgirl.

Oh no.

"Are you all right?" he asked.

"Hmm? Yeah, why?" I asked, in a completely normal, totally not high-pitched voice.

His hand slid down my arm until his thumb traced circles along my wrist before pressing against my pulse. "This is beating faster than a war drum. Do you need to rest?" The attention only caused my heart to race faster.

No. Nooo, fuck! I ripped my arm out of his grasp and scooted as far away from him as the saddle allowed. "I'm fine. Just a little hot."

"Are you sure?" His tone turned teasing, and I could practically feel the smirk on his face. "You humans clearly aren't a hardy bunch. There's no sign of a storm coming yet, so I promise I won't hold it against you if you need a break."

I want to ask about your day and create a shared playlist on Spotify so I can learn your music tastes. No, *dammit, Dory! You weak bitch, this was supposed to be fun alien sex. Why do you always equate good dick with relationship material?*

CORRELATION DOES NOT EQUAL CAUSATION!

"Dory?"

The devil on my shoulder giggled at the concern in his voice, and I mentally grabbed the evil little bugger and threw her under Blossom's feet. A crush on Sol was not a part of the game plan. The plan was to get to the research center, punch the department head in the face, and see about stealing a ship for the ride home.

. . . after figuring out if there were gas stations in space.

It was probably just a trick of the serum anyway. If we were back on Earth, and he was just another guy in a coffee shop, I absolutely would not look twice at that strong jawline. His catty attitude was annoying and not endearing in the slightest. Nor were his weird-ass golden eyes that shimmered with the warmth of a thousand sunsets . . . *FUCK. MEEEEEE!*

"I said I'm fine!" I snapped, then fanned myself to drive home the lie. "This heat, it's just getting to me, that's all. How long until we reach the cul-de-sac, Intern?"

The Biwban jumped up and struggled on tiny wings to lift himself higher in the air. He peered past the hill we were climbing, then fluttered back down to his perch. "About four more Earth miles. You should be able to see it once we clear this hill."

"That's a relief." I sighed.

"Hey, Stardust, what's that one say?" Lok shifted back on Beast's saddle and pointed to a billboard in the river. His demeanor was back to that of the carefree flirt. How easily the wolf slips into his sheepskin.

At some point I'd need to sort out how far Lok's possessiveness went. With any luck, he was simply a wolf in the sheets. If so, hell yes, be still my raging heart. But if I actually had to do something about this, I was gonna be fucking pissed.

Still, I was beyond grateful for the distraction and peered over my shoulder, then snorted at the image of a shark with piano keys for teeth and read it aloud. "Accordion Acid Academy: Squeeze the Noise!" He barked out a laugh and pointed to another. "Fizzy Pickle Parakeets Tickled by the Brine!"

Behind me, Sol let out a sound that had me whip around to see his face, confirming it was still him and not some doppelgänger. "Sol," I asked slowly, "was that a laugh?"

His jaw clenched. "No."

"Well, fizzle my brine, maybe you can do more than scowl and run your mouth."

He smirked. "You weren't complaining about my mouth earlier."

I bit the inside of my cheek. "I . . . all right, you win that one."

Starting tomorrow I only ride with Lok. Sol is dangerously my type and a girl has to have her wits about her when traversing an alien planet. Lok was a danger all on his own, but at least his playboy style of flirting didn't make me fantasize about cosigning a lease.

So long as I played the part of an agreeable mate, he'd keep taking me toward the research center. For all he knew, I just wanted revenge against the department head. I made a mental note to tell Toto not to spill the beans about the escape plan, or the birth control.

Deep down I knew there was no chance in hell I'd be able to fly an alien spaceship back to earth, but living in la-la land, where I wasn't permanently trapped here, felt comforting. Besides, miracles happen on occasion; look at a Hallmark movie. I had to at least try to get home.

Right?

Of course I'm right. I'll enjoy my little alien vacation, go home, sell the videos and notes I've taken to the highest bidder, and live the high life for the rest of my days. Simple.

Damn I miss TikTok.

"What's got your mind in a rush?" Sol asked.

I shrugged. "Just wondering when I'm gonna learn to stop lying to myself."

"Ah. Did you come to a conclusion?"

I turned to look at him, drinking in that mind-numbing tonka-bean smell until I grew dangerously close to trying to decipher what his zodiac sign was. "No. I think I'll live in my fantasy world a little longer."

"Hmm. Let me know when you return to reality."

"What if I don't want to? It's nice here in denial land. I might set up shop and stay awhile."

"Then you are a foolish creature with fits of fancy."

I snapped my fingers. "Virgo."

"What?"

"Nothing, it's not important." Of course he'd be Virgo to my Cancer. I remembered Intern mentioning something about the Biwban using an algorithm to match pairs based on compatibility. Not that a race of highly intelligent beings would base their research on a star chart from a solar system they weren't even a part of, but still. He seemed like a Virgo. Which meant I was fucked.

Thwack.

Something wet and sticky slapped against my side, nearly yanking me off Blossom when it retracted. I flailed, grabbing the front of the saddle to avoid falling off. I looked around wildly for the source. "What the hell was that?"

Behind me I heard Lok's booming laughter. He pointed to a green boulder on the side of the hill. The boulder suddenly grew eyes, and a long tongue shot out to grab at me again with a loud *thwack*, but its stickiness was only strong enough to jerk me forward. My mouth hung open when the giant frog bellowed in disapproval.

"That's an American bullfrog the size of a cow," I said, pressing my palms to both sides of my temples. "An American . . . bullfrog . . . the size. Of. A. Cow."

Sol peered over at the scientific anomaly with bored interest. "So you mentioned."

Lok clicked his tongue and steered Beast closer to us. "Did you want to eat it? The legs are delicious over an open fire."

I swung my legs to one side and slid down Blossom. "I don't think you guys are hearing me." My arms flung out to the bullfrog to emphasize my point. "It's a giant . . . frog. This doesn't happen. That's nowhere near the size a frog is supposed to be."

Intern lifted his arm and scanned the creature. His screen came up with a little beep and a holographic image of the frog pulled up. "Hmm. It says it's a common Earth species. Could it be another one of your dinosaurs?"

"No, it cannot be!" I said, fully freaking out. "Never, in the history of frogs, has there ever been a species more than ten pounds. TEN! Not even the Beelzebufo, the KING DADDY of frogs, got to be even a third of the size of that thing!"

Lok nodded slowly, eyeing me as if I'd grown a second head. "All right . . . Do you want to find out what it tastes like or . . . ?"

"I just . . ." Mind reeling, I put my hands on my hips and moved closer. "No scientist in the entire world has ever recorded a frog of that magnitude. Yet there it is. Trying—"

Thwack.

"And failing to eat me. How am I supposed to move on from this?" I asked the frog. "How are you even alive?"

Its only response was to slap me with its tongue again.

"We've already established that doesn't work," I said, running a hand down my face. "Which leads me to ask again, giant frog, how are you alive?" My question ended on a shout that had the behemoth amphibian squatting lower in his place in the dirt.

"Why is she yelling at the frog?" Lok asked Sol.

The hunter shook his head with a smirk. "She does this. Just let her have it."

Intern scoffed from his place on the saddle. "Dory, never mind the frog. We should get going—"

I held up a finger, cutting him off. "We're not going anywhere until I figure this shit out!" I marched up closer to the frog and began snapping pictures with my phone. When I got a good ten feet away, I beckoned Lok closer with a wave. "Hey, Lok, sweetheart, you want to earn some good mate points, grab your spear and come help me."

The larger Sankado dismounted and came to my side. "What do you need, gorgeous?"

Not bothering to look back, I moved in closer to the frog. "If it eats me, stab it until it doesn't."

Sol let off a frustrated noise before jumping off Blossom. "No, no, don't get near it. It's still big enough to swallow you whole!"

I stuck a hand to my hip and whirled to face him. "I know that." Smiling, I nodded to Lok. "That's what he's here for."

Terribly smug, Lok crossed his arms over his chest and looked down his nose at Sol. "Yeah, that's what I'm here for."

Growling, Sol grabbed my shoulder to stop me. "That doesn't mean you go sticking your strange little head into a predator's mouth just because it's big. We've already established that those Biwban took a few creatures from your planet you're not used to seeing. This is no different."

"You don't understand!" I squeezed his biceps and shook him a little bit in my excitement. "It should not exist. Based on the fact that its tongue isn't strong enough to pull me to it"—I paused to run a hand up my body before gesturing to the frog—"a creature which, by all accounts, it should be able to eat due to the increase in size, then . . ." I released the hunter and ran around the frog to capture its full size. "This is my white whale. This is a mystery." I snapped another picture, then looked at my much calmer companions. "Why is no one else freaking out?"

They stared at me blankly, so I moved on to more important matters. The bullfrog's body was half sunken into the dirt. A layer of dried crust around its lower half told me it had been there for a while at least. Drag marks appeared in the dirt behind it and headed toward the river not far away. "So you must have dragged yourself here instead of hopping. Your legs don't appear to be any different from your Earth counterpoint. Which would mean your body hasn't adapted enough to your new size to maintain your mobility. But your tongue didn't get stronger either, and you didn't gain any extra muscle mass to be able to lunge after prey, so just what are you eating, you giant slimy marvel, you?"

The frog's body lifted slightly, so its large eyes could focus on me. One large webbed forefoot came out as the frog shifted its weight to its side.

"Oh! Yes, yes! Come chase me!" I said, running into its sight line and backing up. I patted my knee with one hand and held up my camera in the other. "Come on, big guy. Show me those moves."

Lok glanced at the hunter and gestured toward me. "Should we be jealous?"

"I refuse," he replied instantly.

The frog's forelegs shot out and dug into the ground a few steps from my feet; then with a grunt the frog slowly dragged itself toward me.

"Get away from the blasted frog!" Sol snapped.

The poor giant made a few pitiful attempts at trying to gobble me up. But all I had to do was back up another step to avoid it. There was no way this thing hunted anything bigger than a house cat. Yet it had grown to adulthood, and if those groaning noises coming from the lake were any indication, there were enough of them to warrant a breeding population. What could have caused frogs, of all things, to blow up like this? My mind was so deep down the rabbit hole of this ribbit mystery that I didn't even notice Sol dragging me away until he pulled me in front and forced me to look at him.

"Do you want to die?" he asked, vexation evident in his dark eyes.

"Not particularly."

"Then why are you offering yourself up to a frog?"

"I wanna know what it eats." The words came out a little more clipped than I'd meant them to. "Thought that would be pretty obvious at this point."

"You," he barked. "You and any other wandering creature foolish enough to stick their head in its mouth."

Thwack.

Sol jumped with a yelp, then shot the frog a glare. He closed his eyes on an inhale. "Look, it's not like you can ask it."

I stared wordlessly at him. "OH! I CAN KISS IT AND ASK IT!"

"No!" Sol lunged, catching me around my waist. He brought an arm around my neck, bringing me flush against him. His breath fanned across my ear as he took a measured breath. "You are not kissing the fr—"

Thwack.

I watched as that tongue globbed onto Sol's face seemingly in slow motion; every emotion from surprise to horror to grim acceptance flashed across his face. His cheek pulled away before snapping back on a ricochet.

I couldn't stop the laughter if I tried. Sol threw me over his shoulder and brought me to where Lok was doubled over in the grass. "Watch her," he said, dumping me next to him. Sol left to wash his face off in the river as Lok and I tried to get it together.

"Fly!" bellowed a voice.

The frog's tongue shot out and caught a microraptor flying overhead. Poor thing never stood a chance.

"Oh . . . well, that answers that."

In seconds the frog's meal was no more than a few blue feathers trapped around its mouth. "Ack!" it croaked. In a long confused-sounding bellow, it shouted, "Answers . . . that?" It tilted its head, then blinked rapidly. Then fixed its eyes on me and asked, "Fly?"

Keeping my voice soothing, I answered, "No, buddy. Not a fly."

The frog shuddered at my words, then leaned back and watched the sky. "Not . . . fly."

"Nope."

Its eyes darted to me again, then away. "I . . . not fly." The frog blinked rapidly again. A look of shock crossed its face. "I . . . I can . . . think?" The frog fell very still. Then it just started screaming and didn't stop.

I pulled out my phone and added a note not to grant sentience to any other animals.

CHAPTER 10

WHEN WE FINALLY REACHED THE EDGE OF THE FOREST, my jaw fell open at the sight. Not at the cluster of houses dropped in the middle of nowhere, but the rainbow mountains that surrounded them. A kaleidoscope of colors swirled around the peaks while rocks splattered bits of blue and yellow through the valleys, as if a struggling artist had grabbed buckets of paint and a handful of shrooms and just said, "Fuck it."

The colors were so vivid and fantastical that they seemed to belong to another dimension. Fiery reds and blazing orange raced against waves of ocean blue, creating a swirling pattern that almost looked like it was about to swallow the houses nestled in the center.

"Well?" Intern asked, flying to my side. "Did we get the houses right?"

"Forget the houses. Look at those mountains!" I crept forward on Blossom's back, grabbing her shoulder to get a better look at the way the grass beneath her bled into the first wave of yellow rock.

"What is this place?" Sol asked, looking just as awestruck as I did.

"You've never been here?" I asked.

Lok rode to our side. "Of course he hasn't. The Night Ridge clan are harvesters. If you dragged them too far from the safety of their borders, they'd probably faint."

Not even Lok's gentle ribbing was enough to take Sol's eyes away from the sight before him. But that didn't stop his smart mouth. "Yes, forgive us for not charging headfirst into dangerous unknown territory for the chance to shave a yix."

"Ah, but you don't even know what beautiful dangers you're missing!" Smiling wide, Lok sped ahead of us and gestured to the painted landscape. "Welcome to the Mirage Mountains!"

"It's incredible," I said, snapping a picture. I tucked my phone back into Blossom's saddle, leaving just enough of the solar-panel case exposed to pick up a charge.

Intern groaned and waved impatiently at the cul-de-sac. "Yes, yes, sandstone mashed together by tectonic plates makes a lovely picture. Now the houses, go look at the houses!"

"All right, we're going. Don't molt over it," I said. I gave Blossom a gentle kick, and the duckbill resumed her march.

Lok pulled a waterskin from his pack and took a long drink before tossing it to me. "If you think this is nice, just wait until you see the Fuchsia Grove on the other side. That's where we'll rendezvous with my men tomorrow to hand off the herd. A word of warning, though: there are dangerous predators out here. Be sure you stay close to me, Stardust."

"Worse than the velociraptors and the pink T. rex?" I asked, taking a sip. The water tasted sweeter than candy on my parched throat, and I guzzled down more of it, only to choke on it. I covered my mouth and tried to rein in the coughing fit before water spilled all over my shirt.

"What's a T. rex?" Sol asked.

"Oh right, you two were too busy fighting to see it." I turned around in my seat and stuck my arms to my sides, mimicking a T. rex's tiny arms. "It's the giant raptor dinosaur with tiny arms and huge teeth. A pink one sniffed at me this morning, then walked away. Nearly had a heart attack when it snuck up on me."

Sol looked ashen; his voice was barely above a whisper. "Was it missing an arm?"

"Yeah, do you know it?"

"You've seen the Gruulorak."

I shrugged. "Guess so."

His eyes widened. "You guess so? Dory, I've been hunting the Gruulorak for weeks. That gluttonous monster slaughtered ten of our best warriors and feasted on our cattle until it grew fat." He looked me over as if he were speaking to a ghost. "How are you still alive?"

"I don't know. She sniffed my hair and it made her sneeze, so she left."

"You made her sneeze?" he asked incredulously. "You get approached by the terror that stalks the dreams of my clansmen at night, and you live because you made her sneeze?"

"I don't know what to tell you, man. She's not a fan of hair in her nose."

He ran a hand through his hair and let out a breath. "Why didn't you call us for help?"

"You were busy punching each other in the face. A lady never interrupts."

Lok roared with laughter, nearly falling off the saddle in

his hysterics. "A woman who looks death in the face and shrugs it off. Gods above, you've stolen my heart already."

I flashed him a thumbs-up. "I do my best."

Behind me, my dour companion looked ready to give up on the world entirely. "You two are going to be the death of me."

MY EYES LINGERED ON THE BEDROOM, TAKING IN THE ECcentric decorations with a mix of amusement and confusion. It was as if Intern and his little friends had spent too much time scrolling through a witch's Pinterest board and running with every bizarre idea they found. The walls were a dramatic, deep shade of purple, adorned with hanging pentagrams that added to the overall occult aesthetic.

It was certainly an improvement over the gaudy cowboy chic design of the neighboring house. Despite the different exterior appearances, each house shared the same floor plan—marble countertop kitchens, oversized flat-screen TVs that were really just metal boxes with still images of a football game, and the giant bedroom that took up the entire second floor of each home. Which led me to my latest frustration. "Intern, all of these houses only have one bed."

"Correct," he chirped happily.

I searched the ceiling for the patience that escaped me. "Why do all of these houses only have one bed?"

"Our research shows that the 'only one bed' method is a tried-and-true way to get humans to mate! Thankfully you've been rather agreeable when it comes to mating, but we've added a few incentives to hopefully trigger more obstinate pairings to come together."

Lok clapped his hands together. "It's perfect."

"Of course you think so," I hissed. "Look, I know this is a breeding program hell-bent on getting me pregnant, but I'm going to need some privacy from time to time."

"Do you think you're pregnant yet?" Intern asked, eyes sparkling.

"No, I do not."

"Pity."

"I'm so scared to ask this, but where did you find that research?"

"We found one of your planet's mating guides. Cost a fortune to find a linguistic team skilled enough to make sense of it, but what's a pleasure cruiser's worth of credits in the face of scientific advancement?"

With a deep breath for fortitude, I asked, "What mating guide?"

He pulled up his screen, flipped through a few tabs, and read aloud, "*Romanceopedia: A Guide to Writing the Ultimate Romance*. It references something called an 'only one bed' trope no less than six times."

I nodded. "Sure. Why not, right? It's got 'romance' in the title. Must be true."

His head tilted to the side, large lime-green eyes studying my face intently, and I couldn't help but wonder if this was how the meerkats felt when I studied them. Unnerving to realize that I was now on the other end of the camera. "Your tone suggests that it is sarcasm. Which, from what I understand, means you do not actually agree and are making a jab. Why do you jab? This was said to be very well received on your internet forums."

The hopeful look on his face was as irksome as it was adorable. As easy as it would be to light this house on fire just to spite the research team, I could tell Intern was genuinely proud of his involvement with this project. It wasn't his fault he was tasked with re-creating the homes of an alien life-form with nothing but three days' worth of data. My hand sank into the bedding, and I pretended to take great care in testing the level of softness, before wandering around the room with a critical eye.

Toto shouldered past Lok and leapt on the bed before stretching out. "Oh yes. I like this. This is nice." The lion flopped down onto the pillows and settled in.

Intern watched, unblinking. Each stop I made was mirrored by shuffling feet or the occasional twitch of his crest. "You know what? This is pretty good, Intern. I'm impressed."

"YES!" he shrieked, flapping his wings. He froze midair with a shocked look and fell to the floor. He patted down his feathers before clearing his throat. "What I meant to say was, I'm glad you like them. We at the Biodiversity Conservation Initiative strive to make your planet as habitable as possible."

Damn my love for small animals.

"All right, well, fellas, you enjoy this one. I'll be in house number 5. Let's go, Toto," I said.

Intern froze. "What? No, you have to sleep together. That's the whole point!"

Lok caught my arm as I headed out the door. "I agree. Stay here with me tonight. The bed is plenty big for the three of us. Right, Sol?" He motioned toward the bed, where Toto was already snoring. "Or four," he amended.

Weariness deepened the shadows under Sol's eyes. He pushed himself off the doorframe he leaned against. "I've no interest in sharing a bed with you either. Let her sleep where she wants."

A sliver of annoyance crossed Lok's face before it was smothered away. "Don't be that way. As I mentioned, there are dangerous predators in this area. It would be safest for her to stay with us. Who knows what could wander inside in the middle of the night."

"Yes, yes! Dangers abound. Everybody stay in the same bed!" Intern demanded.

"I'm sure she can figure out how to lock a door," Sol deadpanned. He put an arm around my waist and led me out of the room.

"But—"

Sol cut him off. "Don't be clingy."

"It feels like you three have NO concern over the success of this project." Intern let out an aggravated squawk and flew out the window.

Once outside, Sol walked me into the next house and closed the door behind us.

The tension in his shoulders made me think he had something to say, so I kept quiet. He peered through the window, looking to see if Lok had followed. When the coast was clear, he crossed his arms over his chest and leaned against the wall. "We need to talk."

"Mmm. That's never followed up with good news. Are you breaking up with me, Sol?"

He checked the window again, then ran a hand down his face. "Please, be serious for a moment."

The tension in his voice made the hair on the back of my neck stand up. "What's wrong?"

"Lok isn't a Roamcrest. He's General Ghoszi Lokbaatar of the Singing Arrows, one of the most notorious war generals back on Sankatul."

Great. Cool. Of course he is. 'Cause why would anything ever be easy? I swallowed the lump in my throat and asked, "How notorious?"

"He's said to be the mastermind responsible for the flooding of Tynfo and turning the tide in the Broken Plains War. I'd assumed he and the rest of his ilk died in the Calamity when the spaceship crashed on Dulrock. The continent's decimation was all over the paper for weeks. I have no idea how he survived or why he's posing as a Roamcrest, but I need to know now if you want to stay with him. If not, we wait for him to fall asleep and run. I won't be able to save you if it comes down to a fight."

"Are . . . are you sure it's him?"

Sol nodded. "I had my suspicions as soon as I saw the arrow tattooed on his throat. It wasn't until he summoned his Beast using the call of the Amdora bird that the pieces fell into place in my head. That call was the greeting card used by his war band before laying waste to whatever fools got in their way." His eyes took in my trembling form, and he pushed off the wall before placing a comforting hand on my shoulder. "I'm not saying this to frighten you. But you have a right to know who you're traveling with."

"I . . . Wait, but you two have been trading blows all day. What makes you so sure he'd win if it came down to it?"

"A warrior that powerful could have killed me thrice over by now. If he decided he didn't want to share you, he could have tossed you in the air, slit my throat, and caught you before your feet ever hit the ground. Our morning spat was merely him toying with me. Notice how he never once resorted to his fire? I was hurling everything I had at him to no avail. I'm not foolish enough to think I stood a chance if he was actually trying to hurt me. Tell me now, do you want to leave?"

"Leave?" Lok's deep voice cut through the air like a blade.

My head whipped around to see him draped along the windowsill, his chin resting in his palm. "Without so much as a goodbye? Dory, you'll break my heart."

"Lok," I gasped, and took a step back.

He tensed as if I'd struck him, and the ever-present grin on his face faltered. "Now, now. Don't be that way. I haven't done anything to hurt you, have I?" he asked with deceptive calm.

"Were you eavesdropping?" Sol hissed.

Lok took on an innocent face and shook his head. "No. Well, yes, but I have a good reason." He placed a bundle of neatly wrapped cloth on the windowsill, then grinned. "Darling, I brought you dinner."

"Is it true?" I asked. "Are you really a war criminal?"

"Criminal?" he asked, cocking his head to the side. "Depends on who you ask, I suppose. I've done what needed doing in order to win. But the same could be said for the other side as well."

"Sol just said you flooded a city!"

"Did he, now?" His smile returned as he eyed the other Sankado.

Fear, stark and vivid, showed in Sol's eyes, and I kicked myself for opening my big mouth. Lok brought his attention back to me, still wearing that deceptive grin. "It's true. I did. But not without due cause, you see." He crossed his arms over his chest and sighed. "Osid, the cowardly king that he is—er, *was*—set fire to my people's capital, Uslanknot. All because I was beating him at the war *his father* started, if you can believe that."

He shrugged, like he was recounting office gossip instead of a war. The feigned indifference he used as armor shone brightly. "War is as war does. He burns down my city, I flood his, and on and on we fight and kill until a giant spaceship drops down right on top of us."

"You are very nonchalant about all this," I said.

He barked out a laugh as the armor cracked. "Why wouldn't I be? I spend my life fighting an unwinnable war, finally turn the tide, and then . . . the world ends." He ran a hand through his hair, still chuckling like it was the funniest joke in the world. "And now I herd yix and got mated to a stranger and an alien."

He laughed harder, and it was infectious and heartbreaking. "And now I'm taking that alien on a quest to punch a bird alien who may or may not be partially responsible for the end of my old world, while in the company of her talking predator friend, yet another bird alien, and—" He paused and looked at Sol. "Sol, what did you do before the Calamity?"

"I was a lawyer."

"A lawyer? Of course. No wonder you're wound so tight. So I'm traveling with three aliens and a lawyer to punch a bird in the face."

Sol chuckled, then laughed so loud and wide that it spread to the rest of us, and once it started, it didn't stop. The giggle fit was hysterical and uncontrollable, and for some reason it was the most at ease I'd felt since I crash-landed. But Lok was right. The whole thing was absurd.

"So, what do we do now?" I asked, reining in my giggles.

"I believe you wanted to take a shower. Then sleep on your own, instead of safe and sound in my arms, where you should be." Lok outright pouted as he crossed his arms.

"And what then? We just wake up tomorrow and keep going like everything is normal?"

He snorted. "What's normal on this planet?"

"Point taken," I amended.

"Are you going to kill me?" Sol asked.

Lok raised a brow, then rested his chin on his hand like he was thinking about it. "Do I need to?"

"No," Sol replied carefully.

Lok nodded, then bid us both good night and left. Sol and I stood in the living room watching him retreat to one of the other houses. I broke the silence first. "He didn't answer the question."

"No." Sol sighed. "No, he did not."

CHAPTER 11

NOTHING RUINS THE BLISSFUL AFTERGLOW OF A SCALDING-hot shower like a saber-toothed tiger in your bedroom.

Water dripped from my red curls to the hardwood floor. My hand stayed frozen on the doorknob while the cat pinned me with a chilling glare.

"You have no business being in this climate."

She snarled.

I shut the door.

Resting my head against the doorframe, I tried to fight off the impending mental spiral of why in the world an ice-age megafauna was in such a hot landscape. Clearly the Biwban just dropped every animal they made wherever they wanted, but did no one question the reason for the double coat? The damn thing must be so hot. "Stop it, Dory. Focus," I whispered to myself. "How does one get a *Smilodon* out of one's bedroom?"

For a moment, I decided to pretend that the *Smilodon* and

I came to an agreement where we both just decided the other didn't exist so we could move on with our lives in peace.

Bam!

"I'm sure that was nothing."

The *Smilodon* roared and threw herself against the bedroom door. Which probably meant she'd decided to try to eat me after all, instead of allowing us to delude ourselves into a mutual peace. Shame, really. Why does no one else want to live in delululand?

I calmly walked over to the window next to the staircase, opened it, stuck my head out, and screamed bloody murder. The reaction was immediate: Toto leapt up from his spot resting in a patch of grass and looked around wildly. My two aliens burst from their respective houses and bolted toward mine.

Help on the way, I pulled my towel tighter around my body and descended the stairs. By the time I reached the bottom, the *Smilodon* had smashed a paw through the bedroom door and was frantically clawing at the wood to get out.

My trio of protectors burst through the front door while the *Smilodon* broke down the other. I shouldered my way past them. "Take care of that, fellas. I'll be in house 1."

"Great fireball in the sky. She is a *vision*." Toto's voice held the reverence of a prayer. I turned back to see the lion staring at the enraged *Smilodon* at the top of the steps. He crept forward. Fangs the size of daggers glinted as she snarled at him.

"Toto, I don't think she wants to talk," Sol warned.

He slinked closer, never taking his eyes off her as he reached the staircase. "She . . . she can talk, snarl, or spill my blood on these steps. As long as she tells me her name."

The *Smilodon* roared when his paw reached the first step. He froze.

"Toto, are you insane? Get away from her—she'll kill you!" I moved to stop him.

Lok blocked my path and said, "Let him handle this."

"If she were a cobra I'd beg for her poison every sunrise and sunfall." His forward advance was met with a dangerous swipe from her claws. He backed to the bottom of the steps and sat down. "It's too soon, you're right. What would we tell the cubs if we rushed things? You luscious thing, our sons will be giants."

She didn't swipe at him again, but she did jump out the window.

Toto darted up the steps to watch her retreat to god knows where. "I'll see you tomorrow? Or tonight? Just roar when you want some company. Or worship. Everlasting adoration." He sighed, so struck with wistful pining that he couldn't keep his mouth shut and kept going. "Oh, darling, why are we fighting this? I want to swim in your eyes and die defending your lands!"

We dodged out of his way when he ran out the door after her. "She's going to eat him," Sol said.

"Probably."

"No faith in either of you." Lok shook his head in admonishment.

"Well, as much as I love standing around dripping on claw-marked hardwood, I'm going to get dressed and snag one of the other beds." I held a hand up to Lok when he opened his mouth. "No, not yours."

The bedroom in the first house was on fire. Which was odd, as when I first explored the house some two hours prior, it was definitely not on fire. Stranger still, the roof of the second house collapsed just before I stepped inside. I glared at Lok, who held his hands up in surrender. "I swear, it's not me."

Sol motioned to the third house. "There's still two beds left. Sleep in house 3 and Lok and I can share 4."

"Oh, thanks, Sol, that's real—" My words were interrupted by a loud rumbling, causing me to lose my balance and fall to the ground. Lok quickly grabbed me and pulled us away from house 3 just in time for two massive brontosaurs to come crashing through it.

The force of their collision was so strong that I could feel the ground shake beneath my feet. One of them swung its long neck at the other with such force that I worried it might have given itself a concussion. The second brontosaur stumbled and crashed into the neighboring house, sending shingles flying to the ground. But the larger one wasn't finished yet; it let out a fierce cry before charging toward its rival and slamming into it once again, chasing it off into the darkness of the night.

Which left us with one house and one bed.

I turned to see the intern perched on the mailbox of the final house. The little blue bird innocently cleaned his feathers, refusing to look at me. "How did you even do this?" I asked him.

His feathers poofed like he was shocked at the accusation. "Me? I . . . I didn't do anything."

"I know it was you, okay? Today is not the day I get gaslit by a *bird*. The bedroom did not just spontaneously catch fire."

He flicked a piece of fuzz off his talon before inspecting it. "Must be faulty wiring. I'll send in a work order to the maintenance team when we get to the research center."

"And the roof?"

His crest flattened against his head as he shifted on his feet. ". . . Water damage."

"The rampaging dinosaurs?"

"Mating season!"

I clicked my tongue. "Intern, what's your name?"

His eyes widened. "Why?"

"What do you mean 'why'?" I shrugged nonchalantly. "I'm just asking your name."

Tiny fingers tapped nervously on his leg. "You've never needed my name before this moment. What would cause you to need it now? I'm fine with you just referring to me as my title. Why are you coming closer? Stop advancing!"

I spread my arms wide and smiled. "Why do you look so stressed? I'm just asking for the name of the creature who is lying straight to my face." The last few words came out in a rush as I lunged at him. My fingers brushed soft tail feathers before he darted out of the way.

"I'm not lying!" he shouted, then flapped for all he was worth when I jumped up to grab him. His tiny wings weren't meant for hovering, but they damn sure tried in the face of my wrath. "These are all just highly unfortunate coincidences that have nothing to do with— Ah! Stop trying to grab me! That have nothing to do with my chances at promotion!"

"Aha! So that's your game!"

"No, it isn't."

"Bullshit, we all heard you."

"Oh zorblax!" he cursed. Intern ducked behind Lok, using the larger Sankado as a meat shield before trying to placate me with a friendly grin. "Look, Dory, I misspoke. Remain calm, everything is fine."

I stomped my foot. "Everything is not fine! You purposely orchestrated these events to get us to sleep together, admit it!"

His cheeks puffed before he let out a shrill cry. "All right, fine! I admit it. I lured the *Smilodon* into your room, I compromised the structural integrity of that roof, and yes, I set the bedroom ablaze! Happy?"

"No! Why are you going so far just to get us to sleep in the same room? We're already fucking. Your work is complete."

It was his turn to stomp. "Physical attraction isn't enough. You're supposed to fall in love with each other so the pairings last! The guidebook clearly states that this trope sets the stage for tension, humor, *and* romantic developments. You've been with them all day and your affection meter has barely risen.

"There's an affection meter?" Lok asked.

"Yes." Intern reached into the feathers in his neck ruff and pulled out a little egg-shaped pendant. He removed the necklace to reveal the screen on the back. He pressed a button and the screen lit up with a jaunty little tune. Two pixelated characters danced next to a couple of bars.

I took it from him and inspected it more closely; Lok and Sol both peered over my shoulder as well. The background was a gradient of yellow and turquoise, with four star-shaped buttons lining the bottom. Both characters did the same little dancy dance, but the meters next to them were mostly empty. The green liquid on the slightly smaller character's meter filled up only three of the ten notches, while the other had two. "Is this Tamagotchi supposed to mean anything?" I spat out.

"Of course. That shot I gave you also had a little chip that lets my affection meter keep track of your hormonal levels and biometric data. I expected this thing to be half-full by now. Sol's is a little higher, but these numbers are terrible. Terrible! So stop being difficult—"

"DIFFICULT?"

"YES, DIFFICULT. Now, go sleep in the bed!"

"OH, I COULD JUST THROTTLE YOU." Before I could make good on the threat, Sol hooked his arms under mine and began dragging me to the final house.

"There's been enough destruction for one day, Dory. Let's just go. Intern, stay out of the house tonight. We'll see you in the morning."

The Biwban glared back at me, feathers puffed up in a sorry excuse to make himself look bigger. *I will pluck those feathers off one by one.* "I will never forget this slight," I seethed.

"Come on, darling," Sol drawled.

"Do you hear me?"

"Good night, Intern," Lok called.

"NEVER!"

I RUMMAGED THROUGH THE DRAWERS OF THE BEDROOM, looking for any kind of garment that could pass for a bonnet. If I had to hazard a guess, I'd say the clothes and items inside the house were also AI generated based on what an AI thought would be in a human house. Shiny metallic catsuits took up an entire drawer, and another was filled with Renaissance-style clothing. There was a pair of men's boxers made of silk that might've worked, but I just couldn't bring myself to put them on my head. The curls must be protected, but at what cost? I sighed, throwing the boxers back in the drawer. "There will be no tension," I said coldly.

Lok combed out his hair next to the full-length mirror in the corner. "Of course, my heart."

"No humor or romantic developments either." Another drawer revealed the bright, flowery aesthetic of 1970s disco. Still nothing I could really use as a bonnet, but disco clothing would be a lot less hot than the Renaissance clothes or the catsuits. My own T-shirt and cargo pants smelled like ass after days of running around, so there was no way I was putting them back on tomorrow. Instead, I laid out a gold backless halter top and a pair of bell-bottom pants. Not the best travel clothes, but beggars can't be choosers.

Honestly, I gave the AI props for having clothes in my size. It may not have known what time period I was from, but I guess it also had no idea what the American standard of beauty was either. The clothing size ranged from toddler to sumo wrestler. And by that I mean I literally found a sumo wrestler outfit.

"Wouldn't dream of it," Sol murmured. His hair was wet from the shower, and the pants he wore hung low on his waist. I did my best not to stare.

Okay, fine. I stared.

A frustrated chirp came from outside the window. "But that just defeats the purpose—"

"Intern, I swear to god."

"All right, fine."

"What are you looking for, Dory?" Lok asked.

"My hair has been a nightmare with all this adventuring. I'm trying to find something I can use for a bonnet. You wouldn't happen to have an extra sash made of yix wool, would you?" It was a pity and a crime I wasn't given a moment's notice before getting shipped off into an alien breeding program. They could've at least let me bring a carry-on bag. I had no hair supplies, no lotion, no laptop filled to the brim with movies, nothing.

I'm gonna punch that guy twice.

"I should have one in my pack over there; check the front pocket." He pointed to a bag in the corner.

I made my way over and plucked a roll of yellow fabric from the front pocket and rolled it out. The material was unbelievably soft in my hands, and I breathed a sigh of relief. "Lok, I'm gonna be honest here. You scare me a bit, but, dammit, you're growing on me."

"Scared? What for?"

"Oh, I dunno, the general warlord business and the 'you're mine' attitude. Lest we forget, your and Sol's little 'will they / won't they kill each other' dance."

"Come on, that was funny."

Sol stared at him. "For. Who?"

"Calm your fire, harvester. I was only kidding around."

We'll see about that.

Lok held a hand over the tip of his right horn and bowed slightly. "From now on, I'll be on my best behavior. There. All better now, right?" When the room fell silent, he let out a huff. "What is it?"

"I mean, you've still seen battle," I said.

"So?"

I rolled my eyes. "By show of hands, who in this room has killed someone?"

Lok and Sol both raised their hands.

"WHAT?"

Sol scratched the back of his head, looking not nearly contrite enough for the admission of murder. "Your morals have to be set aside in the apocalypse. Things are more stable now, but when we were first dropped on this planet, there was a lot of infighting."

His words rocked me. Of course he'd told me about the destruction of his planet before, but for some reason it never truly hit home the horrors they must've faced on a dying world. It was a miracle Lok was as nonchalant as he was.

"And he's a lawyer," Lok said in a low, conspiratorial voice.

Sol's posture straightened and his arms crossed over his chest. "And what does that have to do with anything?"

"I'd say it means you probably let evil men back on the streets every now and then. Who's to say you haven't released anyone far worse than me? At least the viscera I carved had a purpose." He nodded at Sol and whispered to me, "He's clearly a villain, this one. I say you just kick him out now."

His rival snorted. "So much for art needing to be shared."

"Things have changed," Lok shot back.

"You're just jealous that I'm higher up on the affection meter than you."

"YES!"

"Calm down," I said, getting into bed. "I've known you a day and Sol a fraction longer. Don't expect any insta-love from me."

Lok sighed dramatically and climbed into bed. His weight dipped the mattress until I rolled into his side. He settled me to rest my head on his arm. "Fine, Sol wins today. I'll make up ground tomorrow."

"Don't get your hopes up," Sol replied. He slid into the other side and rested his hands behind his head, a smug grin on his face. "I'm sensing this might be a recurring theme."

"Pride comes before a fall."

"Whatever you need to tell yourself."

"That's it." I slapped my hands on my thighs and sat up. "Intern, toss me the Tamagotchi." I caught it easily enough and pressed the center button. When its theme song started to play, I focused my attention on Sol's meter.

"Wait, what are you doing?"

Through the sheer power of spite, I focused on every little annoyance I could think of.

Sol sucked in a breath when his meter began to drop. "Stop that!"

Lok's roaring laughter shook the bed, and it took all my focus not to grin. When the meter dropped down to one bar, Sol snatched it from my hands and threw it across the room.

"There, it's over," I said, settling in. "Now, both of you, shut up. I'm going to sleep."

CHAPTER 12

I AWOKE TO A FRUSTRATED BIWBAN STANDING ON MY chest. "Why hasn't your meter risen?"

Sol's head was buried in the crook of my neck, while his arm was slung over my waist. Odd. I would have pegged Lok as the resident snuggler. Yet my large companion merely slept on his back beside me, snoring softly. Somebody's tail was wrapped around my leg, but it was too much effort to sort out whose limbs were whose so early in the morning.

Eyes still heavy with sleep, I blinked at Intern a few times, then let my head fall back on the pillow. "Release my tit."

He stared down at his talons, which were clamped firmly on my left boob for purchase. He shuffled back to my belly and said, "This is serious. If the meter falls below zero, the department head will want to take corrective action. What's it going to take to raise your affection level?"

I was about to tell him to fuck off back to his space pod, but a thought wormed its way into my coffee-less brain. Intern had no idea how humans acted. I could tell him anything. Literally anything.

"Mmm. I'll need my own sleeping space."

"But the book—"

"The book is only half-right. The 'only one bed' trope can work, sure. But we also need time apart to sort out our feelings. It's called pining."

He repeated the word. There was a soft green flash and suddenly he was typing on his little floating screen. "Time apart needed for pining. What else?"

"Coffee and chocolate."

"Food?" He tilted his head. "We have plenty of food on this planet. I'll do a scan of the local fauna to see what's edible."

"No, no. This is specific food. Coffee helps keep our minds focused, and *chocolate*"—I stressed the word, filling it with as much desire as I could. "That's the real game changer. Some say love is impossible without it."

"Really?" His eyes sparkled.

"Of course. Chocolate is one of our most important foods. We have an entire holiday dedicated to love, and the sacred food is chocolate. Normally, potential romantic partners give each other chocolate, and Cupid, the god of love, blesses their union."

"And this chocolate triggers love?"

I nodded. "Oh yes. I'm no scientist, mind you, but I remember reading an article that said chocolate helps stimulate the chemicals in our brains responsible for love and bonding."

He was practically vibrating with excitement now. His little fingers flew across the keyboard, jotting down every word of my bullshit. "I may not have the means to acquire this chocolate now. But as soon as I get to the lab at the research center, we should be able to find examples of this chocolate and re-create it."

"Perfect. There's still hope, then."

"I wonder if there's anything in my database that I could use." The feathers on his crest flicked, mirroring his rushing thoughts. With a beep, his screen faded away. "I'll need to look over my notes. When you finish resting, I'll be downstairs." He dashed out of the room with a quickness.

"I thought he'd never leave," Sol murmured.

"Oh, you were awake."

"Mostly." He untangled himself from me and rose with a stretch. My tired eyes fluttered closed as he shuffled about the room, only opening again when I heard a creak on Lok's side of the bed. Sol put a finger to his lips in a shushing motion. His free hand held the red ropes I'd seen on Lok's clothing. Very carefully, he lifted the other man's wrists and tied them to the bedpost.

"What are you doing?" I whispered.

A mischievous chuckle was his only answer. He fetched something from the corner of the room and placed it on the side of the bed. Hair slightly tousled from sleep, an irresistibly devastating grin on his face, he trailed his fingers along my ankle. "Good morning."

My measly mortal brain melted in the face of such boyish charm. "Good mor— Oh!"

He dragged me by the ankle to the edge of the bed and guided my knees up with gentle authority. With a fluid yank, the sweatpants I'd been using as pj's vanished. My heartbeat sped up as his finger tenderly traced the line of my hip bone. His grin deepened at my shudder. He hooked the hem of my panties beneath his thumb and slowly dragged them off me before kneeling at the edge of the bed. His lips played down the expanse of my inner thigh, sending tremors of anticipation to flutter in my belly. Just before I expired from want, he buried his face between my legs.

I moaned softly, then bit my finger to keep from crying out and waking Lok. The ridges of his tongue glided along my folds. Oh Mylanta, I forgot his tongue had ridges. Every tongue should, if this is the pleasure it could bring, slow, languid licks that teased my aching flesh until I quivered.

Muffled cries filled the room as he flicked his tongue against my clit. My back came off the bed when he covered the little bud and sucked. The bumps along the side of his tongue rolled against it, before he licked the expanse of my pussy. Groaning, he threw my leg over his shoulder and drove his tongue deep inside me.

"Fuck," I cried out. My hands found his horns, holding on for dear life as I fucked myself on his tongue. His fingers dug into my ass as he held me tighter to him. That damnably long tongue rolled inside me, letting the nubbed bumps massage my sweet spot in a rapture so good it had to be sin.

My body shook; desperate whimpers fell past my lips as my orgasm climbed at a breakneck pace. Then he vanished, turning my whimpers into an indignant half snarl. "Wha? Why did you stop?"

Sol grinned up at me, licking my wetness from his lips. He nodded to the corner of the bed and said, "Give me my rating back."

"Huh?"

He removed my hand from his horn and kissed my wrist. "You took my higher rating away. Give it back."

Still confused, I looked to the edge of the bed to see the fucking Tamagotchi. Sol's icon danced next to his meager one bar.

Men and their damn pride.

"Are you kidding me?"

His lips twitched; he was clearly having the time of his life. "Do you want to come or not?"

"Yes, I want to come," I hissed, "but if your goal here is to win my affection, pissing me off is not the way to do it."

"Oh really?" He nipped the sensitive skin at my thigh, then ran a finger lazily around my clit. "You think I can't see the way your body tremors when I tease you?" He shoved a finger inside me, roughly stroking my sweet spot. His tail latched onto my clit; slow movements cast aside, Sol set a delirious pace. Stars danced behind my eyes as my hips bucked against him. He shrugged off my thigh, pressed his forehead to mine, and whispered, "I think you like being toyed with. Don't you, darling?"

My breathing was quick and shallow. My pulse thudded in my ears, beating faster and faster every second this sadistic fucker didn't let me come. "Not even a little bit."

He chuckled. "You're a cute little liar, you know that?"

My heart fluttered.

The Tamagotchi dinged.

We both froze, then looked over to see the proof of my lie in the form of Sol's affection meter. Now back to three. The pixelated version of Sol danced happily to its cheery theme song as fireworks exploded around the bar. A rush of warmth flooded my cheeks, only made worse by the knowing grin on his face.

"Shut up."

His laugh was aggravatingly rich and warm. And despite my embarrassment, pride wormed its way into my chest that I was the one to draw it from him.

Another ding.

"Oh, fuck off, Tamagotchi."

A growl came from behind me. I heard the headboard shatter before Sol's eyes widened. In seconds, Lok had shoved Sol away from me and took his place kneeling between my legs. He tore off the red tie around his wrists with his teeth, then shot Sol a dirty look and pointed to the door. "You, out."

Two Tamagotchi dings and a sore coochie later . . .

"Are these yix eggs?" I asked. The biggest poached egg I'd ever seen sat in front of me. Slices of buttered bread lay next to it. I was half-tempted to ask where the butter came from but wasn't sure if I'd like the answer. I gathered a spoonful of egg, sent a small prayer to the stars that dinosaurs didn't carry salmonella, and took a bite. A bit gamey, but rich.

Lok took a moment to swallow before answering. "No, they won't lay until early summer. I found these near Fujilly Rock."

"'Spose that makes sense. Any idea what they were from?"

He shrugged. "Not a clue. Why do you ask?"

Sol cut off another slice of bread from the loaf in the center of the table, then slabbed a generous portion of jam on it. "She likes to scream at every beast and leaf she sees."

"I am not *screaming* at them."

"Could have fooled me," he said. Then yelped when I kicked him under the table.

"I'm cataloging them. And it's not every leaf. Just enough to get a sense of the genetic diversity."

He nodded agreeably as he chewed. Unfortunate that the man was allergic to actually being agreeable. "Of course. My mistake. She just needs to scream at every leaf she sees until the proper amount of genetic diversity is found."

"I know you're saying that to be catty, but you've stepped into a huge pile of my hyperfixation, so listen up."

He fetched another slice of bread from the center of the table. "Oh joy."

I studied the piece in his hand before asking, "Are you carbo-loading or do you just not like eggs? You've already gone through half the loaf."

"He needs the yeast if he wants to replenish his fire," Lok said, and slid the rest of the bread over to Sol. "Go ahead and take the rest." His voice turned low and smug. "Unlike you, I don't go around wasting fire. You fight like you'll never run out."

Sol rolled his eyes as he downed another slice. "Forgive me for not spending my days learning proper battle techniques. Setting your enemies on fire is generally looked down on in court. No matter how deeply satisfying it would have been for a few of them."

I held up a finger. "Um . . . quick question: how does bread make fire?"

The two men looked at each other, confused. Lok blew out a breath and ran a hand through his hair.

"You don't know?" I asked.

"Of course we know," Sol said. But the way his brows knit together suggested otherwise. "It's just . . . been a while since health class."

"Their bodies naturally produce ethanol as a metabolic byproduct." Intern spoke up from the couch. His eyes were still glued to the screen as he typed away. "When their bellies are full of yeast, they can ferment the ethanol into methane and store it in the gas chambers in their tails."

Sol drummed his fingers on the table. "Yeah, what he said."

"AHA!" The three of us jumped at Intern's outburst. The Biwban had forgone breakfast in favor of sitting on the couch in the living room engrossed in his notes. If it hadn't been for the faint sound of his typing, I would have forgotten him completely.

"Find something good, Intern?" I asked.

He jumped to his feet and flapped over to our table, snatched the Tamagotchi off Sol's belt, and flew out the window.

"I'll . . . take that as a yes, then."

"Excitable little thing, isn't he?" Lok remarked.

Sol shrugged and nudged my arm. "Never mind the bird. Tell us why you scream at leaves. I'm waiting with bated breath over here."

"Thank you. Enthusiasm is encouraged." I shoveled a few more bites of food into my maw, then pulled out the pictures on my phone. "I know y'all don't have any frame of reference for the plants and animals of my home world, but the fact that this planet has so many species from different geologic time periods is madness. Look at this stegosaur eating dandelions. Those two things existed millions of years apart from each other. Yet it's just munching away. Don't even get me started on the ground sloth."

Lok rested his chin on his wrist and flipped through the pictures. "What if I wanted to get you started on the ground sloth?"

"I was so hoping you'd say that. I have a lot of feelings about this."

Taking the phone from Lok, Sol looked at the picture of

the sloth, then his eyes widened in recognition. "Are you talking about the duviff you were yelling at the day we met?"

"You screamed at a duviff?" Lok asked incredulously. "Why? They're as peaceful as can be so long as you leave them alone."

"I'm sure they are. But the point is, they don't belong here either. They're from the last ice age on my planet. I'm pretty sure I also saw a reindeer running around yesterday. None of these animals belong in a warm climate like this. Yet, Sol, you mentioned your people were dropped on this planet over ten years ago, right?"

"Give or take," he said.

"I just don't understand how these creatures are still alive and coexisting with each other like everything is normal."

"Dory, what did you do before all of this?" Lok asked.

"I was training to get my degree in wildlife biology."

He cracked a grin before covering his mouth to avoid laughing up egg all over the rest of us. "No wonder you had so many questions about the yix. Still, I had no idea most of this world's creatures came from your world. What planet do you hail from?"

"Mine was called Earth. You know, now that I think about it, I never asked what this planet is called."

Then men paused, then looked at each other in confusion. "Did your clan ever decide on a name?" Sol asked Lok.

He shook his head, took the time to swallow, then asked, "You?"

"No. Nobody wanted the responsibility after the last guy."

"Really?" I asked. "Nobody came up with a name?"

"Oh, there were plenty of names thrown around when we first landed," Sol began. "The problem was, every remaining world leader—"

"Or any sap in middle management or above," Lok interjected.

Sol nodded and continued. "Basically any idiot with a thirst for power decided that whoever came up with the planet's official name became the ruler of it. It was called Bulcovar for a while. Then it kept changing."

"Why didn't it just stay Bulcovar?" I asked.

Sol chuckled. "Bulcovar ended up with his head on a pike next to the destroyed sign."

"Oh."

"Do you want to name it?" Sol asked.

I swallowed thickly. "No. I don't think I do."

"Don't fret. No one's going to kill a woman on this planet. You're too rare."

"Comforting," I said dryly.

Lok pounded a fist on the table. "She could probably name it after her right ass cheek and the men in my band would praise the name as scripture."

"You know, for once I agree with you." Sol leaned back in his chair and eyed me expectantly. "Well, Stardust, what will it be?"

The nickname threw me for a loop. "Since when do you call me Stardust?"

"What, he's the only one with nickname privileges?" he asked, pointing his thumb at Lok. "Hardly seems fair."

"Okay, fine. Stardust it is, I guess. Hmm. Never been asked to name a planet before."

"The pressure's on," Sol teased. "Make it good, lest Bulcovar's spirit haunt you for the rest of your days."

Lok flicked a piece of egg at him. He pinched his fingers next to another bit of egg, ready to fire it off. "Be nice."

"You're no fun," Sol grumbled. He turned to me, grabbed the end of my chair, and flipped me around to face him. "Quick, don't think. Say whatever word pops into your mind. Now."

Fuck, the pressure of being put on the spot. How does anyone name anything? Do I even speak English or have I been trapped in a fever dream my whole life where everyone was just pretending to understand what I was saying?

"Stop thinking. Any word. Go!"

Somewhere in the panicked recesses of my mind, a word sprang forth. "Waffles!"

Waffles?

Sol released his hold on my chair and crossed his arms over his chest. The men shared a look, then nodded. "I can get behind a name like that."

Lok picked up his water and raised the glass high. "Long live planet Waffles!"

I scooted my chair back in place, then let my head fall into my hands. *I just named a planet after a breakfast food. A once-in-a-lifetime opportunity, and my dumb ass said "waffles."*

There was a scratch at the door. Sol got up and opened it, then nearly took a door to the face when a frantic Toto burst through. He was covered in mud, his mane half-stuck-up like he'd slept on his side.

"Dory!" His paws slammed into my chest, sending both of us to the ground, along with my breakfast.

"Good morning, Toto," I said flatly.

"Never mind the time of day! Get out your captain's log. I have important information."

"I just showered, man."

"What does that have to do with my important information?" he growled. "Wait, is that food?" He sniffed at the egg splattered all over my face, then licked it.

"Ew, gross! Get your sandpaper tongue off me!" I shoved at his face and rolled from beneath him. He ignored my complaints and gobbled up the egg on the floor.

Lok reached out a hand and helped me up. "How did it go with your new woman, Toto?"

"Incredible." The word came out muffled around the egg in his mouth. He swallowed and continued. "I barely escaped with my life."

"Oh shit, are you okay?" I asked, and noticed the claw marks on his back.

"No, I am not okay. I'm so in love I could cry. I just want to settle down with her and any sisters she may have and raise a whole mess of cubs. Now, open up your log!"

Sol returned to his spot at the table. "What's this about a captain's log?"

"I'm keeping a research log of all the things I see here, in case I get rescued or something and go back to Earth."

"You want to leave?" Lok's question came out in a tone that sucked the heat out of the room, but I was in no mood.

"Don't start with the crazy mate shit. It's too early." I pulled out my phone and set up a new recording. "I'll need to make one for yesterday anyway; we'll just pretend we recorded this last night. All right, you start us off," I said, holding the phone out for Toto.

Toto cleared his throat, and his eyes sparkled with a wistful gleam. "I fell in love today."

"That's not research, Toto."

"It is to me!" he snapped. He breathed deep, then sat down to settle in for his tale. "I saw my reflection in the gleam of her fangs and knew I was nothing without her. Our daughters will expand our territory far beyond where any lion has laid claim before. When we return our bodies to the ground, the land will see my love for her reflected in the might of the sons we leave behind. Let this day mark the first step of our courtship, and let the wounds on my back bear witness to my oath. I will have her!"

Why is the lion more romantic than the last three of my exes?

Sol kneeled next to him and inspected his back. "You just love wasting my med supplies, don't you?" He shook his head and moved to dig through a pack he'd left on the couch. "Go rinse yourself off. There's no point cleaning a wound covered in mud."

"What, this?" Toto asked. "It's just a scratch. A love mark. I'll be—"

"Dead of infection in a week if that wound is not properly sanitized," Sol insisted impatiently. "Do you have any idea how many workplace negligence cases I've won because an employer didn't insist a worker clean the wound after they got injured on the job and it got infected? Too many. Go rinse off."

Toto's face scrunched and he looked to me for help, but I merely shrugged. Seeing as I slept through most of my mandated first aid class, I wasn't really in a position to argue over which wounds would result in a negligence lawsuit. "Go wash off, I guess. I can't help you."

"Fine," he huffed. "How?"

Right. Lion.

"I guess . . . I will be the one washing you off."

Toto took to the bath about as well as anyone would expect a lion to take to a bath. Which was very unwell and full of thrashing. The pet shampoo I'd managed to find was meant for puppies above six weeks of age, but anyone in hearing range of Toto's caterwauling probably thought it was pure acid.

I slipped on the wet tiles of the bathroom floor and fell on my ass. Toto raised his head and prepared to shake and I held my arms up to shield myself. "Toto, no!"

My cry was ignored and the lion shook water and soap everywhere. When he tried to get out of the tub, I clambered my way up, grabbed him in a headlock, and forced him back in. "Oh, you jerk! Be happy I knew to put this shower cap on. If you messed up my hair—"

"What?" he snarled. "You'll keep bathing me with that foul-smelling slop? Get OFF!" He jerked back, falling onto his back when I let go. Water splashed out of the tub and all over my front.

I wiped the suds from my brow, grabbed him by the front leg, and furiously scrubbed at the mud caked onto his belly. "No, I'll shave you! I'll shave your whole stupid mane off and then you'll be a naked loser the next time you see your big-ass girlfriend. Hold still!"

"Get off me," he sobbed, pushing against me. "Let me be dry, you vile witch! I'M CLEAN!"

"You're covered in suds. Just let me rinse you off and this can be over!" He jerked away from me, and I slipped on the tub and into the water.

Somewhere in the mix of soapy water and lion slaps, I thought I heard Intern scream my name. I shoved Toto off me and pulled my head out of the water. "Did you hear that?" I asked.

Toto paused from his whining and sniffed. "The sour bird's screams? Yes. You should leave me immediately and go check on him."

"Nice try," I said, grabbing the shower hose and spraying him.

"NOOOO!"

I kicked the drain loose, letting the disgusting water pour out as I hosed the last of the suds off Toto and then myself.

Intern screamed my name again, much louder, accompanied by the Tamagotchi theme. The jaunty tune grew closer, followed by loud stomping.

"Ugh, what now?" I returned the showerhead to its holder and shot Toto a warning look. "Don't move." Of course, as soon as I got out of the tub, he made a mad dash for the door, leaving a trail of water all over the damn floor.

"Dammit all." I opened up the window to the bathroom and stuck my head out. Then I immediately found myself back on my ass when Intern slammed into my face.

"She's gonna eat me! She's gonna eat me!" The bird's high-pitched wail echoed through the room, and he buried himself against my neck, as if I was going to be able to save him from whatever impending doom he'd just brought to my door.

I shoved him off me and got to my feet. "Slow down. Who is trying to eat you?" My gaze followed his quivering hands as it pointed toward the window. Dread crawled up my spine as I saw it. A colossal yellow eye, framed by pink scales, peered at us through the window.

The T. rex's gaze lingered on Intern before she shifted her massive head to sniff at us.

The warmth of her breath lingered on my skin. Panic set in, but I fought to maintain composure. "What do we do?" Intern's voice trembled, mirroring the fear we both felt.

Slowly, I crept backward toward the door. Something bumped my foot and I froze. The dog shampoo.

How sensitive is a T. rex's nose?

No time to second-guess my theory. I picked up the bottle of shampoo and sprayed as much of it as I could at the T. rex's nostrils. She let out a cry and withdrew from the window. She sneezed, the rolls on her neck jiggling as she frantically shook her head back and forth before attempting to rub her nose against the dirt. It was then I noticed the missing arm. "That's the Gruulorak. Did she follow us?"

Intern swallowed thickly. "I . . . may have tried to milk some of her venom."

"You tried to milk a T. rex?"

"For your chocolate!" he cried. "These animals had to be crossed with an arachnid-type species from the Sankado's planet. They produce a numbing agent to paralyze their prey, and if my theory is correct, it could be used to make a similar taste to chocolate."

"YOU TRIED TO *MILK* A T. REX?"

"For science!"

Fire cracked against her side in a sickening boom. Sol shot out from the smoke and launched a spear at her throat.

The T. rex dodged with agility that was downright terrifying. Beady eyes locked on as she swiveled around to face Sol. She paused, her head tilted slightly, before bobbing up and down as she scrutinized his presence. Her pupils dilated, then she chattered like a cat that saw a bird in the window.

Sol's palm lit up and he slowly waved his hand in front of her in wide movements, holding her rapt attention with the allure of a snake charmer. She stepped forward. He shot a fireball directly at her snout and received nothing for his effort. The embers sparkled uselessly across her thick hide.

She crouched low.

A fist closed around my heart. "SOL, RUN!"

The Gruulorak lunged. Their forms disappeared when Lok threw me over his shoulder and took off down the stairs. I raged against him, screaming at him to go back and help Sol. "Wait, we can't just leave him!"

The usual mirth was gone from his voice, replaced by a startling hardness. "We can, and we will. Sol is a hunter. He'll prove his worth or he won't."

"That's insane. Put me down!" I yelled. I thrashed against his hold, trying to break free. "Look, we may not have to fight it. She backed off when I squirted this shampoo in her face. If their noses are as sensitive as I think they are, we might be able to use it to chase her off."

He ignored me and ran toward the rope fence he used as a makeshift yix stable. In quick movements, he threw me onto Blossom's back and cut the rope. Intern flew to a pocket on her saddle and tucked himself inside. All at once, the yix panicked and took off running. I peered back toward the house to see Sol fire at the Gruulorak's head before darting toward the house with the broken roof. He plastered himself against the wall, only diving out of the way in time for the T. rex to crash into it. The house groaned before chunks of drywall and wooden beams fell. I heard Sol cry out, but I couldn't see him through the cloud of dust.

The Gruulorak stood and shook herself off. Her head snapped to Sol pinned under a chunk of drywall. Dread pooled in my gut and I pleaded to the man hauling me onto the saddle. "Lok, listen to me! We can save him!"

He jumped on behind me and kicked Blossom into a run, then pulled me against him when I nearly flung myself off. "No, you listen. The Gruulorak will snap you up faster than either of us can blink. Whether or not you believe you are our Zhali, you cannot die."

"Dammit, Lok, we can't just leave him!"

"If you die saving him, I'll kill him myself," he said darkly. He pulled me farther against him. "You want to help him so badly, be still and let me protect you."

Listening to him would be the smart thing to do. The correct thing to do. I honestly couldn't tell which one of us was more surprised when my feet hit the ground. It made no sense. If someone asked me any other day if I'd ever run headfirst at a T. rex with nothing but a bottle of dog shampoo as a weapon to save a man I'd met two days earlier, I would have laughed in their face.

I freed the cap from the bottle and flung it. Blue goop splattered across the Gruulorak's snout. She recoiled in disgust, turning away from Sol in her sneezing fit. His arms were straining to lift the drywall off his leg, and I ran to his side and pushed at it with all my might.

Confusion flicked across Sol's face at the sight of me, but only momentarily, and then he reverted back to the grumpy bastard I'd decided to risk my life for, for some ungodly reason. "By the sands of the shifting desert, what do you think you're doing?" he shouted.

"Ordering a fucking latte, what's it look like I'm doing?" I snapped. My poor excuse for muscles strained for all they were worth, barely managing to lift the drywall another inch off him. The T. rex rubbed her face on the ground. No telling how much time she'd need to remember her prey.

"We're about to die and you want to have an attitude? Stop wasting time and get out of here!"

I gritted my teeth and shoved harder. "You have such an off-putting way of saying 'thank you.' Work on it."

Because this planet was a giant wad of "fuck Dory and the ship she crashed in on," it started to rain. Pour, actually. My feet slipped in the newly formed mud. Sol lurched with a pained gasp as the drywall slipped from my grip. Cursing, I braced myself and shoved, damn near falling forward when the hunk of debris lurched away from me.

Lok lifted it over his head with a grunt and threw it to the side. He grabbed Sol by the front of his coat and threw him onto Beast's back. I barely had time to squeak in surprise before I, too, was slung, over Blossom. Lok whistled, and the beasts took off at a run.

The T. rex roared and shot after us. Fat bullets of rain pelted against my face, obscuring the wall of teeth that snapped far too close to my side.

Heat radiated from Lok before the world flashed with each blast he fired off. The balls of fire peppering into her side did nothing but enrage the T. rex, which forwent Sol entirely to focus on chasing us.

Lightning flashed bright enough to blind us all. Blossom tripped on something in the confusion, and Lok and I were flung off her back and into the mud. I landed hard on my side, head spinning from the fall. The duckbill let out a bloodcurdling scream as fangs sank into the base of her tail. The Intern struggled out of the saddle's pocket and tried to fly away. The T. rex's focus shifted immediately, releasing Blossom to snap at the Biwban. Intern shrieked as he dodged. The Gruulorak stomped on Blossom's side in an attempt to catch the intern. Blossom wheezed out a panicked call before thrashing desperately underfoot.

A spear planted itself in the Gruulorak's neck. Not deep enough to kill her, apparently, but just enough to cause the Gruulorak to stumble back, allowing room for Blossom to wiggle free.

Sol appeared out of the rain like a phantom to plant another blade in the T. rex's neck. From his enraged shout, I knew it wasn't deep enough. Her hide was too thick. He yanked the spear free and aimed to plunge it in her eye, but the Gruulorak shifted her weight and kicked Sol off. He rolled into the fall, then shot to his hooves. Instead of aiming another attack, he turned and ran toward me, scooping me up and flinging me back into Lok's outstretched arms. "Get her out of here," he shouted over the chaos.

With the pounding rain all but rendering my senses useless, I could do nothing but cling to the saddle for dear life until the angry snarls of the Jurassic horror faded into the distance.

CHAPTER 13

LOK CUT AN IMPOSING FIGURE AT THE MOUTH OF THE cave. He stood with his arms crossed, glaring out into the storm. When lightning flashed for dramatic effect, I half expected him to spin around and regale me with evil plans of world domination. Instead, he scowled at me.

Which shouldn't have been effective enough to have me curl into myself like a naughty child, but it was. The blatant disapproval in his silver gaze was cold enough for my brain to helpfully recount every single mistake I've ever made on a stage until my skin scrawled with the need to apologize. The flash of lightning became stage lights. The water dripping from my clothes morphed into the sickeningly sweet chunks of apple pie I'd spilled on myself after a juggling trick gone wrong.

Dorothy the disappointment.

Probably shouldn't have fired that therapist.

"I—"

"Don't apologize. You don't mean it," he said sternly.

"I don't?" My words came out as a question, but we both knew the answer. "I don't," I said again, stronger the second time. I balled my fists, spine straightening with the practiced mask of a woman who actually has her shit together.

But I didn't and he knew that. He had to. I could see it in his eyes. Hell, everyone could probably tell what a wreck I was if they just took two seconds to look and see that there was something wrong with me. My clothes were always wrinkled or covered in fur, my hair was dry, I'll never be as skinny as I was in my pageant days, I'll die before I get my degree, I couldn't even drive a stick shift.

I bit my lip to keep it from quivering. "He could have died."

Seeing as he was still out there, he might die anyway. Sol, Toto, Intern, most of the herd, it was anyone's guess who made it out fine. Blossom rested against the wall of the cave, occasionally sneaking glances at the world outside. I didn't need years of study to guess what she was looking for. Her mate was out there. So was mine.

"Are you aware that you are very small?"

"I mean . . . by human standards I'm actually pretty tall."

"You are small."

"Relatively speaking."

"And yet you charged at a full-grown billjaw, the Gruulorak no less, with no hesitation. Which, and I do want to be clear on this, was the sexiest thing I've ever seen in my life." A hint of admiration crept into his voice, but it was quickly overshadowed by concern. "But more importantly, it was monumentally foolish."

I bristled again at his censure, feeling defensive despite knowing he was right. "Sol was trapped. He could have died," I repeated stubbornly.

"You could have died!" The force of his shout reverberated off the walls of the cave, making me flinch. He must have caught my reaction, because he took a deep breath and visibly reined in his anger. After a moment, his posture relaxed on a long-suffering sigh. His hand scratched at the back of his head as he regarded me with a mix of frustration and tenderness. "I don't know how things work in your species," he began, his voice more gentle now. "But as a Sankado male, I need you to be safe. If you get hurt, this world and everyone in it will turn to ash beneath my hooves."

Hot.

"That seems like a bit much, even for a war general."

Promises flashed in his silver eyes. "Let me assure you, it's not."

". . . How passionate."

"Dory, I'm serious. You are my Zhali. My reason for being. I'm not letting you run off in a storm to look for a dead man."

"He's not dead!" I yelled. He wasn't. I could feel it in my bones. From the moment Intern shot me with that dart, maybe even prior if I was honest with myself for once, something in me was drawn to the both of them like a moth to a flame. No matter how much I tried to ignore it. Maybe if I'd run from them at the start, it wouldn't have gotten this bad. If I'd let Sol walk away from me on the beach, then I might have been spared the festering ache of his absence. But I didn't. Instead, like an *idiot*, I'd told myself it'd be fine just to have a taste and be on my way. Then I'd shared my body, my bed, and banter around a breakfast table. Now I knew the crooked curve of his smile and how fucking good it felt to be the one to put it there.

He couldn't die now. Did the poached eggs mean nothing?

Our bond was sealed, and the need to go to him pricked scalding needles into my heels until I wanted to run headfirst into the rain. Sol was alive, and the thought of him out there alone made me sick. "He's not dead, but he could be hurt. We need to go look for him."

Lok's mouth formed a thin line, but he remained steadfast in blocking the entryway.

"Lok, please." When he ignored my plea, I clenched my fists. "You spoke your piece as a Sankado male. Here's mine as a human woman. We don't take kindly to hostage situations."

"You are not my hostage; you are my Zhali."

"One of those is debatable. The other is changeable."

"As your man, I am duty bound to protect you. Even from yourself. Erase any notion you have of looking for the lawyer."

"Don't just call him 'the lawyer,'" I sneered. "His name is Sol. You know, the guy you had your dick in not long ago? Don't tell me you feel nothing about him still being out there."

Lok sighed, his expression hardening as he responded, "His loss is unfortunate."

I could feel my frustration rising. "He could still be out there! We have to try and find him."

"And what good would a search do, hmm? Blossom's too tired to take another step. That leaves me, you, and the storm. Can you track him in the rain? Are you trained to track him at all?"

"Lok, we have to try."

"No, we don't."

"What if it was you out there?"

"Leave me."

"What?"

"Leave. Me," he said slowly. "A rescue is only worthwhile

if the rescue party comes back. If I were out in a storm with the Gruulorak, do you really think I'd want my Zhali risking life and limb to save me on the off chance she doesn't slip off a cliff and bash her pretty skull on the rocks? If you are that adamant about finding him, then you will wait for morning when it's clear and not a second before."

"I—" Countless arguments clawed at my throat, but what good would they do? He was right. All I had were the clothes on my back and the gut feeling that Sol was still alive. Neither was gonna do shit where it mattered.

I looked past Lok into the storm, hoping for some miracle *Homeward Bound* situation where Intern, Sol, and Toto came running over the hill into my waiting arms. But the rain was so heavy I couldn't even see past the mouth of the cave. Let alone any miracle hills for them to bound over.

Tears pricked at my eyes. "This is such bullshit."

He gave my shoulder a comforting squeeze, then let me sulk in silence as he checked on Blossom. The bite mark thankfully wasn't too deep. With a good healing salve and bandages, it wouldn't cause any lasting damage. Much like the cave Sol took me to my first night, this one had been stockpiled with firewood and a few supplies.

I sat by the firepit as Lok carefully blew at the embers until the kindling caught. "Are there a lot of supply caves like this?" I asked.

He nodded and tossed more dried moss into the growing flames. "Resting spots are built all along the paths we use to migrate our herds. Most of them were made by drovers, but anyone that passes through is welcome to use them as long as they restock."

"Even those of the Night Ridge clan? You and Sol didn't exactly seem on friendly terms when you met."

He chuckled. "They're the ones that seem to have a problem with everyone else, but yes, them too. As sour as tensions can be between clans, this world is far too dangerous to be stuck out in the wild. I'd much rather they take shelter than end up the dinner of a passing billjaw."

"That's generous of you."

"Well, don't sound so surprised," he teased.

"Sorry, I just thought you might be at war with them or something."

"No—well, not on this planet anyway. I don't know where the rest of his clan hailed from before we were all dropped here, but judging from Sol's accent, I'd say he's from Ibemili. That's halfway across the world from my old home, and they were far too removed to take part in the Broken Plains War."

"What was the war about anyway?"

Grinning ridiculously, he took a seat beside me. "So many questions. Are you finally taking an interest in me? Where's the Tamagotchi?" he asked, looking around.

"I can go back to silence, if you prefer," I warned.

"Testy." He laughed. "You know, I don't recall. We'd been at war with the Dulba Empire for most of my life, and the fighting started well before that," he said, staring into the flames. "My homeland of Sumduul was a vast grassland, home to four major clans. The Dulba Empire sat in the eastern region, my clan ruled the northern plains of Tarssego, Stormforge had the mountain ridge that separated us from the rest of the world, and the Roamcrest were nomads that kept to themselves when they weren't trading."

He paused to add another log to the fire. "Tensions were on and off with Stormforge, but we've always been at war with the Dulba Empire. I may have turned the tide, but who knows how long that would have lasted. Not that it mattered after the crash anyway.

"Unfortunately, the surviving members from all four major clans were brought in on the same cargo ship and dropped in the same spot. I'm guessing only one ship was assigned to the area. As you can imagine, things got violent fast. Besides the Roamcrests, mind you. They took one look at the big wide world and left the crash site on the first day. I thought they were cowards at first. Who would turn down an opportunity to seize control in a perfect blend of chaos like that?

"I could've seized that moment. Exploited the infighting among the clans to forge a new empire under my rule. My father fell in the Calamity, which meant I was head of the Singing Arrow clan. To rule is what I'd been trained to do since I could hold a spear. King Osid was dead, and King Towei's about as useful as wet firewood in a fight. That left both Dulba and Stormforge weak to attack. I could have brought my two biggest competitors to heel and then . . ."

He trailed off, seemingly lost in the flames. "And then?" I asked.

"Exactly." He chuckled. "And then what? Rule over a bitter and broken people? Spend my days fending off assassination attempts? I finally killed that bastard Osid, and the world ended. That's the real kick in the teeth: none of it mattered. He burns my city, where my family stood for centuries, to the ground, and it doesn't matter. I flood his city, wiping out anyone in it and everything he held dear, and it doesn't matter. The blood on my hands holds no purpose other than to stain my dreams.

"Once I really sat and thought about it, I realized it would never stop. And I'd rather throw myself off a cliff than keep fighting. At least then it would be a quick death. Sankatul had been consumed by conflict long before I ever took my first breath, and I carried its scars, both seen and unseen. So I found myself at a crossroads: continue chasing my own tail in an endless cycle of violence, or take the coward's way out."

"Was there no one you could pass the crown to?"

He shook his head. "Kings don't retire; they're beheaded. If I told my men what I was thinking, they'd label me mad. And a clan with a mad king is a weakness just waiting to be exploited. No. It was better for them if I vanished. As luck would have it, dry season brought the first Rumbling, which meant the entire crash site was thrown into disarray. Everyone was far too busy fighting off the monsters of this world to pay attention to me. So I decided I couldn't take it anymore and it was either the cliff or the yix and just vanished. I left my armor near the Glyph Stone in the Fuchsia Grove and never looked back. Eventually I caught up with those yix herders and asked to join them."

"What's the Rumbling?" I asked.

"Have you seen a titanstalk yet? Giant creature with a long neck, shakes the ground when it walks?"

He probably meant some kind of sauropod. "No, but I think I know what you're talking about."

"Well, imagine a herd of them as far as the eye can see. Not just them either; horncrest, billjaws, all manner of beasts just came at us in droves out of nowhere. They completely trampled most of the encampment we had managed to scavenge together. It was enough to temporarily get everyone to stop killing each other to defend the rest of the supplies we had on the ship."

"Do you regret your choice?"

"Not for a second. I would have liked to have been able to

say goodbye, but a farewell note kind of defeats the purpose of disappearing into the night."

"Yeah, I could see how that would be counterintuitive."

"Get some rest," he said, tending to the fire. "We'll look for Sol at first light." His tone gave nothing away, but it didn't have to. I knew as soon as he avoided my eye contact that he had no intention of looking for Sol in the morning.

UNDER NO CIRCUMSTANCES SHOULD MY BLACK ASS BE creeping around an alien planet by myself. Even as I left the cave, I could feel my ancestors calling me a stupid bitch. But dammit, I was really worried about Sol. I gave one last look behind me to ensure that Lok was still where I'd left him. The larger Sankado was sprawled out next to the embers of the fire, one arm slung over his eyes as he snored the morning away.

I made my way back to the cul-de-sac and tried to pick up the trail of my other companions. Hell, I'd even settle for T. rex tracks if it meant I'd get closer to them.

"Dory!" came Intern's voice. I looked to see my avian companion perched on the mailbox of the decimated house waving frantically at me.

I let out a breath of relief and ran toward him. "Intern! Oh my goodness, I'm so happy to see you!"

Thwack.

CHAPTER 14

MUFFLED VOICES PULLED ME OUT OF MY SLEEP. PAIN raced up my side when I moved to rise, and I gasped before giving up on getting up and rolling to my back.

"You ever just wanna bite somebody?" I recognized Toto's voice and tried to blink away the rest of my sluggishness. I was trapped in a wooden cage just big enough to sit up in. Straw lined the flooring, with tufts of it bunched together around the entrance, showing the aftermath of my capture in the form of drag marks along the dirt. The room was bare, save for the other cages and a hanging rack on the far side of the room. Outside I could hear muffled voices speaking in Sankado. Toto was in the cage to my right, half sprawled out on his side as he chatted with the occupant of the next cage.

The annoyed voice of a woman piped in. "No, strange talking lion. I've never been struck with the urge to bite someone."

"Well, if you're going to be judgmental, I'll shut up."

There was a pause followed by a long-suffering sigh. "I'm sorry. Continue."

"It's like an intrusive thought. Ya know?"

I snorted, finally managing to raise my head. "Toto, you've never had an intrusive thought in your life. You just have a thought and then act."

"Oh, Dory, you're alive!" The lion padded over to the wall of wooden bars that separated our cages and rubbed his body against them.

I reached out and petted his mane. "I'm so glad you're all right. What happened to you? Are Sol and the others okay?"

"Really?" the feminine voice asked. "You wake up in a cage and the first thing out of your mouth isn't 'why the fuck am I in here'?"

My body groaned in protest, but I ignored it and struggled to sit up to where I could finally see the last cage. In it sat a dark-skinned woman with a purple Afro and a cat eye so immaculate I got the deep sense that I could trust her with my life. She wore a white tank top with black jeans and dark purple boots with an excessive array of spikes. Claw marks littered one of her pant legs, and I could see her leg had dried blood on it as well. Silver chains rattled below the tattoo of a fanged animal skull that spanned her throat. Long red nails drummed along her knee as she eyed me curiously. "Are you real, or am I having the longest acid trip of my life?"

"Real as can be, unfortunately," I said.

The woman tsked. "Positive? 'Cause I'm pretty sure I just spent the last few days wandering around a dinosaur zoo before getting snatched by some freakishly tall goat people. Then I get attacked by a lion who starts talking."

"I did not attack you," Toto hissed. "I just needed to lick your face so we could talk to each other."

She blinked at him, then lifted her scratched-up leg.

"You kept struggling."

She opened her mouth to speak, then just shook her head before turning to me. "Yeah . . . so as I was saying, all signs point to acid trip or hell."

"What's an acid trip?" Toto asked.

The woman grinned. "Come here and I'll show you."

"What?" I shouted, then reached through the bars to grab Toto's tail before he could make his way over to her. "Are you crazy? Do not give the lion drugs!"

She rolled her eyes. "You got a better idea, *Dory*? What kinda name is that anyway? Your folks super into Disney or something?"

"No, it's from the mathematician at NASA. But whatever, that's beside the point. Who are you and how did you get here? I thought I was the only one that escaped the ship."

"Heh, yeah, not quite. My name's Blair, and I saw you back on the ship running around like a chicken with your head cut off. All those bird freaks were so distracted they didn't even notice me slip away. Didn't plan on my pod crashing me in the middle of some pink flower field, though. The next day I got snatched by those goat bastards."

"And they kept you in this cage the whole time?"

She nodded, then jerked a thumb to a neon-green punk rock jacket with various pins from bands I could only assume I wasn't cool enough to recognize hanging on the wall. "Don't suppose you're wearing a belt? I'm trying to lasso my jacket to me, but mine's not long enough. I've got a knife and revolver in there we can use to break out of here."

"You have a gun?"

"I will once we get my jacket. So, what's it gonna be? You got a belt or are we letting the lion trip on acid on the off chance he Hulk smashes his way through the bars?"

Toto's eyes widened at her words. "Will the acid make me stronger?"

"Maybe."

"NO!" I shouted, then glared at Blair. "We are not resorting to animal cruelty. Just give me a second to think."

She let out an exasperated noise and crossed her arms. "Well, damn, girl, hurry up. They haven't let me out for a break since they dragged that gray guy off, and that was *hours ago*. I have to pee."

"I also have to pee," Toto added.

A sudden *boom* shook the ground beneath me. Shouting followed the sharp screech of splintering wood. Through the doorway, I saw men armed with spears and arrows rushing toward the source of the disturbance. Discordant bellows vaguely reminiscent of enraged hippos during mating season sounded off after them.

Blair merely rolled her eyes at the display. Toto pushed his snout through the bars of his cage and gave the air a sniff but lost interest soon after and lay back down.

"So . . . anyone want to tell me what that was about?" I asked.

"Probably just another breach in the fence," Blair said. "The place is surrounded by this megaherd of dinosaurs, and they keep knocking the fence over. You should have been here yesterday. A triceratops rolled in like a bull in a china shop and nearly gored somebody. It was good fun."

Toto's eyes lit up. "Oh, that does sound fun!"

"Yes," I said slowly, eyeing my two bloodthirsty companions. "Who doesn't love a good triceratops skewering? Wait, we're getting distracted; go back. Blair, you said they dragged off a gray man. Toto, is Sol here?"

"Yeah, the Intern too. That giant crocodile thing chased us all the way to Fuchsia Grove, where the other gray men ambushed us. They don't speak like your mates do, though."

Blair quirked an eyebrow before sitting up a little straighter. "I'm sorry, her *what*?"

"Her mates," Toto said slowly. "You know, for the breeding program you were brought here for."

Blair's eyes grew as wide as dinner plates. "THE *WHAT*?"

I took a moment to share with her what I knew of our situation. To say that she didn't handle the news well was an understatement. Blair raged against the bars of her cage with enough ferocity to have Toto back himself into the corner farthest away from her. A white-haired man with long curved horns opened the door to our room to check on the commotion. Her boot met his face and he fell to his back. When another came to check on him, he was treated to a slew of colorful and creative insults.

"Blair, calm down," I said, trying to get her attention over her hysterics.

Her freak-out was drawing the attention of more of the men outside. They dragged their unconscious friend away and tried speaking to her in hushed tones. Without the translator symbiont, none of us could understand them.

The men in the doorway made way for a newcomer who stood a head taller than the rest. He wore a mask of blue and reddish-orange lines that hooked over his curved horns. The mask added another pair of horns behind his natural set that curved toward each other to form a half circle pointing skyward. Elaborate yellow and orange tattoos raced up his forearms to create a circular pattern on his left biceps. The same markings on his tattoos repeated on the staff in his hand and the wrap he wore around his waist. A red arrow was tattooed on his neck, the same one Lok wore.

My heart leapt at the sight. If he was one of Lok's men, maybe I had a shot at getting out of here alive. He waved off the onlookers and barked an order at a younger-looking man in nothing but a loincloth, who ran away to do whatever was asked of him.

"CALM DOWN?" she screeched. "We've been locked up by some evil goat bastards to pop out babies with FUCKING HORNS. HORNS, DORY! How would that even work, pregnancy-wise? Am I gonna be knitting a sweater for li'l baby Lamb Chop one day, only to have her stab my fucking spleen? No, I will not calm down."

The tattooed man approached her calmly and attempted to place his hand on her cage, then snatched his hand away when Blair swung at him. She crouched low, muscles tensing, before she rammed herself against the bars. They creaked under her weight, and the sound was enough encouragement to spur her on. "I am not!"

Slam.

"Pushing out!"

Slam.

"A FUCKING GOAT BABY!" With the final slam, the bars finally caved, and she kicked the splintered wood out of the way. Before she could step outside the cage, a bolt of fire shot at her feet. Something akin to ice coated the air as we looked to the newest man standing in the doorway.

I noticed his eyes first, piercing blades of green that caused the hair on the back of my neck to stand on end. He wore plated armor along his shoulders, decorated in black-and-red patterns, with a feathered necklace adorning the bottom. The belt around his waist held the face of a four-eyed creature with razor-like teeth.

The tattooed man fell to his knees, forehead planted firmly on the ground in total submission. The green-eyed man ignored him completely and knelt before my cage. His sharp gaze raked over me, head to toe.

"Is your name Dory?" His voice was low and commanding. He held my gaze without blinking.

"Yes?" I said, voice wavering. "How can you understand me?"

"Check her Zhali."

The tattooed man stood and approached me without a word. He tapped his staff twice on the ground and his tattoos began to glow. The light from them rose in his body to form a bright orb of orange gas in the center of the horns on his mask. With a light pop, the orb split into three. The center orb turned blue, while the remaining orange ones began to orbit around it.

The leader gave the display a passing glance before he tilted his head to the side and considered me. "Well. That's interesting." He looked me over again before scratching at his chin. "Bring him in."

Two men dragged in a beaten and bloody Sol. His arms were tied behind his back. Muffled insults were gagged by the cloth in his mouth. The leader nodded to him. "Do you know that man?"

I swallowed thickly, unsure how to answer. His hand shot out, grabbed me by the throat, and pulled me flush against the bars of the cage. Sol thrashed, desperately trying to fight off the hands holding him still.

"Get your hands off her!" Blair yelled. She stole glances at her jacket on the wall but made no move to retrieve it.

The leader smiled, showing off gold fangs. "Hmm, he certainly knows you. Now, are you going to tell me the name of the man responsible for that second orb, or do I need to make this meeting even more unpleasant?"

Sol tried to shout something to me, but the words were lost against the gag. The leader flicked a hand, and his lackeys dragged Sol back out of the room.

"Wait, where are you taking him?"

"Asking questions before you answer my own?" The hand around my throat tightened. "I'm afraid that's not how this works, Doll."

"Do as he says, Dory," Toto said flatly. There was no mirth in the proud lion's words. Just a coldness that reflected how fucked I was.

My vision spotted as my lungs started to burn. ". . . Lok."

No sooner had the name left my lips than he released my throat. I gulped in air greedily, then coughed and backed away from the bars. When I looked up, the leader was smiling.

"Now, see? That wasn't so bad, was it?" He stood and addressed the tattooed man. "Bring me the Biwban." He turned his attention back to me and pinned me with a stare so intense, goose bumps raced along my arms.

Bravado was never my strong suit, but I gave it a go anyway and did my best to fix him with a steely glare. "I answered your question. Now answer mine."

He smirked. "So there is some fight in you." He wagged a finger at me before pulling an empty cage over to sit on. "I like that. Hate to imagine the mighty General Ghoszi saddled to a simpering welp of a woman. So tell me, Doll, how is the bastard?"

"Sol?" I stressed.

"Right." He chuckled. "You've got nothing to worry about,

I promise. We may have had to be a little rough with him when he first got here, but that's all over now."

"And why is that?"

His eyes flashed. "Because you're going to behave. Aren't you, Doll? And to answer your previous question, your little Biwban friend explained everything after he pecked one of my hunters on the mouth. Naturally, when an alien bird and a man with a Zhali bond showed up on my doorstep, I had a few questions. Lucky for me, that little bird loves to sing."

Dammit, just what did Intern tell him? "How . . . how do you know Lok?"

He put a hand over his chest and gasped. "He didn't tell you about me? Oh, I'm so hurt."

Awareness pricked at the edge of my mind and my eyes widened. "King Osid."

My reaction seemed to amuse him. "Ah, so he did talk about me. And here I was thinking this grudge was one-sided."

"He said you were dead."

"I'm sure he said a lot of things. Never could keep his mouth shut, that one. Tell me, where is my favorite broken arrow?"

"He . . . Look, he doesn't want to fight anymore—"

"I know," the king interrupted. "I mean, at first I thought he was just ignoring me. He didn't even have the courtesy to join in on the fun when we all landed here. Every remaining Sankado worth their salt dropped on a ripe new world and a power vacuum just wide enough for anyone willing to fill it. I thought for sure that would be enough to lure his sorry carcass from whatever rock he crawled under. Yet imagine how hurt I was when he never showed up. Not only that, I find out from one of his men that he renounced his title and abandoned his armor in a flower field. Then takes up yix herding of all things?" He leaned toward me; his gaze was ice. "But of course, it isn't enough of a kick in the teeth for that bastard to flood my city, decimate my best war party, and fuck off to a life of leisure. No, on top of all that, he still gets the girl in the end? Now, that just doesn't seem fair, does it?"

Before I could answer, the tattooed man returned with Intern in his arms. Despite all his annoyances, relief flooded me to see that the little guy was unhurt.

"Do it."

The tattooed man dropped Intern, who flapped rapidly to avoid smacking into the ground as he landed. "You . . . you should know, there's no guarantee on who she bonds with. She may not even bond with anyone here."

There was a lethal calmness in the king's eyes. "For your sake, you better hope she does."

With shaking hands, he cast a worried glance at me before he pulled out his dart gun and shot Blair.

The purple-haired woman screeched, backing as far away from the bars as she could before ripping the dart out of her leg. "What the fuck is this? What did you do?"

A dark laugh brought my attention back to the man in front of me. I watched in horror as his horns began to grow. He smiled as he answered her but didn't take his eyes off me. "Just leveling the playing field is all."

Panic like I'd never known before welled in my throat. I smoothed my shaking hands down the front of my pants, letting my nails pinch at the skin underneath in the vain hope that the pain would be enough to distract my pulse from beating any louder.

"Nah, fuck this." Blair stepped out of her cage and dusted hay from her pants. "The talking bird just mated me to someone I wouldn't even swipe right on Tinder for. I'm out; I'm done."

Intern pulled out an orange Tamagotchi covered in a beehive-type pattern. His beak fell open in shock when he turned it on. "Oh, that is low."

"Did I give you permission to speak freely?" King Osid asked.

"Do I look like I give a damn?" Blair asked. "'Cause I don't."

Intern chewed nervously on his finger as the Tamagotchi gave off an angry-sounding series of beeps. "Headquarters is not going to like this."

Blair ignored him. "I don't put up with men with mommy issues or overly dramatic dreams of vengeance." She put a hand to her hip and cocked her head. "What did this man even do to you aside from handing you what you wanted? He left." She stressed the last word with a clap of her hands. "That means you won your little war, so now you can go be king of all the other little goat people and leave us the fuck alone."

"He doesn't get to just walk away from me. Lokbaatar and I—"

She scoffed. "Scrape my ass with a cheese grater, just stop. Stop. It's embarrassing for me to be with you right now."

"What?" He chuckled.

"I don't stutter. And if what they told me about this mating-bond thing is true, I'm probably stuck with you. That means your actions reflect on me. I have a brand to maintain and you are bringing it down right now."

The orange Tamagotchi buzzed angrily, making Intern's feathers stand on end. "It's in the negative." He looked between the pair with obvious panic before holding his hands up. "Now, Subject 12, you and your mate clearly got off on the wrong foot. Why don't we both just sit down and—"

"SHUT UP!" the pair said in unison.

Blair took a confident step away from her cage and looked the king dead in the eye before crossing the room to her coat.

"And where do you think you're going?" King Osid asked.

"I'm getting my jacket. Got a problem with that?" With a level of venom I'd only ever seen in a banded krait's kiss, Blair swiped her jacket off the rack and put it on with a spin so she could look directly into his soul and hiss out, "This is the only warning I'm ever going to give you, *mate*. Never throw a fireball at me again."

The king smirked as he stood to face her. His eyes raked boldly over her, before he spit a ball of fire past her face. The flames licked at Blair's cheek before bursting against the wall behind her.

"You seem intent on testing my boundaries. So be it." She reached into her coat, then flicked her wrist with a click.

Pop.

King Osid hissed in pain and brought a hand up to the side of his face. His eyes widened as his palm came back red. The tattooed man stumbled away from the spot where the bullet dug into the wall past the king's head. "Now, that's a neat little trick. What is that?"

"Conflict resolution," Blair said, pointing the gun at him. "The next one's going right between your eyes."

High-pitched screeching broke through the air. Intern's head whipped wildly between Blair and the bullet in the wall.

His feathers fell flat against him as his screech morphed into a rushed cry. "Humans can *hurt* their mates?!" His rapid and shallow breaths echoed through the silence, punctuating the air with little gasps of panic.

"Damn right we can. Now, you, Osid, move out of my way." Blair shoved past the stunned king, flipped the latch on my cage, and held a hand out to me. When I reached out and took the offered hand, she pulled me upright and clapped an arm around my shoulders, relaxing into my side as she fixed the men in the room with a confident grin. "You should be happy I was able to convince Little Miss Bloodlust over here it was worth hearing you sorry idiots out before we decided to leave. If she had it her way, you'd have been spending the day peeling your goons off the walls. Now, return her man to her before she decides to paint the town red."

King Osid looked at his bloodied hand again before looking to the wall behind him in disbelief. He turned to one of his men and asked, "Didn't I tell the druid to check their supplies for weapons?"

At his side, the tattooed man visibly tensed.

"This isn't right," Intern stammered. "This can't be right. What hope do we have of successfully building breeding pairs if the humans can kill their mates?" The little bird called up his screen with shaking hands and frantically flipped through the pages of his notes. "There has to be something in here that explains this. None of the training modules mentioned anything about projectile defense mechanisms."

Blair's face scrunched in annoyance. "Why are you freaking out like you've never heard of domestic violence? Of course we can hurt people."

"Not people," he stressed. "Your mate! What kind of pair-bonding species is capable of this?"

"He shot fire at me," Blair snapped. "Why aren't you shocked about that?"

"*At* you," he said. "It never touched you."

"So?"

He made a frustrated noise and wailed, "You were never in any danger! The fire didn't touch you because it can't. He can't hurt you!"

Raising a fine arched brow, she turned back to the king. "Is that right? Well, unfortunately for you, *dearest*, my species doesn't share the same compulsion."

He held a hand up to her. "In a moment, darling. It seems like there was some kind of miscommunication with my orders." He came beside Blair and leaned against the cage. Crossing his arms over his chest, he clicked his tongue as he scanned over the men in the room. "You see, when you first arrived here, I could have sworn I told my druid Sarek—that's him there with the funny mask. Wave to my wife, Sarek."

The druid raised a slow fidgeting hand and gave Blair a curt wave.

King Osid scratched his head. "So your ears do work. Odd." He turned his attention to Blair and nudged her shoulder. "As I was saying, I could have sworn I told Sarek to check your items for weapons. Yet here we are. My only question now is, are my orders mere suggestions to be ignored at his convenience, or is that red arrow on his neck still clouding his mind?"

Quick as lightning, the king snatched the gun from Blair's hand and shot Sarek. Blair and I screamed and backed away from the king. Toto snarled and retreated as far back as his cage would allow. The druid hit the ground with a pained cry and clutched at his leg.

King Osid turned the gun around in his hands, running his

fingers over the cylinder before inspecting the trigger. "What a neat little toy." Sarek moaned in pain, but the men around him made no move to help him. King Osid rolled his eyes and pushed himself off the cage before lazily crossing the room to squat in front of the bleeding Sarek. He stared at him for a moment before lifting the mask off Sarek's face. The king tutted. "Pity, with all that moaning I thought I might have gotten a tear from you."

Sarek's face clouded with rage. He opened his mouth to speak but was cut off when the king shoved the barrel of the gun in his mouth. "Ah-ah. Before you go spouting off more of your nonsense, remember that the only reason that you still draw breath is that my last druid got himself eaten. Your talents for medicine are hard to come by. Not irreplaceable. Remember that the next time you get an idea for a half-baked assassination attempt." King Osid removed the barrel from Sarek's mouth and patted his cheek before standing. With a wave of his hand he said, "Get him out of my sight."

My fingers dug into my sides as I watched two men drag Sarek out of the room without a word. I swallowed hard. If what Intern said was true about Sankado not being able to harm their mates, then that was great news for Blair. But I was still very much on the chopping block. And it was my mate he was after. From what Lok had described, King Osid was a power-hungry madman with no qualms about doing whatever needed to be done to get what he wanted.

The king turned to face us and offered an apologetic smile. "You'll have to forgive the unpleasantness. Some men take to new management better than others."

Blair curled her lip. "Yes, I too shove guns into the mouths of everyone who disagrees with me."

Osid laughed. The blood dripped down his face and fell to

the floor, mixing with the hay and dust beneath him. He took a step toward Blair and ran his knuckles against her cheek. "Oh, I *like* you. Your friend reads like an open book, but you, I can't tell if you're bluffing or ready to spill my guts on the floor." The purple-haired woman went stone-faced as he traced the path his fire had nearly grazed, then turned his attention back to me.

There was a darkness in his eyes, a deep, festering rage that chilled my spine, but when he spoke, there was a lightness in his tone.

Like we were old friends.

Like he wasn't contemplating the best way to rip my throat out.

And it terrified me.

The king stepped closer to me, and the hand that had just touched Blair went to my shoulder. He squeezed, digging his fingers into the meat around my collarbone until it was numb, confirming my suspicion that his inability to hurt us only extended to Blair. He smiled when I flinched, then leaned in to whisper, just loud enough for me to hear. "You have a fire in you that's worth tapping. If I didn't know better, I'd say that was Lok's influence."

His grip suddenly loosened, and he backed away. I rubbed at the bruise forming, watching him. "But fine. You caught me," he told Blair. "Not even I'm a cold enough bastard to hurt such a pretty face." He clapped a dark-haired man on the shoulder. "Volen, have the cook prepare a feast."

"We're not staying," Blair said.

A smile pulled at his lips. "Oh, don't be so hasty. A good meal is the least I can offer after treating my Zhali so terribly. Enjoy a nice dinner with my council while I chat with your friend. I have a proposition for her."

"And why should we bother listening to anything you say?"

He chuckled, then glanced at Volen before nodding to Blair. "Cute, isn't she?" The king spoke in a casual, jesting way. "It's just as the bird said, love. *I* can't hurt you. But I have well over two hundred men that don't share the same compulsion."

CHAPTER 15

I WAS GETTING REAL TIRED OF LIFE HANDING ME LEMONS. As far as alien abductions go, I felt like I'd done at least a passable job at surviving. I was on day four, after all. I'm sure some would cry, "Dory, that's not very long at all! Stop patting yourself on the back while you eat dinner with a madman." But I choose to believe those people are stupid and would have died out on the first day.

They didn't get bitten in the neck by a lion. Nor did they get mated to two weirdos or chased by what was possibly the chonkiest T. rex in existence with nothing but a bottle of puppy shampoo and a dream. I did. So if I wanted to accept my fate and enjoy my last meal, then maybe they could get off my fucking back.

My fork stabbed into the meat on my plate before I shoveled it into my mouth. It tasted a bit like jerk chicken, but the meat was more like venison. A drop of juice fell from it and splattered against the dress King Osid had provided for me. It was made of the same yix silk as most of their clothing, with a plunging neckline that disappeared into the sash wrapped around my waist. Red arrows sat boldly against the dark blue of its sleeves, while a green-and-red bird soared along the bottom of the dress.

King Osid was my only dining companion, despite the grand table we were at. He sat at the head of the table, casually sipping from an amethyst cup. The tribal patterns lining the cup's rim repeated in the grand mural decorating the wall behind him. My focus drifted past him to take in the intricate work of art. The scene depicted a man holding a staff high above him. A bright orange orb floated in the center of his horns. Blue and purple flames blazed behind him, trapped inside a banded diamond shape.

Above the speared man, a one-eyed centipede creature peered down at him. Petals as vibrant as a peacock unfolded from the center of its head in a mesmerizing pattern, revealing an eye at its center that seemed to pierce through the fabric of reality. Skinny blue arms ending in six-fingered hands sprang out from its long, coiled body. Many of them reached toward the speared man with ravenous intent. The bottom of the mural was nothing but bones, piles of skulls trapped in eternal screams, and an array of smaller bones tied together in weblike circles that lined the bottom corners.

"Interesting artwork," I offered. "Is there a story behind it?"

King Osid raised a brow, then looked behind him. "Ah, Yashvara and Laju the World Eater. You're unfamiliar with the story?"

I swallowed my food, then pointed to myself. "Alien, remember?"

"Right." He chuckled. "Funny, you probably had to pass by her on the way here."

"Pass by a giant world-eating centipede? I sure hope not."

He smiled and leaned back in his chair. "It's said that Laju lives trapped in the Kavithran Whorl, a constellation seen from our old planet. Legend says that the Kavithran Whorl was created by the gods themselves to contain the World Eater, a monstrous being born from chaos and destruction with countless arms and a never-ending appetite. Yashvara, the greedy bastard, sought to take some of the gods' power for himself and plucked a single star from Laju's cage and used it to grant us our fire." He lifted his palm, letting flames dance around its center before they floated to the ceiling in little wisps of smoke.

"Let me guess. His hubris caused the World Eater to break free and wreak havoc?"

"Ah, so you have a similar legend on your home planet?"

"Let's just say the audacity of men is universal."

"I won't disagree with that. Many bookish types use Laju as an allegory for insatiable greed and ambition. But great change as well. After all, it's Yashvara who granted us all the power of fire. Though I wonder if the change was worth the cost."

"So, tell me how it all ends. Did Yashvara fix his mistake?"

"Not before Laju's hunger drove her to devour entire civilizations. The only thing she understands is hunger, and Yashvara used that to his advantage. Using the last of his magic from the stolen star, he lured the beast with illusions of endless feasts and guided her back to her prison. Just before Laju's last leg could enter, he sliced it from her body and used it to form a new lock on her cage. And that's where she stayed. Locked safely away until she finds a new path to freedom and resumes her quest to devour the world."

"Illusions of a feast, huh?" My eyes roamed over the banquet table, filled to the brim with various meats and fruit. Far too much for our mere party of two. "Do you plan on cutting my leg off and throwing me back in that cage?"

He threw back his head and let out a great peal of laughter. "That would send a message, I'll admit. But there's no need. I've got just about everything I need from you. And it's a little too macabre for how I like to run things. The end of the world doesn't have to turn us into animals." He plucked a berry from his plate and tossed it into his mouth. "Besides, if the conspiracy theorists are to be believed, Laju already escaped her prison and took the form of a spaceship that swallowed the world in poison. Now all that's left is to bring order to the era of change she left in her wake."

"And I suppose you're the man for the job?"

"Should I have left it to your runaway coward? While he was off rolling in yix shit, I built a fortress for our people to escape the rabid beasts that infest this land. Try the wispfruit; it's a delicacy in these parts." King Osid pointed to a bright green fruit about the size of a pineapple, its swirled leaves wrapped around the base like a dragon fruit.

I reached a tentative hand toward it and looked back at him. "It's not poison, is it?"

He didn't bother to look up as he sliced off another chunk of meat. "Would I tell you if it was?"

"You sound like someone I know." I plucked the fruit from the table, then dropped it with a scream as the swirls along the leaves shot out like spikes. The fruit fell to the ground in a sharp *tink* as it bounced on its spikes and rolled out of view. "What the fuck?" I snarled, clutching my wrist.

I heard the scrape of his chair before the king grabbed my wrist and lifted it above me. He wrapped a white cloth around my injured hand and pressed it in the center of my palm.

Blood soaked the cloth. He watched the white fabric bleed into red before a chilling smile lit up his face. He released my wrist, holding up the bloodied cloth like it was made of solid gold.

"What the hell was that?" I asked.

"The last thing I needed from you," he said, snapping his fingers. A soldier came from the next room and collected the bloody cloth without a word, before retreating. King Osid slid back into his chair. "That wooden saucer next to you contains a healing cream. Rub it on your palm to stop the bleeding."

I stared at him wide-eyed. "Why would I believe you after that?"

He merely shrugged. "Use it or don't. If it were me, I'd rather not bleed all over my plate. But to each their own."

I gritted my teeth, unsure of what to make of him. But the pain in my hand was murder. Frustrated, I snatched an unused spoon and poured a generous portion of the white paste on my palm. A coolness eased out the pain and I breathed a sigh of relief. "At least you weren't lying about that."

"I haven't lied at all. Wispfruit is a delicacy; you just don't know how to open it." To prove his point, he grabbed another wispfruit by the top of its leaves, separated them with his fingers, and peeled back the skin like a banana. The flesh inside was a deep blue with flecks of red. King Osid sliced the flesh free from its stem with a knife, placed it on a small plate, and slid it over to me. "Try it."

"No!" I slammed my fists on the table and stood, the chair screeching against the wooden floor before toppling over. "I don't want to eat your damn fruit. I want my friends back and I want you to let us the hell out of here. Now!"

He rested his chin on his hand; a glint of amusement

flickered in his eyes. "Now, why would I go and do a thing like that right before I get everything I want?"

"I . . . You can't just keep us trapped here!"

"Oh, I think I can. Get comfortable, Doll. You barely touched your food. I won't have Lok screeching about how I starved his woman. It's bad for morale. You understand."

"I don't give a damn about your—"

"Sit down."

"I—"

All amusement faded from his gaze. "Sit. Down."

I picked my chair up off the floor and sat.

"Better," he said, refilling his glass. "Tell you what, I'm a reasonable man. When the general comes in, fire raging to save his stolen love, I'll let you say goodbye before I kill him. In the meantime I'll gift you a home with your alien friends and your other mate. What was his name again? Saw?"

The nonchalant murder plot sank beneath my skin like ice. "Why are you doing this?" I asked breathlessly. "Lok abandoned his post; you won. There's no need to keep going after him, let alone keep the rest of us here. Just enjoy your victory and let us go."

"Let you go?" He chuckled. "Don't sell yourself short, Doll. You and my darling new wife might just be the most valuable people on this planet. The first two women most of us have seen in a decade, and what's more, the promise of even more women once we find out where the rest of your kin were dropped off. To be honest, I can't fathom why you'd want to leave my care in the first place. In here you'll be safe and protected. With a snap of your fingers, you could have just about any man here on bended knee swearing fealty just to be a part of your harem. Doesn't that sound nice?"

"A gaggle of horny men following me around at all times?

No. No, I can't say that it does." I barely had enough stamina to keep up with Lok and Sol as it was. "Maybe Blair or one of the other women will be more open to the idea of wrangling her own personal football team, but I'm good. So, if you could just let us go, I'd be more than happy to go find Lok and tell him to never darken your doorstep again and we can all go our separate ways. Sound good?"

The king shook his head. "And therein lies the crux of the problem." He got up from his seat and motioned for me to follow him. "Walk with me. If you're not going to eat, you can at least see what this is all about."

I stood and quickly followed him out of the room. He led us out of the feasting hall and into the fortress itself. I shielded my eyes from the bright midday sun and followed him closely. Towering wooden walls encircled the fortress, adorned with weathered banners that fluttered in the brisk wind. A group of men were patching a destroyed section of the fence. Beside them lay a dead triceratops. Scorch marks coated the beast's hide. An elder Sankado carved meat from the carcass with practiced ease. Beyond the wall was a cacophony of noisy animals. The only ones I could see for sure were some type of sauropod. Their long necks reached far past what a mere fence could block out. One good tail swing from one of those giants and this whole fortress would be busted right open.

The men repairing the wall stopped to peer at me curiously as we passed by. I noticed a sharp intake of breath and turned to see two of them eyeing the bird along my dress. They whispered to each other in hushed voices. One took a step toward us but was yanked back by his white-haired friend. So distracted by the bird on my dress, the men failed to notice the ankylosaurus poking its head through the gap in the fence. The armored dinosaur grunted and began trying to shove the rest of its body through the gap. When that didn't work, its head disappeared from the hole, followed by a splintering *crack* as its clubbed tail slammed into the fence. The blow shattered the wooden plank, nearly taking the white-haired man's head off in the same swing.

In a flash, the group jumped into action, pelting the ankylosaurus with fireballs. King Osid rolled his eyes at the display and kept walking.

"How often does that happen?" I asked.

"It's been never-ending for the past few days," he said tersely. "The same bloodthirsty beasts attacked us last year while we were building. It took weeks to fight them off last time, and we lost some of our best people. We need every able-bodied man ready to fight these monsters off in order to secure our home. Yet some of my men would rather chase dreams of the past and divide us. That's why I can't let you go. You see, as much as I loathe to admit it, General Ghoszi Lokbaatar is one of the finest leaders to ever live. His men worship him with an almost cultlike reverence." A muscle in his brow ticked. "Even the fact that he abandoned them in a new world wasn't enough to sway his most stalwart supporters."

"You sound like you envy him."

"I do." He chuckled. "Who wouldn't want blind devotion from their men? In the wake of his absence, the Singing Arrows fell almost as fast as clan Stormforge did. Though that's not saying much. King Towei was a miserable cretin. If I hadn't taken his head, I'm sure one of his men would have done the honor. With those two out of the way, I was finally able to unite the three great clans under the Dulba Empire. Or what's left of it. A feat no king before me managed."

"Your journey of conquest is inspiring," I drawled. "What does that have to do with Lok?"

"Everything."

We came upon a crowd of men jeering at something near the lake. As we approached, the rhythmic splashes reached my ears, and a feeling of dread settled over me like a heavy shroud.

A man with long arching horns and black hair cropped short stood on a wooden platform with his hands on a lever. The muscles in his arms strained as he pulled the lever back. A long wooden pole rose from the water. I gasped as I saw the man trapped in a cage at the end of it. He coughed up water, heaving desperate gulps of air before wheezing into a coughing fit. He paid no mind to the crowd jeering at him, but through the haze of his wheezing, he locked eyes with King Osid. Rage, white and hot, flashed in his eyes. The man stood on wobbly legs and let off what I could only assume was a stream of Sankado cusswords.

King Osid raised his voice to carry over the crowd. "Yengro, are you ready to speak, my friend?"

Yengro curled his lip, then spat at the king. "USINDULA!"

The king glanced at the man working the lever, who nodded and dunked the cage back underwater.

A gasp caught in my throat. My hands trembled, and I instinctively pressed them against my mouth to stifle the horrified sound threatening to escape.

What should I do? What can I do? There was no way I'd be able to fight my way through a crowd of alien warriors to save the poor guy. Hell, if I stepped in, King Osid might just put me in the cage with him. Sickening helplessness twisted in my gut. The cage rose again, before stuttering coughs gave way to another splash.

"Please stop this." I reached out to the king, but when I caught sight of the impassive look on his face, I nearly retched.

King Osid merely glanced at me with a cold indifference that sent a shiver down my spine.

The king smirked down at me, then tilted his head toward the dunking. "First time?"

My eyes widened. "You're joking about this?"

He laughed as the cage rose. "If you can't have fun at work, you've got one hoof in the grave already."

"You are insane!" The crowd around us continued to revel in the torment. He didn't give a shit. None of them did. I drew closer but was stopped when King Osid pulled me to him, draping an arm around my shoulders.

"You know, he's in there because of you."

Splash.

"What? I've never seen him in my life. I swear, Lok and Sol were the only two I—"

"Doesn't matter." He slid a hand to my back and guided us forward. The crowd around us parted like a school of fish in the path of a shark. "Didn't I tell you, Doll? You rack up just enough bad luck to be stuck with Lokbaatar, unquestioned leader of the merry band of intransigent dogmatic idiots who insist on making every little thing so difficult." He spat the words out contemptuously.

The cage rose, its sole occupant wheezing for life-giving air. Yet Osid had no reaction. With a creak, the cage jerked down a notch when the torturer prepared to dunk him again. The man in the cage fell to his hands and knees. His arms strained in an attempt to push himself back up, only to collapse beneath him.

King Osid held up a fist, halting the man on the platform. "That man has just enough bad luck to be loyal to that stupid bastard. Which I've come to understand means"—he paused, nostrils flaring in an ill-suited attempt at hiding his anger—"it doesn't matter that your king has shed his armor and fled. Nor does it matter that I so graciously allowed you to live instead of slaughtering the lot of you insufferable bastards. You still scream for a revolt every time you think that man takes a shit. You want to see him again that bad? Fine."

He pulled me onto the platform with him, placed his hands on my shoulders, and raised his voice to address the crowd. "Listen up! I want every remaining Singing Arrow still loyal to your old king to hear this. Here's King Ghoszi's Zhali match. I've confirmed it with your druid Sarek himself. As we speak, my scouts carry this message to him. 'General Ghoszi Lokbaatar, I regret to inform you that your wife has been poisoned with wispfruit.'"

The man in the cage slammed his fist against the bars.

"No, no," I repeated, shaking my head. "Why is the crowd murmuring? I don't like that. That's not the life I'm trying to live right now."

"Then this next part will be good or bad news for you. 'The barbs of a wispfruit release a toxin potent enough to fell a titanstalk in six days. You'll be a lucky son of a bitch if she gets three. If you want the antidote, return to the grove where you so easily cast off your honor and don it again. At sundown tomorrow I will meet you there. Let us finish this feud once and for all.'" Cheers erupted from the crowd while Yengro slammed against the bars with a roar.

"Are you kidding me?" I screamed. "That shit was actually poison?"

He smirked down at me. "Did you think I cut you because your blood was pretty?"

I smacked him hard across the face. "Don't fuck with me, Osid. I'm not dying because you and your men can't get your shit together. Give me the damn antidote!"

The king merely smiled down at me and rubbed at his cheek where I'd just slapped him. "My, my, the Singing Queen has some fight in her after all. That's good."

"OSID!"

He patted my shoulder. "You'll get your antidote as soon as I take Lok's head."

My heart thudded in my chest as all thoughts drove to the cut on my hand. I ripped off the wrap and inspected the cut, hoping any signs of discoloration would clue me in to what kind of toxin the plant held. Yet the cut merely looked a little aggravated. No discoloration or numbness had set in. I'd researched countless plants, both poisonous and otherwise, in my studies. Which meant FUCK ALL on a goddamn alien planet. "Shit, shit shit!"

His eyes flicked to the man in the cage, before he lowered to whisper in my ear. "He's shouting about how he'll save you. Beat me to death and return his king's queen to him, yada yada."

"You think a battle to the death is going to get his men to listen to you after this?" I said, voice quivering with unease.

"Of course. Singing Arrow warriors take an oath to serve their leader with unquestioned loyalty. After I remove Lok's head, his title will fall to me."

"And they'll just go along with it? After you've murdered their leader and tortured them? That's insane!"

"Like I said, dogmatic idiots."

"It won't matter. I've seen Lok fight. He'll make mincemeat out of you."

The king nodded as if considering. "Yeah, in a fair fight, I suppose he would." He brushed a curl behind my ear and whispered, "Good thing I coated his armor in Aetherrot toxin."

"What?"

"Did you think I'd leave the fate of my empire up to chance? Oh, you adorable little fool. Lok will suffocate on his own spit before I even have to lift my sword."

I shoved away from him. "You have the gall to call him a coward, then you go and poison his armor? That's not an honorable match at all."

"True. But who's going to tell them? By the time the match is over, there will be nothing anyone can do about it."

His words hung heavy in the air, until their meaning rocked me back on my feet. The king was the only one with the translator symbiont. With Sol and the others locked up, there'd be no way for us to transfer it to anyone else. Desperate, I turned toward the crowd anyway. "Listen to me, King Osid poisoned Lok's armor! This challenge isn't valid!"

The cheering continued, undisturbed. A few men in front called to the torturer behind us, making pulling motions toward the lever. "Dammit, stop with the medieval torture bullshit and listen to me!"

King Osid chuckled as he patted my shoulder. "Save your breath. You know they can't understand you." His laughter disappeared behind a scowl as he glared at the man in the cage. "Oh gods, he's started a poem. Dunk him. Dunk him now!"

The torturer pulled the lever.

"STOP!" Driven by a surge of desperation, I couldn't stand by any longer. The cage descended once more, and without further thought, I rushed forward, shouldered the torturer away from the lever, and threw my weight against it. The cage breached the water once more and I fell back, panting.

The torturer reached for the lever, then drew back his hand when I slapped it away. "No! No more dunking." I pushed myself to my feet and glared down at the laughing king. "You've made your point. Going any further is just barbarism. Let him out."

The king crossed his arms over his chest and turned to the man next to him. "It's incredible how many demands she makes without any leverage." Several members of the crowd snickered, but there was a notable edge in the air that wasn't there before. I scanned the faces in the crowd. The people enjoying the spectacle threw up their fists, cheering for another pull of the lever. Past them, on the outskirts of the revelry, I spotted the two men I'd seen whispering to each other earlier.

One wore a scowl as he leaned down and spoke softly to his companion. The second nodded and turned his attention to the men beside him. Their eyes were fixed on me, but I could feel them studying the scene around me. The tall one tapped the other on the shoulder. I couldn't make out what he was saying, but his body language read urgency.

King Osid smiled, and the hairs on the back of my neck stood up. "You're right. Perhaps I have made my point." The air shifted, and a familiar scent hit me. The scent of fire and smoke.

He held out a hand to the cage, embers igniting in the center of his palm. Before I could react, the king fired a shot at the cage, only for the fireball to explode before it reached its target. The world went white, and I felt my body skitter across the water before going under.

CHAPTER 16

AH. I'M DROWNING AGAIN. *IT DOESN'T HURT, WHICH PROBably means I have a concussion. Which is not ideal, clearly.*

But the water cradled me like an old friend, and my body was just so tired. For a moment, just a sweet, blissful moment, I let my eyes close. Sunlight warmed my skin as I sat with Toto under that oak tree. I ran my fingers through his mane.

"Is this how far you want to go?" he asked.

I leaned my head against the tree, letting go of the weight of my burdens until I felt nothing but that beautiful sunlight. "Spare me the pre-death parables, would you? I was ready to give up and die on the beach but you insisted on seeing how far we could go. I went. Now I'm tired. Lemme rest."

The lion stretched, letting his head loll on my lap. "I'm not stopping you."

I bit my lip. "Why would you say it like that?"

There was a trace of laughter in his voice that ate at me. "I didn't say it like anything."

"Liar," I snapped, sitting up. "You think I'm giving up too early. Like I give up on everything else."

"Do you think you're giving up too early?"

"So what if I am?! What difference does it make? If I opened my eyes right now, I'd still be drowning on an alien planet. I'd still be trapped with a madman who poisoned me while Sol gets the snot kicked out of him and Lok is god knows where about to put on poison armor. Even if I swam to safety, what then? I don't have a way out of here, and the only people who can understand me are either locked in cages or a damn villain! I'm not the hero type. This isn't my big moment where I find out I have witch powers or I'm the child of an adulterous god with no concept of safe sex and magically save the day with a sassy comeback."

"Who said you had to be?"

"I . . . Nobody. But that's not the point. The point is, I am not built for this shit. If the Biwbans wanted a test subject that was willing to solve political disputes, they should have abducted a CIA agent or something. Instead they got the girl that films the dramatic retellings of the lives of meerkats."

"All right. Lie back down."

"Maybe I don't want to lie back down, ever think about that?! And you know what? This is all Osid's fault anyway! Of course you need every hand on deck just to keep the herds out. Who builds a settlement right in the middle of a migration path—oooooooh." The realization came flooding in all at once. If the Rumbling, as Lok called it, happened once every year, then this settlement was probably just in the way of a yearly migration. Animals as big as sauropods probably couldn't graze in the same area for long without depleting their food source. If they were also dealing with triceratops and other herd species, then it was probably similar to the great Serengeti migration, just on a much larger scale. I had only gone to see the event once before, but I couldn't imagine trying to build a camp right in the middle of a million-strong feeding frenzy.

Toto merely grunted.

"Shit!"

"About time."

"You know, I could do with less judgment, Toto. You could have just given me the answer in the first place."

His side-eye was scathing. "Dory, this isn't real. I'm literally a figment of your imagination. You're drowning, remember? Wake up and tell that idiot king to move his settlement."

CHAPTER 17

WATER RUSHED IN FROM EVERY DIRECTION, AND AN ARM came around my waist and hauled me upright. I gasped for air as soon as my head broke the surface.

"What the fuck?" I cried out. My hands fisted a familiar green coat, and I nearly sobbed in relief when I recognized the gold stripes of Sol's horns.

"Stop squirming," he called over his shoulder. He elbowed a soldier out of his way and ran through the crowd like his heels were on fire. Toto tackled another man to the ground when he lunged for us.

A sharp whistle rang through the air, and the next thing I knew, the area was swarmed with men in red armor. They bulldozed through King Osid's men like a group of linebackers on steroids.

Sol dodged to avoid an oncoming spear. The air was knocked out of my lungs when his shoulder dug into my stomach. Wet hair slapped right into my mouth. I spat it out and tried to call over the chaos but was drowned out by a scream as a body was flung over my head. "Wait, stop!" I tried again. "Sol, tell them to stop! We don't have to fight, I know how to fix the fence iss— Ack!" My words were cut off when Sol swung me around, my knee connecting with the jaw of a soldier. With a sickening pop, his jaw dislocated.

Wasting no time, Sol threw me back over his shoulder and took off down the street. "Did you just use me as a weapon?" I yelled.

"They took my knives," he said petulantly.

"Still, though!"

"Be angry later. Intern flew ahead to find Beast; they're set to meet us at the front gate. Lok's men won't be able to hold off the bastards forever. We have to go!"

"What about Blair?" I asked.

"We got separated during the breakout." Sol rounded a corner with Toto following closely and was met with the towering walls of the village border. "This would be easier if I knew where I was going."

A shout drew our attention to four soldiers advancing down the alleyway. Sol turned to escape down the other path, but that, too, was blocked, by another soldier.

"What do we do?" I asked.

"Hold on, I'm thinking."

"You don't have a plan?"

"The plan was to break out and grab you. So far, it's going great. We're just in the middle of a little hiccup and need to find a way out, that's all."

"And an antidote."

"Antidote?"

"Yeah, I kinda sorta got poisoned by wispfruit."

His jaw dropped. "You were poisoned. How? You were out of my sight for no more than a few hours!"

"Really, Dory, you are not making this rescue easy," Toto chided.

"Don't gang up on me! How am I at fault here? A lot of things happened in those hours, all right?! I learned the king's evil plan, had dinner, saw a torture, and . . . OHHHH! That's right, the fence!"

"Dory, now is not the time to keep screaming about the blasted fence. We're in the middle of a situation."

"Which makes it the perfect time!" I snapped. I slid off Sol's shoulder and faced our assailants, my hands held up in surrender. "Have any of you gotten the translator yet?" I asked. "Or be willing to hold still long enough for a quick smooch?"

"What are you doing?" Sol hissed.

"My job, kinda." Conflict resolution wasn't an uncommon job aspect when it came to being a wildlife biologist. It was often up to us to figure out how to develop strategies to mitigate conflicts between humans and wildlife, whether it was building an electric fence so the wildlife stopped eating crops, or even teaching scare tactics to countryfolk to stop them from shooting any predator that came near their sheep. I can't say any of those countryfolk have ever held a spear to my throat or poisoned me, but life's a bitch and then you die. So I may as well give it a go.

A spear embedded itself in the wall next to my face.

"You know what? You're right, it's not the time." I bent down and tore at the laces of my left boot.

"Finally, you begin to see sense—" His body tensed when my hand gripped his shoulder to keep myself steady. "In the name of the old gods, what do you think you're doing? They're about to run us through!"

With a yank, I pulled my foot free of the boot, ripped off

my sock, then raised my foot toward our assailants and screamed, "Hoof rot!"

The reaction was immediate. The faces of our attackers twisted into horrified grimaces. The two charging forward skittered to a halt; one slipped on the cobblestones and frantically crab-walked backward to get away from my foot.

For extra effect, I wiggled my toes and hopped closer to them.

The guard in the rear retched and took off running. I turned to wiggle my toes at the man in the alleyway, only to find him long gone, his spear clanking against the stone floor as if it had been recently dropped. The man on the ground looked up to see that he had been left for dead in the face of my disease-ridden foot, scrambled upright only to slip on his friend's vomit, vomited himself, then tried again and took off. If he hadn't just thrown a spear at my head, I almost would've felt bad for him.

Sol stared ahead blankly. "I . . . I can't believe that worked."

"Yeah, y'all got some serious issues with feet."

CHAPTER 18

THE WEATHER ON THIS PLANET WAS A VIOLENT, FICKLE thing. During my march to the dunking, the sun shone bright on the horrors basking in its rays. Almost as if it was delighted. Hungry for its Sankado sacrifice. Robbed of its meal, the sun hid away behind festering storm clouds and lashed out with claws of lightning and the hiss of pelting rain.

Sol did his best to shield me from most of it. Despite my protesting that he was obviously more banged-up than I was, his yix wool coat was thrown over my head, its water-resistant material keeping the worst of the freezing rain's bite from my skin. With a snap of the reins he urged Beast faster, hell-bent on putting as much distance between us and the king as he could. The normally ornery duckbill snorted but did as he was told. His heavy hooves sank deep into the mud, leaving an obvious trail for any pursuers to follow, but in the mix of the giant migratory herd that surrounded the fortress, it was unlikely anyone would be able to distinguish one set from another.

Behind us, I heard Toto groan and looked back to see that the poor lion was hanging on for dear life. His claws tried to dig into the beast's hide, but the dinosaur's tough, scaly skin proved too tough for Toto to get a good grip. The arms around my waist sagged, and I had only a fraction of a second to grab hold of my alien before his weight slumped and pitched to the side. I pulled the reins from his loose fingers and pinned his arm to my stomach with my free hand. "I can't hold him up forever. Tell me you've found a place to rest."

Intern toyed with his screen. "My scanner picked up a human enrichment building not far from here." With a ding, the screen shifted into a floating yellow arrow. It spun in circles before pointing toward our right. I steered Beast to follow it.

When we finally reached the location indicated by Intern's scanner, a storm-ridden pink grove unfolded before us. The relentless tempest had already plunged what I could only imagine was a normally picturesque scene into disarray, with swirling petals and bending branches creating a chaotic dance amid the ongoing downpour.

We quickly sought refuge in the looming Renaissance-style chapel that stood as a silent sentinel amid the storm. I guided Sol's head to rest on Beast's back before sliding off the dinosaur to force open the heavy double doors. It was only by sheer force of luck that whichever Biwban designed this thing was so extra that they thought a whole-ass Sistine-style chapel was a human enrichment toy. But the doors were big enough for a duckbill, so I wasn't going to complain. I ushered Beast inside and Toto immediately jumped off the dinosaur, violently shaking the rain out of his precious mane.

Inside, the atmosphere was as tense as the violent storm that echoed in the stone walls. Rain battered against stained glass windows, and the fractured patterns of pink and gray they cast were the only light we had—and that wasn't saying much.

The duckbill knelt down, making it easier for me to slide Sol gently out of the saddle. Dizziness struck me out of nowhere and I slipped on the wet floor; he came crashing down on top of me, knocking the wind out of my lungs. My vision blurred as I stared up at the ceiling. I forced my eyes shut and shook my head, trying to force it away. When my head stopped spinning, I slid out from underneath him. When I tried to stand, my heart thudded in my chest and my body pitched to the side, and I found myself on my back staring at a spinning ceiling once again.

Shit. Nausea was not a good sign. Heart palpitations were not exactly ideal either. Nor did they give me any real hint about what kind of poison I was dealing with.

All right, think. King Osid said I'd be lucky if I got three days before whatever this shit was would kill me. It had been a few hours since exposure, and I was only beginning to see initial symptoms. That should rule out cyanide or any other fast-acting poison. Unless I was about to drop in the next few minutes. *No, can't think like that.*

If it was a slow-acting poison, something like oleander, then the Biwban research center could probably sort out an antidote for it after we grabbed Lok. I pulled out my phone and jotted down my condition, as well as a description of the fruit. I'd need to keep a running log of the effects to maximize my chances.

Sol's lashes fluttered and he regarded me through bleary eyes. "Did we make it out?"

"Barely." I sighed, stuffing my phone back in my pocket. The ground thudded and I looked up to see that Beast had taken a page from our book and plopped down.

"Why are we on the ground?"

"You're heavy."

"Noted."

"You're not gonna die, are you?"

A smile tugged at his lips. "The compassion in your voice is truly heartwarming. You know I've always longed for a mate that would question my continued existence with the same nonchalance of someone asking to pass the garlic bread."

I sucked in a breath. "There's garlic bread on this planet?"

"Do you even realize how much wonder is in your eyes right now? This is the happiest I think I've ever seen you, and it's directed at neither me nor Lok." He took my chin in his hand and tilted it up to face him. His voice was low and purposefully seductive. "Yes, my star, we have garlic bread on this planet."

"I see they didn't beat out that sassy attitude." I laughed.

"Just a tooth."

"Oh no, really?"

He hooked his finger on his lips and pulled back, revealing the missing molar on the upper right side.

"Oh, you poor thing." I reached out and brushed his hair out of his face, taking gentle care not to brush against the dark bruise forming above his eye.

He pulled me to him and his kiss sang through my veins. "See now, this is better. This I can get used to."

I could too.

The thought was involuntary. As was the way his name hummed in my chest. *Damn. Is this what love is? It feels good.*

The Tamagotchi went off like a church bell around the Intern's neck, blaring the tune of my embarrassment to echo through the halls of the cathedral. Intern pulled it out, his face brightening when he saw the screen. “Seven notches! Oh, this is a wonderful development. You know, the manual did have an entire chapter based on near-death experiences. I’d hoped we’d get to at least a four after today, but this?” He jumped up with a loud chirp, then paused when he noticed neither of us was celebrating with him. “You two need time alone. I’ll just . . .” He paused and looked around. “Be over in that general direction,” he said, flying off.

Even with the distance, I could hear the Tamagotchi’s jolly little tune peal out between the rumbles of thunder. “I’m gonna break that thing.”

Sol seemed rather pleased with himself. “Look at you. Besotted.”

I smacked his shoulder, trying to stifle the laugh building in my throat.

He merely grinned with smug delight. “Oh, don’t feign an icy demeanor now. You’re obsessed with me.”

“You’re insufferable.”

“You love me.”

“You’re all right.”

“Sing as many lies as you like, Stardust,” he said, pulling me to rest on his chest. He tugged his coat over us and threaded his hand in mine. “You forget, before the end of the world, I was a liar’s worst nightmare in the House of Justice, and you, my adorably smitten little alien, read like an open book.”

There was something warm and enchanting in his humor. It provided a sense of safety I wasn’t used to feeling. Even with everything that had happened. Hell, poison coursed through my veins, and by no account were we actually safe at all, but . . . I felt at peace, just lying there with him.

It was not unlike how I felt around Lok. I somehow felt

more at ease lying on a cold cathedral floor here with Sol than I ever did on Earth. I wondered what it would be like if we got the chance to explore this further. Somehow beat the odds, defeat the mad king, get the antidote, and punch that bird in the face. I could still study animals on this planet—a much wider variety than I'd planned to study on Earth. I'd have none of the funding or tools, but on the bright side, no student loans. Take that, Sallie Mae.

Even more than that, I'd get to stay with them.

"Maybe there's something to that Biwban algorithm after all," I said.

"I admit I had my doubts at first."

"And now?"

"You have to ask?" He laughed. "I sang Lok's might and praises to anyone with an arrow tattooed on their neck until I felt I'd retch from embarrassment just to incite a riot, then fought my way through an entire fortress to get to you."

"I'd still like to hear you say it."

"You first."

"Churlish."

"Fine." He sighed. "I love the way you yell at plants."

I snorted. "You jerk."

"I'm serious," he said, and his thumb traced the vein in my wrist in a way that made the room grow quiet. "Watching you comb through every leaf, cataloging their growth and how it's going to affect each creature from crawling bug to flying giant, makes me view the world with a sense of importance I've never had before. Before you, a vine was just a vine. Now I fret over their plans for world domination. You make the mundane precious."

I'm gonna fucking cry.

There was a flutter in my chest, which I hoped to god was

love and not cyanide. I fought the urge to squeeze him to me, mindful of his bruises. Instead, I buried my face in his chest. "Do you think we'll make it through this?"

He didn't answer at first, and when he did, he spoke in an odd, gentle tone. "Why not? After all the nonsense we've had to go through, I'd say we've earned some good fortune. We'll find Lok and warn him about his armor, tell him King Osid poisoned his precious Stardust, and he'll rip the king's throat out and get you that antidote. Easy."

"Just like that?"

"Of course. I won't accept anything else." He said the words with such certainty it made me giggle.

"For some reason, I believe you."

I heard the fluttering of wings before Intern landed on my knee. "What's this about an antidote?"

"Oh right, you weren't there. The king poisoned me during dinner in an attempt to get Lok to fight him. He said it would take about three days to kill me. Which, now that I'm saying it out loud, I'm kinda starting to panic a little," I said, voice wavering. Sol gave my hand a comforting squeeze.

"Well, stop that," Intern said. "You're not poisoned."

"I . . . Yes, I am. I got cut with wispfruit."

"I don't know what *wispfruit* is, but I know there's no need for an antidote. Nothing on this planet is poisonous to humans."

"You know, I'd love to believe that, but based on your track record, I'm going to go out on a limb and say this, too, fell through the cracks."

"You aren't poisoned," he repeated, more sharply this time. "You can't be poisoned; you're far too expensive to be replaced. You cost more than this continent; there's no possibility of you being in any danger."

I sat up and laced my fingers together. "Intern, have we not been on the same journey? We just escaped the fortress holding us hostage."

His tone had become chilly. "You are too expensive to lose. Every plant and creature we introduced from your world was scanned by our finest detection system. It's completely infallible. If you are poisoned, someone is getting executed."

"That's . . . dark and yet strangely comforting." I was more on board with that news than I should have been. *You know what? Scratch that, I'm worth it. Kill that fool.*

"Did you check the plants from our planet?" Sol asked.

The intern halted, stunned.

I showed him my cut, now burning with dermatitis.

All hell broke loose.

Intern's talons latched onto my wrist, his wings flapping wildly as he tried to drag me toward the exit, all the while screaming at Beast to get up. I shook him off my wrist and backed away, but the Biwban flew behind me and shoved at my back. "Stop fighting me and get on the *Parasaurolophus*—we don't have much time!"

I stumbled forward, then sidestepped out of his way when he tried to push at my calf. "Will you calm down? We're not getting anywhere in that damn storm."

"What part of 'too expensive to replace' are you not understanding? Get on the dinosaur. If we ride through the night, we'll get to the research center by morning. We need to get you in the healing pod before the poison runs its course!"

"We can't leave," I snapped. "Lok's as good as dead as soon as he dons his armor. If King Osid is right, then I've got days. Lok doesn't. We have to find him."

The intern squealed indignantly. "Seeing as you still have

one fully functioning mate, no, we don't! Get on the *Parasaurolophus*!"

"What is it with this fucking planet and leaving people to die? We're not doing that. Stop suggesting it! Besides, we're already in the Fuchsia Grove, I doubt it will take us long to find him. We'll look for Lok first thing in the morning, then head to the research center right after. King Osid can follow us if he wants a fight that bad."

"There's no time!" Intern screeched. "Without exact knowledge of how your body is going to react to the poison, we can't take any chances."

Sol struggled to his hooves and collected the screeching bird in his arms. "That's enough of that. Calm down, Intern."

"Calm down?" the bird hissed. "I'm trying to save her life! What are you doing with that rope?" Sol looped a red rope around the Intern. "No, no!" he cried, trying to thrash his way to freedom.

"Find a light, would you? I'll set him in the next room to collect himself." When he turned to leave, the intern kicked at him like a petulant toddler, but Sol merely held him away from his body and kept on.

"It's just one thing after another." I put a hand on my hip and looked around the room. "Toto, help me find a light switch, would ya?"

He blinked at me quizzically. "What's a light switch?"

"Right." I sighed. "Sometimes I forget you're a lion. Okay, I'll find the switch and you . . . just keep doing what you're doing." Running my hands over all the usual spots by the door yielded no results. Nor was there any lever visible. Hmm. If I was designing a playhouse for an animal, I'd put in a rope lever or an obvious pad they could step on. Which I didn't see.

Unless . . .

I clapped my hands, and sure enough the lights turned on. "Are you fucking kidding me? You didn't trust us not to break the button?"

An exasperated male voice drifted from down the hall. "Can you blame us?"

I meant to fire back about him being a cheapskate, but my retort died when I looked at the room. Really looked at the room. I expected the beautiful Renaissance-style paintings. Priceless stained glass windows were also par for the course in an elaborate celebration of reckless ecclesiastical hypocrisy. The subject matter was what threw me for a loop.

"Intern," I called.

"What?" he snapped. Clearly in no mood at all.

"Why do you think we worship Steamboat Willie?"

The paintings were endless, all of them of old cartoons, King Kong, Dracula, and Sherlock Holmes for some godforsaken reason, all locked in battle with Steamboat Willie.

In the center of the room, erected in his honor, was a statue of the glorious mouse himself, sailing his little steamboat over the bodies of his enemies.

"What's worship?" Intern asked.

"What?" I made my way into the next room and found the pew where Sol had stashed him. "What do you mean, what's worship? If this place isn't in service of what you think our god is, then what is it?"

He swiveled his head around and huffed out a response. "It's listed as a communal entertainment building. You can . . . mingle, and stuff."

"I desperately want to be mad at you," I said, gazing up at a portrait of Steamboat Willie choking the life out of Frankenstein's monster. "But this is really fucking funny."

Fits of anger died out from the little bird at my laughter,

not enough to quell it completely. He worked up enough nerve to cease his bitch-pouting and asked, "Did we get it right?"

"You know what? Better. You've exceeded all expectations. I'm incredibly entertained. Follow-up question: why is it all vintage pop culture?"

"I can check the notes if you untie me."

Behind him, Sol lay spread out on the pew, his coat bunched up behind his head for comfort. "I just pulled him off you. If you free him, you're on your own."

"Such a protector."

"And don't you forget it."

I shook my head and turned my attention back to the Biwban, now gazing up at me with innocent wide-eyed adoration. Unfortunate for him that I'd just spent two years handling gaggles of adorable meerkats. All with their own special brand of doe-eyed deception. All of them biters. "How about you just tell me, and I'll decide if I want to risk you scratching up my arm after?"

"Ugh, have it your way." He wiggled his arm until a few primary feathers poked out from the rope. "Press down on the one in the middle."

I did as instructed. This time, instead of using his hands, Intern appeared to be controlling the screen by thought alone. He clicked his beak and a third model of the chapel came on-screen. "Give me a moment to read through these atrocious notes. Novu, you singed-feathered half-wit, why would you arrange this as alphabetical and not categorical? How is anyone else meant to— Oh! Here it is." He pulled up a page all marked with red. The silhouette of a mouse's head popped up on-screen before it beeped angrily, and a crossed-out circle stamped itself over the mouse. "Ahh. That will do it."

"Do what? What does that mean?" I asked.

His tone was solemn and final. "Copyright infringement."

"I can't with y'all," I yelled, half laughing, half crying. "You've got no problem snatching up innocent women, but you're scared of copyright infringement?"

"Intellectual property theft is no laughing matter, Dory. Biwbanian law clearly states that if we are found in violation, the courts could put an injunction on our entire conservation project and shut us down. Not to mention the potential seizure and destruction of all of our research."

"He's right, corporations don't mess around with that," Sol added.

I rested a fist on my hip and regarded the former lawyer with clear disbelief. "You can't honestly tell me that copyright infringement is taken more seriously than human trafficking."

His brow quirked. "How dark do you want to get?"

"Never mind, I'll shut up."

"Smart." He reached out his arms in invitation, and for once, my ever-harried brain decided to stop and smell the tonka beans. I melted into him with a contented sigh, resting my head against his chest. Snuggling in a church pew wasn't the most comfortable thing in the world, a downright blasphemous *scandal* if my grandma were alive to see it. But fuck me, the soothing cadence of his heart would always be worth the scarlet letter.

I loved him.

The realization came without fuss or fanfare. It was pouring outside, my back hurt, and I loved him.

I loved *them*.

The Tamagotchi beeped, and its song started up anew. Sol chuckled beneath me; calloused fingers brushed a curl from my cheek. "Twice in one day? Honestly, Dory, I'm hardly even trying."

My body tensed at the sound of a faint hiss. Some deep primal instinct inside me screamed to run.

"What, no witty comeback—?"

"Hush." I clapped my hands, casting the room in darkness. The stained glass windows were too opaque to see through; instead, I watched the fragmented scatters of light they cast on the floor.

The only sounds were the rain outside and the Tamagotchi's infernal song, yet the hair on the back of my neck rose.

Sol looked around the room before giving me a cocky grin. "Surely you're not still embarrassed? I'm only teas—" I put a hand to his mouth.

There it was again, a low, rumbling hiss. Slowly, I sat up and scanned the reflected light along the ground. Rows of color danced against the rain, before stopping completely at the edge of the room. I swallowed the lump in my throat and looked up, hoping against all hope that the room simply ran out of windows. It did not. There was, however, a dark shadow looming on the other side.

My thoughts flitted to Lok. All alone somewhere outside with that shadow. Possibly poisoned, possibly worse. A fist closed around my chest.

The Tamagotchi beeped.

The shadow moved in an instant, darting in front of the windows nearest to us. Lightning flashed, revealing the stark outline of the last fucking thing I needed right now.

Sol's arm tightened around the small of my back. "The Gruulorak."

Her head snapped up, nose scanning the air, searching for something. When the Tamagotchi's song reached its crescendo, she let out a chattering clack from her maw, the way I'd seen Catzilla react when he caught sight of a bird just out of reach. She shifted her weight to one side and clawed at the window with her foot. A horrible screech filled the air.

I snatched the Tamagotchi from the Intern and sat on it, muffling its noise as much as I could. The Gruulorak's movements grew less frantic. The three of us stayed as still as statues.

A voice pierced through the silence. "Dory!"

Startled, I jumped, and my scream echoed through the room before being cut off when Sol snatched me up and held a hand to my mouth. Without the muffled cushion of my booty, the Tamagotchi's tune rang loud and clear, ending on a cheery note that echoed through the chapel.

Toto's eyes glowed in the darkness as he looked both of us over. "What are you do—"

"Shh!"

"Why?"

I reached out and closed his mouth, then drew him closer to Sol and me and whispered in his ear. "Be quiet, that crazy T. rex is outside."

The lion dislodged my hand with a shake of his head and peered over our heads to see the Gruulorak's silhouette.

An ear-piercing screech filled the room when the T. rex scratched at the window again. Heart pounding, I shut my eyes and hoped against all hope that she'd get bored and leave.

"Hey, Dory?" Toto whispered.

"What?" I snapped back.

"Can my queen stay here with us tonight? She doesn't like the rain."

"Queen?" Sol asked. Shock siphoned the blood from his face when he turned to see a *Smilodon* sitting in the pew behind us.

Toto slipped from my arms to join her. He was only able

to get a good five feet from her before she gave a warning hiss. He stopped his advance and jumped up on the pew to sit as close as she would allow. "She won't eat you, she promised. Right, my darling?"

The *Smilodon* gave what sounded like a noncommittal grunt and lay down. Not the best vote of confidence. But there was a fucking T. rex outside, so I couldn't really muster up the effort to care. "Fine, whatever, just keep quiet."

With the big cats finally appeased, the Church of Cheese fell into a deathly quiet. I watched the Gruulorak pace around the chapel looking for any way inside. Sol held me close until my eyes grew heavy and I fell asleep.

CHAPTER 19

I WOKE UP WITH A TERRIBLE CRICK IN MY NECK. I GOT UP with a stretch, vowing to never again sleep on a bench. The chapel was bathed in daylight as last night's storm had faded into a light drizzle, and as an added bonus, I didn't see any T. rex–shaped silhouettes looming by the windows. Both Toto and his lady love were still sprawled out on their own bench fast asleep. Intern and Sol were nowhere to be seen.

Their voices drifted in from the main hall, and I tiptoed out of the room, careful not to wake Toto and his queen. Pushing the heavy wooden door open a crack, I peeked inside. Intern and Sol were both standing near the Steamboat Willie statue, their voices raised in argument.

"—can't just ignore it, Sol!" Intern sounded pissed. "We need to get her to the research center now. There's no telling how quickly the poison is going to take effect."

Sol crossed his arms over his chest, his expression stubborn. "You don't think I know that? We'll head there as soon as we find Lok."

"No! There's no time to find him. Convince her to go with you now. Make something up and tell her you've seen the poison before and, I don't know, it'll rot her from the inside out or something. She'll listen to you."

An indignant snort. "When has she ever?"

"He's right," I called as I entered the room. "I've never been much of a listener. Seems like you aren't either, Intern. Seeing as I told you last night that the plan is to look for Lok first. Judging by the sea of pink magnolia outside, I'd say we already reached the Fuchsia Grove. Let's just—"

"No!" Intern shouted. "Clearly neither of you understands the gravity of the situation. I gave you until the morning to come to your senses; clearly, that was a waste of time."

"I feel like you're forgetting the T. rex that was prowling around looking for human tartare."

"I would have handled it!"

"How, Intern? How is a twelve-inch-tall bird going to stop a T. rex?"

"Never mind the how. We're wasting time. Both of you get on Beast. We're leaving."

"Dory, maybe he's right."

"Sol, don't you turn on me too."

"I'm not. But we still need to consider the very real possibility that this could turn into a you-or-him situation. Should that be the case, then I know Lok would agree that saving your life is what's best."

"Oh my god, I am so sick of that horseshit! It's my life. Mine! And lately, everyone but me seems to be forgetting that. No one else has any right to tell me how much value I assign to it, and if I want to spend it making sure the man I love doesn't drop dead in some stupid power struggle, then that's what I'm gonna do." I shoved past him to grab Beast's reins. Pausing at the door, I looked back. "Are you coming or not?"

"I . . . I have no desire to force you to do anything, you know that. Enough has been taken from us already. But I am bound to you, you know that, right? If you run off and die, then I will not be far behind."

"Could you live with yourself if we left him? I'm not sure I can."

He crossed his arms over his chest and looked away.

"Sol."

"I'm thinking."

"You are so dramatic."

"All right, fine. If you tell him I said this, I will deny it completely, but this world would be too quiet without the loud idiot. So be it. If you want to play the hero, then I'll stand with you."

Intern flew to roost at the top of Beast's saddle and sighed like he wanted the dino to trample us both. "That was a lovely speech, truly touching. Now get on the dino, it's time to go. I do not want to force your hand with this, but I will."

"It's not going to work, Intern. Our minds are made up."

"Let me ask you a question, Subject 4."

"Dory."

"Of course," he conceded. "Tell me, *Dory*, how long did you study those meerkats before we took you?"

"About two years."

He nodded and replied, "In those two years, did you ever ask any of them what they thought before ensuring that the conditions for their survival were met? Did you check to see how they felt before gathering DNA samples or conducting behavioral experiments?"

"I . . ."

"Of course you didn't. Why would you? Your job was to collect data and ensure the animals in your care stayed alive and well. So I think you know what comes next."

"Intern, you can't just—"

"Just what? What am I doing wrong, Dory? You would do the same in this situation. This entire planet was terraformed with the sole purpose of you and the other test subjects forming a successful breeding population with the Sankado. I admit I didn't think Lok would end up getting himself assassinated when I separated you two, but fortunately you have a spare," he said, casting a quick glance at Sol.

The coldness in his gaze sent my pulse spinning. "What do you mean you separated us?"

He laughed, then pulled out the Tamagotchi, turned it on, and tossed it to me. "Look at your affection meter. You said it yourself, didn't you? Humans need time apart to sort out their feelings. What did you call it again? Ah, that's right. *Pining.*"

I stared wordlessly at the affection meter. Both Lok's and Sol's bars had risen dramatically from the last time I'd seen it. Sol's was nearly full at nine notches, barely beating out Lok's seven.

"Honestly, I was shocked at how well it worked. As soon as Sol and I were separated from you after that vellshoten T. rex attacked us, your affection for him went up three whole notches! Three! I'd be an idiot not to try and replicate that. Especially with that power-hungry Osid so desperate to get rid of Lok. All I had to do was guide you to him, and sure enough, as soon as you began worrying about him, your affection for him shot up. Pining works—far better than the 'only one bed' trope our manual kept harping on."

He pulled up his screen and began typing. "Your cooperation up until now has been helpful. I'd hoped to continue working closely alongside you to better document your progress, but if you insist on doing this the hard way, then I'm afraid I have no choice." With a ding, the screen faded away.

Faint buzzing filled the air.

"Dory, watch out!" Before I could blink, Sol shoved hard at my back, and a net burst through the window and enveloped him in glowing blue rope.

Through the broken window from where the net had burst in, I could see the rain break against the telltale outline of alien saucers. The aliens hadn't just come for me—they had arrived in force.

Intern's betrayal stung. I couldn't tell if I wanted to cry or scream. "You've been in contact with them this whole time?"

With a tilt of his head he replied, "Did you really think we'd risk losing this big of an investment because of a broken hover scooter? You alone cost more than this containment. Your escape from the ship was unplanned, to be sure, but it did present something better. Opportunity. The data I've gathered while traveling with you three is invaluable, and for that, I thank you. But it's time to go."

The net wrapped around Sol tightened until he let out a pained hiss.

"Do as I say and no one has to get hurt."

I bit down on the inside of my cheek, hard enough to taste blood. The net wound tighter around him, and drops of blood spilled from the cuts until something in me snapped.

My fingers wrapped around the phone in my back pocket.

A high-pitched shriek burst from Intern as I threw my phone hard enough at his head to send him flying off Beast's saddle.

"Toto!" I screamed.

The lion burst into the room, paws sliding on the smooth marble floor. He took in the scene with wide eyes. "What's all this? What's happening?"

I stared at the Intern picking himself up off the floor. "Grab your queen. It's time for a hunt."

"Yes!" The lion grinned wide like a Cheshire cat before he charged directly at me. A slight tinge of fear wormed its way up my spine before the lion leapt clear over my head and smacked down a cloaked hover scooter. The force of the blow shattered its windshield, and the green Biwban inside was sent flying out of his craft. Toto landed not far from me, and bloodlust and joy radiated from the big cat in waves. "No need to wake my queen, I will bring her a feast of sour birds and she will know of my devotion!"

Grabbing a chunk of broken glass from the shattered hovercraft, I knelt beside Sol and hacked away at the ropes binding my alien.

"Hurry," he gasped. "I can't breathe."

"I'm going as fast as I can."

The rope fell away and he slumped against me. The smell of iron was thick in the air. "Thank you," he breathed.

"Don't thank me yet; we're not out of this," I said, grabbing Sol by the arm and hoisting him to his hooves. Drops of water fell to the floor not far from us, and without a second thought, Sol raised his arm and shot a fireball. His aim was true, and the craft's cloaking feature fizzled away before the pod crashed against the statue of Steamboat Willie. The room exploded in a shower of debris and dust. I coughed, blinking tears from my eyes.

"You'll pay for that," a voice sneered from behind. I whirled around and saw the Biwban had a ray gun trained at Sol's head.

"No!" Intern shouted. "That's her only other Zhali match. We need him alive!"

Sol chuckled.

Which, hold on . . . was his voice always that deep?

Hello?

"Now, why in Jelrath's name would you tell me that?" He placed a hand on my shoulder and leaned to whisper, "Get to Beast. I'll take care of them."

"Are you crazy? There's a swarm of them."

He rested his forehead on my shoulder and chuckled. "Would it kill you to let me show off a little?"

"Don't do anything stupid."

"When have I ever done anything stupid?"

"I'm not dignifying that with an answer."

He stepped forward, arms outstretched, and the firelight glinted off his horns.

Another saucer fired a net, but my alien dodged with ease. Sol returned the favor, flicking his wrist to send a fireball careening into the spacecraft. The ship spiraled out of control before it slammed against the ceiling and crashed down on the other side of the room.

"Oh, I'm going to enjoy this." He smiled.

Two more craft flew in and took aim. I ducked behind the statue as their ray guns went off.

A scream rang out, followed by the sound of glass breaking and flames crackling.

I peeked out and saw Sol's flames dancing around the room, scorching the walls and the statues and the carpet, but not once did they touch me or Toto, who was happily mauling his way through Biwban.

"Why is this so hot?"

Sol whipped around and sent a wave of fire crashing

against a hovercraft. The Biwban inside jumped out, only to be swallowed up in a ring of fire.

"Move, now!"

Sol's flames cleared the way and I ran back to Beast, Sol close behind. I swung myself onto the saddle and helped him up behind me. "Toto, let's go!"

The lion spat feathers out of his mouth to speak. "Just go, find your mate. These are mine."

I would have objected if the lion didn't look like he was having the time of his life. Toto launched himself into the fray *gleefully*, tearing apart the closest Biwban.

"Are you sure?"

"Of course I'm sure," he said. Toto leapt into the air and caught another hovercraft. "My queen needs breakfast."

With a crack of the reins, we flew out the chapel's double doors. The drizzle hadn't abated and the storm clouds hung low in the sky, but not far off, the sun shone through.

"Hold on!" Beast picked up speed as we galloped through the trees.

"I heard from the other Singing Arrows that King Osid plans to face Lok at the spot where he cast off his honor," Sol commented, forcing my head down with him to avoid smacking into a low-hanging branch. "Do you have any idea where that is?"

I racked my brain for answers, replaying Lok's and my conversation in the cave. "He said something about a shrine, a tall rock pillar with strange writing."

"The Glyph Stone."

"You know where it is?" I asked hopefully.

"I know of it, but I've never been this far outside of Night Ridge territory."

"So you don't actually know where we're going?"

"You could say that, yes."

I sighed. "Perfect. Just perfect."

We could hear the whiz of a hovercraft as it grew closer. Sol shoved the reins into my hands and turned around in the saddle to spit fire in a wave behind us. The flames damaged the ship's cloaking feature, but its pilot was determined and flew up high out of the smoke. Sol fired another shot. The ship dodged the blow but overcorrected and spun out, smashing against the trees.

"They're still gaining on us," I called over the chaos. "Any ideas?"

"None that you're going to like." He sprayed fireballs behind us, taking out a hovercraft and clipping another.

"You said that so ominously, I already don't like it. What's the alternative?"

He pulled me to him and snaked his hand under my shirt and squeezed my tit.

"WHAT THE FUCK?"

Sol buried his nose in my neck, groaning as his fingers trailed a path of heat along my thigh. "If I'm meant to keep my hands off you, why would you let this perfect ass bounce around in front of me? Honestly, Dory, it's cruel to tempt me so boldly. You know I'm injured."

My mouth hung open in disbelief. "We are . . . we are in the middle of a high-speed chase! Why the hell are you choosing now to cop a feel? You are unbelievable." My voice rose several octaves when his hand slipped into my panties and stroked my pussy.

"And you love it, don't you?" he purred against my neck.

My nails dug into his skin as he pushed a finger inside me,

and a hiss escaped my lips. "Sol," I bit out, despite the way my breath hitched as his fingers moved faster, stroking a deep, slow rhythm inside me.

"Go on, Stardust, lie to me." My legs quivered when he nipped the shell of my ear. I bit my lip and fought to keep my eyes from rolling into the back of my head as he curled his fingers; a sharp cry tore from my throat.

"Shove me away; tell me you're not about to come on my fingers for all these Biwban to see. Tell me how much you hate the way I make your knees shake."

"I'm so confused but strangely into this. Continue."

"Do you think the Biwban would like to watch me fuck you? I'm sure the two of us could give them a few more training modules for their manual."

"Mmm, you're losing me on the sex tape."

"I can feel how much you're dripping down my wrist. What do you say? Should we give them a show? Make your tits bounce so prettily the birds can't take their eyes off you, maybe even slip my knot inside you, let them hear how loud you like to beg for it before you come. Say the words, and I'll make you come all over my hand."

"You wish," I gritted out.

Sol laughed. "That's right. My Zhali is a dishonest little thing. Fine, if you're not ready to tell the truth, then I'll start," he said, pushing a second finger into me. My breathing came out in shallow pants as his lips brushed against my temple. Sol placed a kiss on my neck and whispered, "I love you."

Several things happened in rapid succession.

First, that damn Tamagotchi went off.

Second, a hovercraft flew past us, and the bright yellow Biwban inside spun his ship around and readied his net gun. I made a valiant attempt to both tug on the reins to avoid the net and shield myself so I wasn't out here letting every alien trying to capture me get a full showing of my kibbles 'n' bits. That plan was thwarted when Sol's tail knocked my hand away and sucked hard on my clit.

Neither my nor the Biwban's attempts mattered, however, because the damn Gruulorak burst through the trees and chomped down on the hovercraft.

I don't know if it was the adrenaline, the love confession, the alien tail sucking the soul out of my clit, or some combination of all three, but I'd never come so hard in *my life.*

Beast jerked his head, tearing the reins from my hands before veering around the Gruulorak. Sol grabbed me by the hair and kissed me. His tongue delved into my mouth, swallowing the moans that spilled from my lips. His tail released my swollen bud and the thick appendage wrapped around my thigh, holding me steady against him as he rubbed the slick coating on his fingers over my aching clit. When we broke apart, I was left panting, dazed, and wet.

"Now, was that so hard?" he purred, licking the last drops of my juices from his fingers.

"I—that was—what—" I tried to force coherent words out of my mush brain to no avail. Beast slowed to a halt, panting heavily as he tried to catch his breath.

"You're welcome," Sol said, his tone smug.

I punched his shoulder. "I was not going to thank you!"

"You were thinking it."

"Smug bastard. We're in the middle of running for our lives and you decided it would be a good idea to stick your tail down my pants and finger-fuck me. What were you thinking?"

He rolled his eyes and pointed behind us. The Gruulorak ripped another Biwban from their hovercraft and snapped it up like a prized dumpling. Our remaining pursuers fired shots at the massive T. rex, but the pink glutton was undeterred. With a swing of her tail, another ship was down. "I was thinking we weren't the ones she's been chasing this whole time."

A second T. rex emerged from the forest. It was smaller than the Gruulorak, and the blue stripes on its muzzle made it appear younger. Its mother roared, a deep bellow that echoed through the grove. More little ones appeared out of the trees and charged toward the remaining ships. The Gruulorak slammed a foot on a felled hovercraft and used her mighty jaws to pry the top off like a can opener. Her baby made short work of the pilot.

"Oh my stars," I breathed. The last of the ships disappeared in a sea of carnivorous teeth. It wasn't pretty. My stomach rolled, and I swallowed down the urge to gag. Sol was right; we were not the ones being chased. His hand tightened around my waist, and he pulled the reins. Beast took off, and we left the carnage behind.

CHAPTER 20

THE DISTANT ROAR OF THE GRUULORAK FADED INTO THE background as we galloped through the Fuchsia Grove. A coughing fit struck me out of nowhere. The kind that racks your body so hard your lungs slam against your ribs. I covered my mouth with my arm and tried to get ahold of myself. When I drew my arm away, there was blood left behind.

Hello, poison. I wondered when you'd start giving me trouble.

"Everything all right, Stardust?" Sol asked.

"Never better." The lie came out strained and I hid the pain in my throat with the classic art of a subject change. "The fight is supposed to happen at sundown today. We need to figure out how to find Lok before then."

"Easier said than done. It's not like we can just say 'Hey, Beast, find Lok.'"

The duckbill stopped dead in his tracks.

"Wait, are you serious?" I asked.

Beast reared up on his hind legs and blew out a long, low

note from his head crest. Once finished, he closed his eyes and stood motionless. A haunting cry echoed through the air. Beast's head perked up at the sound, and he shot off like a rocket.

"Do you hear that?" Sol's voice cut through the rushing wind.

I nodded, a flicker of hope igniting within me. "It's Blossom. Lok must be close."

Following the echoing cries, we navigated through the forest until I saw a glimpse of a building peeking through the trees. Beast charged through the grove until we came upon a hill revealing a strange marble structure that covered most of the hill. It resembled a series of interlocking curved panels that ascended toward the sky. Intricate geometric patterns were carved into the marble panels; the markings caught what little glimpses of sunlight the cloudy sky provided and cast long shadows along the grass. At the apex of the monument, a large circular hole framed the sky.

"Is that the Glyph Stone?" I asked.

"I'm not sure," Sol replied. "Though if I was a war general who decided to cast off my armor in a fit of melodramatics, this would be the place to do it."

When we drew closer, chanting could be heard from inside. Through the windows I could see Yengro, the man from the cage, among the chanters. Each of them thumped a spear on the ground as they crowded around someone in the center. My heart leapt in my chest when I saw that it was Lok. He stood with his arms outstretched as his attendant tightened the straps of his breastplate. Once finished, he picked up his helmet.

"STOP!" Without hesitation, I dismounted Beast and rushed to Lok's side—or I tried to. A well-muscled wall of a man caught me by the shoulders and refused to let me any closer.

I tried thrashing against his hold but might as well have been trying to bench-press a boulder. "Let go of me! Lok, take that off now!" I jerked an arm free, but the immovable prick just snatched my wrists and pinned them both behind my back. I stomped on his foot, only to scream in pain when I remembered that these guys had hooves, not feet. The injustice.

"Stardust?" Lok called. He dropped the helmet in his hands and rushed toward me. "Let her go, that's my Zhali."

"Yeah, you hear that?" I asked, rubbing at my newly freed wrists. "I'm his Zhali. Watch it."

Lok gathered me into a hug, which would have been so nice if his breastplate wasn't smashing my tits. Oh, fuck, the breastplate!

"How did you get free?" His hand cupped my cheek as he looked me over. "Where's Sol?"

"Here." Sol muscled his way through the crowd.

Lok stared at us both in disbelief before his face broke out into a wide grin. "Fuck am I glad to—"

I shoved away from him and tore at the straps of his armor. "No time for small talk. That psycho king said he rubbed poison all over your armor." The number of straps on Lok's armor was reminiscent of a 2010s cyberpunk nightmare. "There's no fucking way all these straps have a purpose," I huffed and smacked his back. "Well, don't just stand there and watch me struggle. Strip, strip!"

Lok's eyes started to water, and when he spoke, his voice came out in a ragged whisper. "I feel like I've been waiting my whole life to hear you say that."

"Now's not the time to flirt, you oaf." Sol took a knife

from his belt and cut the remaining straps, careful to keep his skin from touching any part of the armor.

Tears streamed down the larger Sankado's face. "What can I say . . . I . . ." His voice faded into nothingness. His face grew an even darker purple than it usually was.

I gasped. "Shit, he's not flirting, he's choking!"

"What?!" cried Sol.

"His throat is closing! Get it off him now!" I motioned for Lok to kneel so I could lift the breastplate over his head and cast it aside. Beads of sweat dotted his brow, and his breathing was labored, each gasp a desperate struggle for air. I called his name, and he blinked up at me from swollen eyes before smiling weakly. "Star—" His voice broke off into a wheeze.

Another Sankado with a sensitive pale gray face came over and started shouting at both of us, and more of Lok's men came forward to fuss over him. "Move back and give him some air!" I demanded. Of course, none of them could understand a word. "Dammit, Sol, you explain to these guys that he's been poisoned with Aetherrot toxin. Ask them if they have an antidote." I guided Lok's head to the floor as he gulped for air. "And tell that attendant guy to wash his hands. Now!"

Sol's eyes widened. "Did you say Aetherrot?" He leaned in closer to the armor, then covered his nose with a grimace. "Gods, how did I not smell it before? Even touching the fruit could cause you to break out in a rash." His gaze turned sorrowful when Lok wheezed. "Lok, I'm so sorry."

"No, no, no, don't say that, he's still alive, we made it, there has to be some kind of antidote. Right?" Panic rioted within me at the misery on Sol's face.

"I'm sorry, Dory."

Bitter grief had me swallowing the sob that built in my throat. I fell to my knees, feeling helpless. "Lok, I'm so sorry."

"Ss my . . . fault," he choked out. "Should have known from the damn trees." He broke off into a coughing fit. "Heard you were poisoned and . . . couldn't think straight." He lifted the letter in his hand, but his strength failed him and his hand fell to the floor.

"Tree? What tree?" I asked. But Lok's eyes became unfocused, and he didn't answer.

Sol repeated the question in Sankado, and the pale gray man pointed to a cluster of apple trees growing on the side of the hill.

"Apple trees?" I knelt closer to Lok, ignoring the concerned gasps of the other men, and sniffed his armor to find the sweet, crisp aroma of apples. "But apples aren't poisonous, so why . . . ?" I looked over his symptoms again, trying to remember all the first aid classes I had to take in order to be cleared for fieldwork. His skin was swollen and flushed, difficulty breathing, wheezing. I put two fingers to his neck and checked his pulse.

"What are you doing?" Sol yelled, snatching my hand away. "Are you insane? You can't touch him!"

"I need a straw!" I yelled back.

His anger bled to confusion, which—understandable. I should explain. Lok reached out and took my hand. "It's all right, Stardust, seeing you one last time was enough for—"

"Shut up!" I snapped. Then I felt bad for telling a man slowly choking to death to shut up, so I took a deep breath and tried to get my shit together. "Sorry, I mean . . . not shut up. But don't talk like that." Turning to Sol, I continued. "He's not poisoned, he's in anaphylactic shock. We need to open his airway as soon as possible. Tell the men to look for any kind of reed with a hollow stem. Check by the river."

Orders received, the men ran off to find what I needed. Lok watched them go with growing concern. "How . . . how will a reed help?"

I tore a strip from my shirt and used it to wipe the sweat from his brow. "I'll have to use it as a nasal tube to open up your airway."

His eyes squeezed shut as he struggled for air. "Nasal?" he gasped.

"Yeah, I'm sorry, love, but I'm gonna have to shove a reed up your nose." Angry dark purple hives littered the skin where the armor had touched. The more I looked at them, the more my own skin burned, as if in solidarity.

"Wait, I feel bet—" He tried his best to choke the words out but fell into a harsh wheeze that racked his body.

"You're gonna be fine. I've done this before." On a plastic dummy under heavy supervision. Admittedly my hands were shaking so badly it had taken an embarrassingly long time to get the tube in the nostril. In my defense, I had two papers due that week and was running on fumes fueled by energy drinks and a crippling fear of failure, but technically I still got it in.

Not that Lok needed to know that. I made quick work of removing the rest of his armor bracers and used a stool to elevate his legs.

A wave of dizziness hit me and I braced my hands on the floor to avoid falling over. I coughed blood into my arm, then shielded the sight from Lok when he tried to see what was wrong. "I'm going to grab something to wash you off with; I'll be right back."

He tried to speak, but it was too difficult and he nodded instead. I rushed to the duckbills and grabbed our waterskins as well as the sash I had used as a bonnet. Kneeling beside him, I wet the cloth and gently washed away the remaining apple juice from his skin. The silver rings on his horns lit up. They were dimmer than normal, but seeing him do literally anything other than wheeze and die was something to be celebrated, in my book. All the while, Lok watched with a grin on his face.

"You are oddly cheery given the circumstances," I said, dabbing at the sweat on his brow.

A small laugh gasped out of him. "Told . . . you to . . . leave me. No—" He paused for breath. "Rescues."

"You did," I said succinctly.

His grin widened. "You didn't . . . listen."

I rinsed out the cloth, then leaned him forward to wash his back. "You can count on that being a recurring theme in this relationship. Get used to it."

He took my arm and pulled me to him. The kiss was slow, thoughtful. When it ended I felt a loss between us both. He brought his forehead to mine and whispered, "Thank you."

Panic like I'd never known before welled in my throat when he went limp in my arms. Sol and the others returned with various reeds, all of them shouting words that only sounded like muffled alarm bells and that stupid fucking Tamagotchi's song. "You're not dying," I whispered.

Shaking hands sorted reeds as I repeated the words. After finding one of a suitable length, I grabbed a knife and cut both ends for a clean insertion. I tilted Lok's head back and took a moment to settle my shaking hands. Every noise but the frantic beat of my heart faded away. Slowly, I fed the reed into his nostril.

His chest rose and the sound of whistling air made the world start up again. It took a moment, but Lok coughed, his lungs expanding and contracting on their own. I could do nothing but sit there and watch. I did it. He was going to be okay.

The next few minutes passed by in a blur. Sol and the other men fussed over Lok, making sure he was stable and helping him drink. With Sol to translate, I managed to convince the lot of them to hold still long enough for a smooch for easier communication.

Yengro was the first to introduce himself and damn near crushed my spine with a hug. He wore his dark hair in an undercut with the top slicked back. His arms were covered in full-sleeve tattoos, and he wore a concerning number of knives on his belt. "Thank you for bringing our idiot back to us! And for speaking up for me while I was in that cage. Couldn't understand a word you said, but the others told me you were Lok's woman and I knew it had to be something ballsy."

"You're welcome," I groaned. Then, when black spots appeared in my vision, I eked out a cry for mercy and he released me.

The pale gray man was named Kizolo; he wore his hair half tied up in a bun and had runes carved into his horns. He shoved Yengro away from me and offered a polite smile before running off to find more water. The tall wall of muscle that had grabbed me earlier was Ruu. Or so Kizolo said. Ruu refused to speak, so I took his word for it.

After what seemed like hours, Lok's breathing evened out, the swelling went down, and the redness in his skin faded. As soon as he was well enough to remove the reed and speak, his men stopped their fussing and stared him down.

Lok sat up and scratched the back of his head. "So, I imagine you all have questions."

"QUESTIONS?" Yengro yelled. "Yes, I've got a lot of fucking questions. First of all, where the fuck have you been?"

"Why'd you leave in the first place?" Kizolo asked. "We've been stuck with that taskmaster Osid ever since you ran off."

Ruu didn't have a question and instead merely uttered the word "Ojenna."

Lok ran a hand down his face with a long-suffering sigh. "I've been with the Roamcrest herding yix. I didn't want to be king." He paused and pointed to Ruu. "You watch your damn mouth. Don't think I won't rip your horns off just because my mate is here."

Ruu came and sat beside him, letting his head rest on the stone slab. "Talk."

I watched the mask of the carefree joker slide from Lok's face. "After we were dropped on this planet, hopelessness plagued me. I couldn't stop thinking about the flooding of Tynfo and all the people who died at my order."

"That's war!" Yengro growled. "Are you forgetting that those savages burned down Uslanknot? You cannot blame yourself for taking the vengeance that was owed to us."

"Yes, that's what I told myself. And then the world ended. All the people I sought vengeance for died in the Calamity. Most of those who managed to flee Tynfo before we struck died in the Calamity. So what was it all for?"

His questions stunned Yengro into silence.

"Now what? I'm expected to continue the same fight, and die for a land my father and my father's father never stepped foot on? No. I refuse. I spend my days spinning wool and herding yix and it's the most peace I've felt in my life."

Kizolo crossed his arms over his chest. "Even so, the leader of the Singing Arrows can't just disappear like that. Everyone was worried about you. They said you went mad."

"I'm not the leader of anyone anymore. Find someone else to do it or follow King Osid."

"Over my festering corpse," Ruu cut in.

Yengro crossed the room and socked Lok so hard his head snapped back. A pregnant pause filled the air before Yengro pulled Lok to his hooves and hugged him. "You should have told me."

Relief melted the tension that coiled around my heart and threatened to suffocate me. I sat and stared at my knees as the emotional toll of the day settled over me, making it feel as if I was wrapped in heavy wool. I let the men and their animated chatter be drowned out and allowed myself time to bask in the moment. A tentative hand touched my back, and I turned to Lok, who held out his hand. I reached up and took hold of it, relishing its warmth as he led me to sit with him away from the crowd.

He looked me over, a small smile on his face. "Thank you again, Stardust."

"You can thank me by never getting close to an apple again. My heart can't take you fainting like that."

He wrapped his arms around me, squeezing tight. "On my honor, I promise to make a valid attempt at avoiding poisonous fruit."

"Hey, you said a whole sentence without wheezing. Maybe there's hope for you yet."

The grin on his face was charged with the sexual magnetism that made him so infuriating and perfect. "You think I'd die after what you let slip earlier?"

I stared at him, confused.

"You said I'd have to get used to you," he said, smug.

"That must mean you've decided to stay. Tell me—it was my cooking, wasn't it? Or perhaps you humans simply can't resist a large set of horns."

I shook my head, laughing. "You are so—"

"Stunning? Virile? So painfully handsome and gallant that you simply couldn't bear to part from me?"

I found myself giggling uncontrollably. The man was just one hoof in the grave and he still couldn't help himself. I brushed a lock of thick black hair away from his face. My breath caught when I noticed just how much his condition had improved. "It's incredible you heal so fast. Your skin is almost completely back to normal."

"It is?" he asked, looking down at himself. He took a long, slow breath. "Well, would you look at that?"

"How is this even possible?"

"It's our bond," he said in wonder. "Didn't Intern say the Zhali match increased our healing abilities?"

"Oh my damn, he did."

He laughed and took me by the waist. "If I had known keeping my hands on you would work such wonders, I'd have picked a prettier place to get my fill of you. Perhaps a meadow? Somewhere surrounded by flowers and some candles for a little atmosphere? A nice view to look out on while I—"

"Keep your reckless ass seated so you don't push yourself into an early grave," Sol interrupted. He sat on the other side of me and handed Lok a drink.

He took it gladly. "Ah, my other savior to the rescue once again." Lok flipped the cap off the waterskin and took a long drink before wiping away the excess water that dribbled down his chin. His face grew somber. "Sol, I want to thank you, truly."

Sol chuckled. "Don't go soft on me now, General."

"I mean it. You didn't have to come save me; you could have taken Stardust and left me for dead, and I wouldn't have blamed you in the slightest. But you didn't. Thank you for that."

Sol reached behind me and clapped Lok on the shoulder. "It was too quiet with you gone. And this one," he said, jamming a finger at me. "On and on, she blubbered. 'Where's Lok? We have to find him! How will I ever go on without my big strong general?'"

His teasing broke into laughter when I hit his shoulder. "Oh shut up, you were worried too!"

Lok smiled and pulled me against him. I laid my head on his shoulder, happily settling into his warmth. "Don't mind his teasing, Stardust. Men like that just use it to hide the fact that they are the sweetest, most altruistic do-gooders around." He reached over and pinched Sol's cheek. "And here I thought you hated me."

Sol knocked his hand away, then reached into his coat pocket and pulled out the Tamagotchi. "Not completely altruistic. Turns out saving you had its perks." He pressed the center button and proudly held it up for us to see. The pixelated version of Sol danced happily next to a full affection bar, while Lok's bar was just behind at nine. With a painfully smug smirk he added, "I win."

Lok grew quiet. He gently took the Tamagotchi from Sol and inspected it closer. Then, as cold as ice, he stared Sol down and crushed the Tamagotchi in his fist. Its chipper song ended in a dying wail, then colored bits of metal fell into the grass.

Sol looked down at the broken pieces, then fixed Lok with an exasperated glare. "You are so—"

"Just stop." I laughed. Having them both back with me felt

like a dream. I was weightless and happy and fucking terrified to wake up. The intensity of that fear made my voice waver. "I love you both."

The humor faded from Sol's face. "Stardust?"

"There's something I haven't been completely honest about," I said.

Lok squeezed my hand, urging me to continue.

I worried my bottom lip. "Well, I know we're technically all in this breeding program, and babies are very much the goal, but how would you both feel if I couldn't give you children just yet?"

"That would be ideal," Lok said.

"Wait, really?"

"Of course it's ideal," Sol continued. "We've not had a day of peace since you landed on this planet. We haven't even discussed where we're all going to live."

"Why would we want to bring a child into this right now?" Lok asked.

"Please tell us you've been on some kind of birth control this whole time."

"Oh. Well, great news. Lok, Sol, there's a birth control implant in my arm, and I'm not ready to ask them to take it out yet."

"Which arm?" Lok asked.

I pointed to my implant. He traced the skin until he found the little matchstick lump just underneath. Then he kissed it. "Thank you for your service."

A loud snapping of tree branches brought him up short, and whatever insult he had locked in the chamber abruptly died off when a thunderous horn blared in the distance. King Osid's war party, riding atop towering triceratops, thundered toward us. At the helm of the charge was the king himself, his red-and-black armor gleaming like polished obsidian in the harsh sunlight. Behind him, a fuming Blair was gagged and chained to the saddle.

The commotion brought the others over to investigate. Sol cursed under his breath. “It just never ends.”

CHAPTER 21

LOK TIGHTENED HIS GRIP ON MY WAIST AND HOISTED ME to my feet, barely a breath before the intruders stampeded their way to the top of the hill. Blair tugged angrily at her chains while swearing muffled curses under her gag. The king kept his cold green eyes trained on us, not saying a word until they rode to the apex of the hill and formed a semicircle in front of us, leaving no route of escape. My spine stiffened. I stared at them with wide eyes, feeling like an ant under a magnifying glass.

With a long look, the king silently appraised Lok. In turn, Lok fixed him with an impassive stare. A hush fell over the surrounding air, tense and filled with an awful, unnameable heaviness that clung to everything.

"You're still alive," King Osid remarked.

"That I am," Lok responded. He took a drink from his waterskin. "You poisoned my wife."

"You wouldn't answer my letters." The king's voice was bored and dismissive.

Lok gave a noncommittal shrug. "I was busy."

"Busy taking the—"

"Osid, you conniving little fuck, you took my wife hostage in order to force me to accept your challenge on the grounds of dishonor, and then you poisoned my armor. If you accuse me of taking the coward's way out by abandoning my position, I will rip your head off and drink from your skull, just like I did to your uncle."

Oh my.

"Fine. Let us speak plainly. I don't give a damn if you want to spend your days knee-deep in yix shit. If our race is going to survive on this planet, we need to work together under a single cohesive rule. One king, one banner, no more warring clans. This is not a matter of honor; this is about saving the Sankado race. We need unity if we want to build a kingdom strong enough to withstand the Rumbling. Your clansmen refuse to see that. Too stuck in the dogmatic ways of the past. Which makes you the last thing in my way." King Osid dismounted from his triceratops and approached and drew the longsword from his back. "I'm going to kill you now. Bid your Zhali a final farewell."

Lok's face hardened into an icy mask. He held out a hand and Kizolo tossed him his spear. "So be it. I accept your challenge."

They circled each other, warily, like two predators sizing up their opponents. As much as I might have wanted to see Osid take that ass whupping, I was not convinced my alien was in any condition to challenge anybody to a fight to the death.

"Wait, hold on," I called. "Neither of you has to fight, I know of a way to fix thi—"

"TEAR HIS HEAD OFF, LOK!" Yengro roared.

Across the circle, one of Osid's men threw up a hand sign and roared back. "As if that sniveling coward has a chance!" The warriors shouldered past me, drowning out my attempts at a less idiotic solution.

Despite still being weakened from the poison, Lok confidently twirled his spear with flashy flourishes, showing off to the crowd. Osid sneered at the display, but underneath the bravado, I could see the hesitation in his eyes. He was expecting a much weaker opponent. Even without his armor, Lok unnerved him. Even better, Lok knew it.

Yet Osid had his pride. As king, he could not back down now. With the eyes of his warriors upon him, he had no choice but to see this through. I held my breath, heart pounding, as I watched the two kings prepare to clash. At some unseen signal, they flew at each other. Spear met sword in a ringing chorus of metal, both striving for the upper hand.

They broke apart, circled, and clashed again in a blur of strikes and parries. Osid knocked Lok's spear aside and landed a gash along his thigh. Lok seized Osid's wrist, pulled him forward, and rammed his face so hard I could have sworn I heard his skull crack. The king stumbled, barely catching himself from falling. His opponent lunged for his fallen spear, then aimed a strike at his neck. Osid recovered quickly, feinting left before sweeping low and slicing a cut across Lok's calf that made him grit his teeth.

With a roar, Osid charged, sword leveled at Lok's chest. Lok spun away, knocking the sword aside with the shaft of his spear, then whipped around to drive the butt of it into Osid's back. The king faltered but quickly recovered, slashing viciously. At the last second, Lok knocked the sword aside, the point grazing his shoulder.

Blair shouted something, and I turned to see her glaring

daggers at me from atop the triceratops. Casting a worried glance at the duel, I slipped out of the crowd and crept over to her. She nodded to a keychain hanging on the beast's saddle.

I grabbed the keychain and quickly released her. As soon as she was free, Blair ripped the gag from her mouth and jumped down from the triceratops.

Rage boiled off her in waves as she turned to dig through a pack on the saddle. "Mad Max me to a fucking dinosaur, will you?" With an evil grin, she found what she was searching for and pulled her pistol from the satchel. "I got something for you, darling."

With the click of a switch, the safety was off and Blair rounded to shove her way past the cheering men. "Move!" Blair cocked her pistol and took aim at King Osid's back as he dueled Lok.

Osid's body went rigid before he spun around to spot Blair. With lightning-fast reflexes, he deftly dodged a strike from Lok and seized him by the horn, yanking him forward as a makeshift shield.

With a guttural scream, I lunged for her arm just as the shot rang out. The blast echoed in my ears until I fell to the ground. Dazed, I reached up and touched my face.

Everything slowed down as my hand came away bloody. The ringing in my ears was deafening. Lok's and Sol's faces blurred as they leaned over me, shouting words I couldn't hear.

I blinked slowly, trying to process what had just happened. The bitter smell of gunpowder hung in the air. Blair stood frozen, the smoking pistol still aimed ahead. Her face was pale with shock.

Lok knelt to examine me, growling in dismay when he saw the blood. He gently turned my head to inspect the damage. I winced as his fingers found the graze along my temple where the bullet had narrowly missed my skull.

The panic and fear in Lok's eyes melted into relief. He pressed a scrap of cloth against the wound to slow the bleeding, then leaned in close so I could read his lips. "It's not so bad, Stardust. Just a scrape. You're going to be just fine."

Blair holstered her pistol, voice shaking as she said, "Dory, I didn't mean to hit you. I—I'm so sorry, I was aiming for Osid."

"You could have killed her!" Lok thundered.

"I was trying to—"

"Enough distractions!" Fury boiled in King Osid's voice behind me, drowning out the screams of the crowd. "Gorvokk, grab my queen and keep her from causing any more trouble." A hulking figure emerged from the chaos and seized Blair, dragging her away as she struggled against his grip.

The bloodthirsty king spat a mouthful of crimson onto the ground and leveled his sword at Lok. "Pick up your spear, *yix herder.* We end this now."

But I couldn't take it anymore. Tears streamed down my face as I pushed Lok's hands away and rose to my feet. My whole body shook with adrenaline and fear as I faced the two opposing rulers. "I'm done," I shouted, voice quivering. "I'm done with all of this shit!"

King Osid sneered, dismissing my words. "This has nothing to do with—"

"Shut up!" I roared, cutting him off. "I'm the one who just took a goddamn bullet to the side of my face, so both of you fuckers are gonna listen to me!"

I ran a hand down my stomach, trying to collect myself enough to speak. "All right, King Osid, your settlement needs to be moved out of the path of the dinosaur migration."

"What?" he asked in confusion.

"You only want Lok's clan to join you so you have enough people to keep the dinosaurs from flattening the place, right? You wouldn't have that problem if you just moved."

The king stared at me as if I'd grown a second head. He looked to Lok for answers, but Lok shrugged and pointed his thumb back at me and said, "She's the animal expert, not me."

"What are you talking about?" Osid asked.

His eyes held the same cold judgment that haunted my dreams. I'm ashamed to admit a small part of me cowered under the weight of it. Lok placed a hand at the small of my back. I closed my eyes and willed away the burning spotlight. Mustering up my best professional boss-lady voice, I answered. "Your ship crashed right in the middle of a migration pathway. Those animals aren't purposely trying to ruin your settlement; you're just in the way of their yearly migration. I'm pretty sure your best bet would be to assign a team to track the herds' movements, figure out where they go and when, then find a new spot well out of their path."

"You expect me to move my entire settlement on the hunch that you are *pretty sure* that we're in the yearly path of these monsters?"

"They're not monsters. They're just animals. And yes, I do. I mean you could build the world's sturdiest wildlife overpass, but seeing as we're dealing with brontosaurs, that doesn't seem like a viable option. So yes, I'd say your best bet is just to move. As a matter of fact— Hey, Sol," I called. "Do you have to deal with any stampeding herds in the Night Ridge territory?"

"We do not," he replied. "The worst thing you'd find in the mountains before the Gruulorak showed up were green billjaw. But at least those predators travel alone."

A murmur broke out among the warriors; some looked skeptical, others who I assumed didn't have the translator symbiont yet just looked plain confused.

King Osid raised his hands for quiet, and the murmurs died. He looked at me, his expression inscrutable. Then he sheathed his sword and walked toward me. I stood my ground, refusing to flinch under his glare.

He stopped a foot away and asked, "How do you know this is true?"

"I'm a wildlife biologist."

A blank stare.

Right. He has no idea what a wildlife biologist is.

"I'm a naturalist, a scholar. I've spent a good portion of my life studying the migratory patterns of animals."

"How?"

"With . . . observation?"

"Why?"

"For the same reason I do anything, because it's interesting. Look, I get that this is a big thing for you and you want your people to stay safe, and I'm trying to help with that. What would it hurt to move? You mentioned earlier that you want to find out where the rest of the women landed so you can integrate them into your empire, right? Well, I doubt most of those girls are gonna be too keen to move to a kingdom that gets into a turf war with dinosaurs every great migration. Find out where the women were left and rebuild there."

Lok threw an arm over my shoulders. He was a head taller than King Osid and used that advantage to look down his nose at him. "We could always go back to killing each other and fight over the rubble."

Osid rolled his eyes. With a sigh, he turned his back to us.

His gaze fixed on something in the distance. I looked, trying to find what it was.

All I saw were endless miles of lush forests, the distant blue smudge of a lake, and the Mirage Mountain Range in the background. "Fine," he said after a moment. "I rescind my claim on the Singing Arrows." He cast an annoyed glance at Lok's men. "You bastards are more trouble than you're worth anyway." The king sheathed his sword and turned back to me. "How would you go about finding the other women?"

"Now, that part is easy." Lok grinned down at me. "Still up for that date to the research center, Stardust?"

"After all this? I can't begin to tell you just how much I want to punch that bird in the face—" The last words ended in a coughing fit. I fell to my knees as blood sprayed from my mouth to paint the grass red. I looked up to see the men staring down at me, wide-eyed.

"So, about that antidote?"

Without so much as a whisper, three Biwban hovercrafts appeared out of thin air above the monument. One of them flew ahead of us and landed gently on the grass. The windshield slid up with a hiss, revealing an extremely miffed-looking Intern. His proud crest was missing quite a few feathers, though one only had to look at the mouth of the lion squeezed in the chair behind him.

Intern's hands tightened his grip on the steering wheel until I feared it would snap. He pulled out the orange Tamagotchi and inspected it with clear irritation. "Negative," he announced before snapping his fingers and pointing at Osid. "Capture Subject 12 and her mate. They are to be delivered to the psych ward for couples counseling."

King Osid let out a cry as a red Biwban zapped him with its ray gun, causing him to freeze in place before being lifted off the ground. I could hear Blair yelling as well before both of them were loaded onto a spacecraft.

Intern cast a searing gaze at Lok, then Sol, then finally settled on me. The little Biwban let out a shaking breath, his voice filled with barely contained rage. "Get. In. The. Ship."

CHAPTER 22

THE DAY ALWAYS LOOKS BRIGHTER WHEN YOU'RE NO LONger writhing half-dead on the floor. And that's on a well-made antidote. Or it could have been the Biwbanian healing pod.

After the intern showed up, they searched King Osid for the antidote, which was then promptly shoved down my throat. Yet the promise of a cure wasn't enough to sway the aggravated Biwban, and my boys and I were promptly ~~dragged~~ escorted to the research center, where I was shoved into a healing pod that looked a bit like a bedazzled egg.

I stepped out of the pod and found Toto waiting near the control panel. The lab's resident doctor was notably missing, not that I minded. Most of the Biwbans here had given the lion a wide berth since we arrived. Toto trotted over to me and rubbed against my side. "Dory! Congratulations on not dying."

"Gee, thanks, Toto." I laughed.

"My darling queen said you'd keel over and perish without

my protection, like a newborn cub. But I told her my pride was made of stronger stuff."

"Such confidence she has in me. Things are going well, then?"

He puffed out his chest. "Of course. I laid enough sour birds at her feet to feed a hyena matriarch and her brood. After she ate, I was even permitted to groom her."

I gasped. "Grooming this early into the courtship?"

"I know! Soon I will have a litter of daughters to begin my empire. Our children will be the first in a line to dominate this planet for generations, I can feel it." The lion's eyes were practically sparkling.

"What it must be like to have a parent who is already so proud of you."

"Don't be so dour. Look around you—you did it! You made it all the way to the research center without dying. Now all you have to do is punch that bird in the face and ride off into the sunset."

He had a point. When I first arrived on this planet, I thought for sure I wouldn't make it this far. I cast a glance out the window to the wide blue sky. Toto followed my gaze, his tone softened as he brushed his head against my hip. "Unless you still want to find out if there are gas stations in space."

I sat down by the window and watched the clouds go by. "It's a bit late for that."

Toto stood beside me. "No, say the word and I'll start attacking sour birds. Your mates won't even know you're escaping till it's too late."

I laughed and leaned against him. "You are always ready for a fight. No, it's not that. As dumb as it is, I think a part of me is still resentful that I won't be able to get my degree. Or at least show what I've learned here. If I could have just seen the look on my mom's face." I let out a breath, aggravated at how much her approval still meant to me. "I don't know. It would have been nice to show her I could do it. Finally have that moment where I could shove my accomplishments in her face and say, 'See! Who needs a rich man to take care of her now?' Maybe we could have understood each other a little better at least." I let out a breath, suddenly feeling exhausted. "Though I guess I did end up marrying a king of sorts. So I guess we both sort of got what we wanted."

Toto rested his head in my lap with a grunt. "Maybe she never would have understood. But fuck her."

"Toto!"

"No, I mean it. You've survived where most wouldn't. More than that, you've faced off against predators thrice your size, protected your mates, and somehow calmed that mad king, from what I was told. Your mother can kiss a mamba. Even without proof, you should hold those accomplishments high."

"Yeah," I said, smiling. "I guess you're right."

"If it's worth anything, if even one of my daughters turned out to be anything like you, I'd be proud to call them my own."

Tears pricked at my eyes as I hugged him. "Thank you, Toto."

"All right, all right, pull it together," he said, his tone teasing. "No need to get my mane wet."

The door opened and a dark blue Biwban approached me and held up a ray gun. "Hold still."

Blue light scanned my body as I did as instructed. Once finished, she checked the screen at the control panel and tsked.

"Something wrong?" I asked.

"Vitals are fine," the Biwban murmured. "The behavioral

observation intern assigned to you mentioned in his report that you mated numerous times."

"I wouldn't say numerous . . ."

The good doc ignored my gripe and continued. "Why have you not fallen pregnant? Are you defective?"

"She's not defective," Toto snarled. "She's—"

TOTO, NO! My body froze as I realized I forgot to tell Toto to keep his damn mouth shut about the birth control.

A sharp voice cut in from the doorway. "Still without her damn chocolate." Sol strode into the room with Lok following; both of them looked remarkably cleaner than when I last saw them. Though seeing as these Biwban saw fit to add a FUCKING SPA to their research center, I couldn't say I blamed them. It was definitely where I planned on going after this.

It was no wonder they ran out of funding. I couldn't even read Biwbanian, but I could tell from the logos that everything in this facility, from the intergalactic arcade to the damn pens, was brand-name.

Sol slid an arm around my waist before focusing his attention back on the doctor. "My wife has been abundantly clear with what she requires. If we are to reproduce, she must be supplied with copious amounts of chocolate and . . . Darling, what was the other thing you mentioned?" he asked.

His nearness sent a delicious thrill through me and it took a moment to realize I'd been asked a question. "Oh, uh . . . coffee! That's right, I need coffee."

"I see," the doctor said, returning to her screen. "Yes, I see his notes on that here. It looks like he managed to isolate the anandamide and the theobromine from the rest of the saliva found in a local predator species, but he lacked something called . . ." Red eyes squinted at the screen. "Cocoa butter. Does that sound familiar to you at all?" she asked.

Sol nudged my side.

"Uh, yes! Cocoa butter and anarassinfrassin."

"Anandamide."

"Yes, that," I said, nodding agreeably. "Important stuff. Can't make babies without it."

Lok snorted beside me and turned his head away to cough.

The doctor thrummed her fingers along the control panel as she scrolled through Intern's report. "I see. Nothing to worry about until we can create a steady supply, then." She fell quiet and the room filled with the sounds of her typing. She looked up from her work to see we were still there. "You are healed. Leave my laboratory, please."

"Right, thanks, Doc," I said. Sol led us out of the room toward the spa. When we were out of earshot I asked, "You knew about the chocolate thing? I didn't even know you were listening to that."

"I'm obsessed with you," he said simply. "Of course I was listening."

"Brownnoser," Lok growled.

Sol clapped a hand on the larger man's shoulder and leaned into him for a half embrace. "Forever live with the knowledge that she loved me first."

Lok's posture slumped. "Fine, you have me there. She loved you first."

"Can't I just love you both equ—"

A sinister grin crossed Lok's face. "But I'm the one that delivered her to vengeance." In a blur of movement, Lok grabbed Sol by the front of his coat, shoved him back into the laboratory, and slammed the door. After that, I was swiftly picked up and whisked away.

I RESTED MY HANDS ON THE GOLDEN DESK OF VEXIL Krynn. As expected, the head of the research department had spared no expense in decorating the west wing he used as an office. Yes, that's right, the entire west wing of the research center was nothing more than an elaborate office.

In order to actually get to Vexil's desk, you had to walk through two separate "welcome" rooms, make a left at the indoor pond, then walk up four flights of stairs. Why were there so many stairs? Why on Waffles did he not spring for an elevator?

I digress.

"Hello, Vexil."

The green Biwban shivered as he shrank farther into his chair. "S-S-Subject 4."

Intern cleared his throat from his perch on Lok's shoulder. "She prefers the name 'Dory,' sir."

Vexil swallowed thickly. "Dory, to what do I owe the honor?"

"I think you already know why I'm here, Vexil."

His eyes widened, then he placed his hands on the desk, half prostrating himself in an attempt at appeasement. "No, wait!"

My fist cracked against his beak, sending him sprawling to the ground. Vexil lay unmoving on the lush carpet.

Behind me, Lok let out a great peal of laughter. "By the son of the red planet, Stardust, I think you killed him!"

"Oh shit, did I?" I asked, running over to the concerningly still bird.

The door burst open, and a panting Sol rushed in. "Did I miss it?" he asked.

"She punched him to death," Lok roared, before doubling over in laughter.

Toto tried to duck underneath Sol's legs, but was too tall and ended up lifting the man off the ground before Sol could hop off him. "She did?" he asked, rushing to the other side of the desk. The lion gasped before regarding me with a look of pure adoration. "Oh, Dory, I'm so proud of you!"

"No, no, he's not dead!" I shouted, more to myself than to the room.

"We should celebrate," Toto said to Lok.

"No!"

"Yes!" Toto shot back. "It's your first kill! This is a huge moment."

Sol gathered me into a hug and rubbed comforting circles on my back. "Dory, darling, he's not dead. Breathe."

"Really?" I asked.

He chuckled before answering. "Yes, love, look at his chest, he's still breathing."

Intern flew from Lok's shoulder to land next to his unconscious boss. "Oh yes, he's still alive. Though, if you wanted to finish the job, Dory, none of us would stop you. I'll tell the next department head it was an accident."

"Do your own dirty work, Intern. I'm not killing your boss."

"But—"

"Intern, do you really think you're in a position to ask favors from me?" I asked.

His feathers puffed up angrily. ". . . Oh, tail feathers."

A boom shook the air, rattling the entire building. We ran to the window to see smoke billowing out from a black tower at the edge of the research center. The windows on one of the lower floors were all blown out from the blast.

"What the hell was that?" I asked.

Intern sighed in defeat. "That would be the Unity Spire. It would appear your friend Blair and her mate aren't taking couples therapy well."

I worried my bottom lip as flames spewed from a corner of the tower. "That blast looks like it took out an entire floor. Should we go help her?"

Just then, the sounds of gunshots and maniacal laughter filled the air, and I caught sight of a tentacled monster throwing itself out a broken window. The giant squid-like creature latched onto the wall of the tower and frantically started to climb down. Blair appeared in the window not long after and opened fire on the creature with a machine gun.

"I think she's doing fine," Lok answered.

"If she's not, that's someone else's problem, I'm sure," Intern said, then flew out the window.

Lok sat on Vexil's desk as he watched the Intern's retreating blue form disappear toward the mountainside. "He just loves to run away, doesn't he?" He tsked.

Everyone who was still conscious looked at the wandering king.

"Don't look at me like that. I had good reasons." He pulled me to him and let his large hands trace the seam of my pants along my thigh. "Besides, I've got something to stick around for now. What do you say, Stardust, should we head to the women's enclosure?"

"In a minute." I grabbed Sol by his belt and tugged him closer. "I've got something else in mind first."

A smirk tugged at Sol's lips. "And what might that be?"

"Toto?" I called.

"Yup, I'm going." The lion snatched up the unconscious Biwban on the floor and trotted out of the room.

With our audience finally gone, I released the clasps of Sol's coat, then paused on the last one. "We should probably lock the door."

Sol traced his fingers gently along my throat before pressing his thumb to my lip, feeling its softness. Eyeing me with a look of scorching intent that was enough to burn the panties right off me, he said, "Or they could learn to knock."

I swallowed, throat suddenly very dry. "Or they could knock."

He chuckled, then focused his gaze on my lips. "Sit on the desk."

I shivered at the husky tone in his voice and did as instructed. Before my ass could even make contact, Lok pulled me into a kiss that sent me reeling. I buried my hands in his hair and returned in kind. Sol's mouth teased the skin of my collarbone, while his hands stroked along the exposed skin of my sides, causing me to quiver. The tips of my breasts hardened at the feel of his rough fingers. Lok groaned, and I slipped my tongue past his lips to taste his fangs. His large hand traced up the back of my neck before grabbing a fistful of my hair, trapping me to him as the kiss turned devouring. I loved the way Lok kissed me. All reckless passion to counter Sol's need for control, and the sweet warfare that broke out between them.

Sol fisted my shirt before tearing it open. I broke the kiss and fixed him with a glare. "I only have so many clothes, you know."

His palm traveled slowly up my front, cupping the pliant weight of one breast through my bra. My anger gave way to a simpering gasp as he ran his tongue in between them. "And you'll have even less after I'm done," he murmured.

Lok continued to devour my lips, his tongue exploring

every curve and sending shivers down my spine. I squirmed against him, my body thrumming with need. Sol's hands traced the outline of my bra, his fingers leaving goose bumps in their wake as he pulled it farther down until the first peek of dark brown spilled over the top. His breath teased over my skin. "I'm tempted to keep this on. See just how hard I can fuck you before these beautiful tits spill free."

"Yes," Lok groaned. His hands trailed down my back, lifting me up slightly off the desk so that I was straddling him. He undid the buttons on my pants and I wasted no time shoving them off. Lok pulled back slightly, his eyes hooded with desire as he gazed up at me. I leaned in to kiss him but he pressed his hand against my shoulder. "Not yet. Let me look at you." His fingers drifted down the outline of my body in a way that sent hot tingles down my spine, yet when I looked into his eyes, there was a pang of sadness there that left me aching.

I took hold of his wrist. "Do you need to stop?"

Sol's movements abruptly halted as he peered down at him. "What's wrong?"

For a moment Lok didn't speak, just took my hand in his before pressing the tips of my fingers to his lips. "I thought he killed you both. When I saw your blood splattered across that letter, I . . . I don't know." He sat up and gathered me to him, leaning his forehead against mine. "Please don't ever run off like that again."

"Yes," Sol hissed in my ear. The hunter cupped my chin and turned me to face him. "Stop running off to your death. It would fix a lot of our problems."

"Hey!"

"Hey nothing. Listen to me, you beautiful, reckless hot mess. Stop running off."

"I saved your life!"

"Technically Lok—"

"No, no," Lok cut in. "That one goes to her. I would have left you to die."

Sol's brow furrowed. "I . . . had a plan."

"You had a plan?" I asked.

"That's right, a plan. A great plan."

I batted my eyes at him playfully. "Oh really? What was it?"

"Wait till the Gruulorak digests you and sneak out her asshole?" Lok asked.

A dying duck honk of a laugh burst out of my throat.

"The fuck was that?" Sol asked with a laugh. The last of Lok's sadness melted away as he, too, fell into a fit. The joy on his face was almost enough to make up for the fact that this was at my expense.

I shifted to get off his lap, but I couldn't keep the smile off my face. "I'll run my ass straight to those escape pods."

"Dory."

"Keep playing with me."

"All right," was all Lok said before he slipped his hands under my thighs, spun me around and lay down to sit me on his face.

I squealed as I felt his warm tongue tracing a line up my inner thighs. I gripped the edge of the desk, trying to maintain some semblance of composure, but failed miserably. Sol's hands found their way to my hips, anchoring me in place as Lok's tongue delved farther. "Oh gods," I moaned, arching my back when he went to work on my most sensitive spot. "This is cheating."

A satisfied smirk crept onto Sol's face as he watched me squirm underneath Lok's ministrations.

Fingers dug into my hips as Sol leaned in close to my ear, his fangs grazing my neck. "Tell me you don't love it." He nipped at the sensitive skin, then his hands squeezed my chest. When Lok's tongue swirled around my entrance just as Sol rolled his thumbs against my nipples, the response was shameless, instant, and total.

"Oh gods, please!" I cried out, my nails digging into the desk for support. "Fuck," I whined, my hips bucking against Lok's face.

Sol chuckled, his fangs grazing my earlobe. Wisps of his red hair teased my neck. "Please what? Do you want us to stop?"

I laughed breathlessly. "You are such a dick."

"Mm-hmm," He ran his lips along a tendon on the side of my neck. "It drives you crazy that you can't even pretend to put up a fight, doesn't it? Not with you grinding this perfect ass on my cock. This body's too honest not to shake every time I dote on this little bud until you scream for me like a good girl," he whispered, twirling a strand of my curls around his finger. "Mmm, yes, you love being praised, sweet thing." That damn tail came out of nowhere and nuzzled against my clit. I shivered when it fell into place and started to suck gently, then lost my damn mind when it closed around it and sucked harder. Which . . .

Hello?

Didn't know that was possible. Could it always work like that or was this man training? First the ridges, then the knotting, now this. How many more sex revelations am I gonna have to deal with? Lok didn't relent either, his tongue and lips working double-time to push me over the edge. My entire body tensed, and I bit down on my bottom lip to muffle a moan. I clenched my fists around the edge of the desk.

"Stop being a fucking brat and come," Lok growled. He swatted my ass and the sharp sting felt so right, I whimpered as waves of pleasure coursed through me, my body trembling as Sol held me close, whispering praise and encouragement until my vision speckled.

"Oh fuck. Oh fuck. Yes."

"You are a needy thing." His expression went feral. His fangs bared, Lok gripped my waist and wasted no time sitting me over his cock and sinking to the hilt. I cried out, back arching off the desk at the sudden fullness. Sol's hands found my breasts again, massaging and caressing as Lok began to move. My body shivered with need and I took deep gulps of air as I adjusted to the feel of him. The modifications the Biwban did on me must have done something to my cervix, because, girl, where are you?

"Oh fuck, oh fuck . . ."

Lok was bigger than most, and when the ridges of his cock flared against my sweet spot it felt so good it burned. I let out a choked gasp as he grunted, slammed me back down, and said, "Your cunt . . . so tight. You feel so good, Stardust."

If there was a brain cell left in my body, I didn't know her. Nor did I see when in the hell Sol got a bottle of lube, but who am I to question that angel? My hips gave a little twitch, encouraging the slick fingers he pressed against my ass. Ragged whispers of sheer need escaped my lips when he thrust them inside. Pleasure and pressure intensified in my core, making me moan louder. My walls clenched around Lok's thick member, urging him to go even deeper. The room was soon filled with the sounds of our pants and wet flesh as we moved in perfect rhythm—their lips on my neck, their hands everywhere. I couldn't take it! It was too much and yet not enough.

"Fuck me harder," I begged. "Please!"

"Hold her still," Sol growled, sliding his cock against my ass cheeks.

Lok's powerful body rippled with tension as he obliged our mate, locking my hips in place as Sol slowly buried himself inside. I gasped as Sol filled me, the sensation of both their cocks inside me overwhelming. Lok's massive length stretched me while Sol's rubbed against my sensitive walls, the friction delicious yet almost too much to take.

"You're doing so well, Stardust," Sol purred against my shoulder. He pulled out to the tip and sank back in with a shudder, his movements languid and unhurried. He worked a hand up my throat and kissed my temple. Moans poured from my lips unbidden; my nails dug into Lok's forearms. The desk creaked dangerously beneath us, but I was too lost in ecstasy to care, my body singing at being so thoroughly claimed.

"Is this what you want?" Lok rasped, his silver eyes burning with lust. He shifted his weight, and the angle changed just enough, and when he moved in time with Sol, I screamed his name.

"Yes! Yes! Please, god, yes!"

Their cocks hammered my sweet spots in tandem and it was all too much. I cried out as they increased their pace, driving into me relentlessly.

The pressure built and built until I shattered, clenching down on them as my climax slammed into me like a meteor. A wave of pure ecstasy washed over me, my body shuddering and convulsing around their cocks. I could feel them both tense, their grips on me tightening as they too reached their climaxes, groaning out their releases. We collapsed into a heap on the desk, panting and sweating, our bodies still joined.

"Damn," Sol murmured. Both of us cried out in surprise

when Lok suddenly shifted us off him to stand, then threw us both over his shoulders, each arm hooked around a set of legs before he carried us out of the room.

"Where are we going?" I asked, far too spent to let my body do anything but dangle in his hold. Instead of answering, Lok walked down the hall to the waiting area and tossed us both in the wide pillow-covered hammock that spanned a third of the room. He climbed in after us and settled in between.

Burying his nose in my hair, he inhaled and admitted, "I'm told I'm too old to be sleeping on a desk."

I giggled into his side and threw an arm over him, settling in. "So, we punched the bird."

Lok peered down at me with a smirk. "One wild first date, right?"

"I vote for the second one to be a more stationary situation." Sol propped his head on his elbow.

"The spa?" I asked hopefully.

His brow quirked before he looked me up and down. "Are you sure you don't want to climb some towering mountain to scream at a flower?"

I tilted my head as if to consider. "There's gotta be some decorative ferns in the spa that need a good talking-to."

Lok chuckled, the sound vibrating through me. "You two are so weird. Never leave me." My eyelids fluttered shut. The last thing I remembered was their heartbeats lulling me to sleep.

EPILOGUE

INTERN

THE NEON LIGHTS FLICKERED ON TO ILLUMINATE MY PATH as I approached the sleek, modern office of the newly hired director of the Biodiversity Conservation Initiative. My hearts raced with anticipation. Dr. Camu Nalari was the most renowned conservation biologist this side of the galaxy, and I would be the first one to meet her!

Gently knocking at the door, I smoothed down my crest and tried to shake off the nervous jitters. "Enter," called an airy voice from within.

I entered to find Dr. Camu poring over a holographic display, her bright yellow eyes focused unblinkingly on a recording of Subject 4 facing off against that pesky pink T. rex. "Dr. Camu," I said, hoping the pathetic pounding of my hearts didn't sabotage my attempts to play it cool before I had even had the chance to begin. "I'm here with the completed field report on Subject 4's progress, as you requested."

Dr. Camu didn't look up from the recording but gestured for me to approach. "Excellent, Intern. Based on the video footage I've already seen, I'm excited to dive into your findings." She extended her K feather and patiently waited for me to present mine as well. I returned the gesture and she immediately began downloading my findings.

As the information uploaded into her core, Dr. Camu's beak fell open as she drew in a breath, and when the transfer was complete she smiled brightly, dark crimson feathers moving up in delight. "Oh, this is most excellent, Intern," she cheered. "Your ability to adjust to Subject 4's needs is commendable. I doubt most others with your experience would have been able to adapt so quickly."

I felt a surge of pride well within me at her praise, and it took all the restraint I had not to puff up my feathers and shrill. "You honor me, Dr. Camu," I said.

Dr. Camu returned her attention to her hologram and passed a wing over it. The hologram changed from the recording of Subject 4 with the T. rex to the live satellite we had watching her movements. She, her lion, and her two mates were well on their way to the female enclosure. The four of them were laughing together. Sol took something out of his pack and threw it at Lok, who only threw back his head and laughed even louder.

Their interactions seemed to please Dr. Camu. "Not only that; our first trio looks to be a resounding success," she said, her eyes sparkling with excitement. "The morning report tells me that we'll be able to introduce cacao plants to their habitat in as little as three weeks."

"That is most gratifying to hear. Is it true they are already setting up a coffee station?"

"Yes, the ground team will finish digging the bed for the coffee river soon. We'll need to account for a longer adjustment period, but the behavioral team thinks we can begin scanning the subjects for signs of pregnancy before the year is out." She clapped her hands excitedly. "More importantly, that's not what I called you in here for. I want to make sure we're taking every possible step to ensure the successful coupling of the rest of our test subjects, and so if you are willing, I would like to offer you a promotion."

There was no helping the poof once it started. I could feel my feathers practically vibrating with excitement. Dr. Camu covered her beak to stifle her laugh and gave me a moment to settle myself. "I won't let you down, Dr. Camu," I vowed.

Dr. Camu nodded, a pleased smile curving her beak. "See that you don't, Agent. Your new position as a field agent is effective immediately. Report to the mechanic bay to pick up your new hover scooter." She held up her K feather once more and transferred the file with all of the information I would need for my new position. At the top of the dossier was my new title accompanied by a code name.

FIELD AGENT 527, CODE NAME: CUPID

ACKNOWLEDGMENTS

To anyone brave enough to embrace your weirdness. And to my agent, Courtney, for not batting an eye when I pitched an idea involving aliens, dinosaurs, and Tamagotchis.

Photo provided by the author

Kimberly Lemming is a *USA Today* bestselling author who is on an eternal quest to avoid her calling as a main character. She can be found giving the slip to that new werewolf that just blew into town and refusing to make eye contact with a prince of a far-off land. Dodging aliens looking for Earth booty can really take up a girl's time.

But when she's not running from fate, she can be found writing diverse fantasy romance. Or just shoveling chocolate into her maw until she passes out on the couch.

VISIT KIMBERLY LEMMING ONLINE

KimberlyLemming.com